CLICK HERE TO START

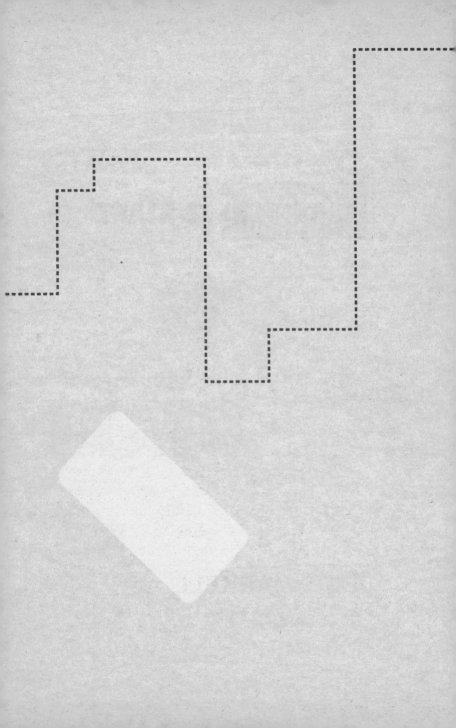

CLICK HERE TO START

a novel

DENIS MARKELL

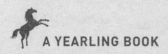

A YEARLING BOOK

Text copyright © 2016 by Denis Markell
Cover art copyright and interior illustrations © 2016 by Octavi Navarro

All rights reserved. Published in the United States by Yearling, an imprint of Random House Children's Books, a division of Penguin Random House LLC, New York. Originally published in hardcover in the United States by Delacorte Press, an imprint of Random House Children's Books, New York, in 2016.

Yearling and the jumping horse design are registered trademarks of Penguin Random House LLC.

Visit us on the Web! randomhousekids.com

Educators and librarians, for a variety of teaching tools, visit us at RHTeachersLibrarians.com

The Library of Congress has cataloged the hardcover edition of this work as follows:
Markell, Denis.
Click here to start (a novel) / Denis Markell. —First edition.
pages cm
Summary: When Ted inherits his uncle's apartment "and all the treasure within," he realizes the apartment is set up like a real-life video game and must solve the puzzles with his friends to discover the treasure.
ISBN 978-1-101-93187-5 (hardcover) — ISBN 978-1-101-93189-9 (glb) —
ISBN 978-1-101-93188-2 (ebook)
[1. Buried treasure—Fiction. 2. Video games—Fiction. 3. Friendship—Fiction.] I. Title.
PZ7.M339453Cl 2016
[Fic]—dc23
2015011782

ISBN 978-1-101-93190-5 (pbk.)

Printed in the United States of America
10 9 8 7 6 5 4 3 2
First Yearling Edition 2017

I dedicate this book

To the valiant men of the 100th Infantry Battalion and the 442nd Regimental Combat team, who fought so bravely for the United States, at a time when their Japanese American relatives back at home were being treated so dishonorably.

And specifically in honor of one of their own, Nicholas Takateru Nakabayashi, soldier, scientist, scholar.

And with all my love to his niece, my wife Melissa Iwai, and our son, his great-nephew, James Takateru Markell.

CHAPTER 1

WHO KNEW A MAN WITH TUBES IN HIS NOSE COULD BE FUNNY?

It looks like something from a science-fiction movie, with so many machines and tubes going into and out of bags hung on poles.

For a moment, it doesn't register that all those tubes and hoses are connected to a person.

I have no memory of what he looked like when I was little, and the only photo of Great-Uncle Ted in our house is from ages and ages ago. It shows a burly man with a crew cut, sitting in a living room in the 1960s. He's got a cigarette in one hand and a lighter in the other. I wonder if he hadn't smoked so many cigarettes maybe he wouldn't be here now. He's looking at the camera with a confident grin that says this is not a man to mess with. The only other place I've ever seen Asian men with kick-butt expressions like that is in samurai or martial-arts movies.

Not that I watch them all that much.

I mean, it's bad enough other people make assumptions about us Asian kids. No need for me to help out.

But I gotta say, that photo can't be further from the old man lying in this bed. The grossest thing is the tube going right up into his nose. It looks horrible, and is attached to a machine that does who knows what.

I go and stand awkwardly by the window, unsure of what to do. I wish Mom had come in with me, but she said Great-Uncle Ted wants to see me alone. Dying man's last wish and all, I guess. I clear my throat and sort of whisper, "Um, hi?"

"Arwhk."

The two veiny sacs of his eyelids slowly open, and when he sees me, he gestures, beckoning me over with one hand.

I gingerly approach the chair next to his bed, careful not to disturb any of the wires and tubes snaking around him. It's hard—I have visions of knocking into some hose or other just as I'm supposed to be having a nice visit.

"Gghhh . . ." Great-Uncle Ted catches my eye and reaches out.

Without thinking, I flinch. I have a flashback to a movie I saw where a guy laid out like this had a monster burst out of his chest and jump on someone's face. I'm not saying I expect that to happen here, but hey, it does go through my mind.

Great-Uncle Ted's eyes change. He points impatiently to something on the table.

A pad and paper. There is spidery writing on it.

"You want me to . . . give you the pad?" I ask.

Now there's a flash of fire in Great-Uncle Ted's eyes. I know when someone's ticked off. The message is clearly *Yes, you idiot. Give me the pad.*

I hand the pad to my great-uncle, who winces in pain as he presses a button on the side of his bed that raises him to a seated position.

Slowly, he writes something and then hands me the pad.

Hurts too much to talk. You Amanda's boy, Ted?

I start to write an answer on the pad.

The next thing I know, Great-Uncle Ted yanks the pad out of my hands. The old dude is surprisingly strong!

BEEP BEEP BEEP

Great. Now the heart-rate machine is going a lot faster. That can't be good.

He scribbles something and hands the pad back to me.

I'm not deaf, you little dope. Talk to me.

I laugh in spite of myself. Of course. Duh.

"Yes, uh, sir . . . I'm Ted." I feel a little weird introducing myself, since *he* knows who I am, but since I don't remember him, it feels like the right thing to do. And I'm pretty sure he seems like a "sir."

The old man writes some more. He's writing with more energy now.

You got big. Do you still like playing games?

"What games do you mean, sir?" I ask.

Kissing games.

What th—?

"Uh, no, sir," I begin. "I don't enjoy kissing games. That is, I've never played them. Maybe I would enjoy them if I did. I mean, you never know about something until you try it, right?" I'm babbling now. Trying to look casual, I lean against something, then realize it's a pole holding some fluid going into my great-uncle (or maybe coming out of him—hard to tell). Gross. I attempt to cross my legs, but I dare anyone to try to do it while wearing these ICU snot-green-colored clown pants they made me wear over my jeans to come in here. It's not so simple. So my leg sort of hovers half hoisted.

Meanwhile, Great-Uncle Ted is scribbling away.

I know you like computer games, you little twerp. I just wanted to see your face.

I laugh, and I see a hint of a smile under all the machinery.

You like the ones where you shoot people?

"I'm not allowed to play those," I say, which is the truth.

I didn't ask if you were allowed to. I asked if you liked them.

I smile and nod. This guy is pretty sharp. "Um . . . yeah, I play them sometimes."

Great-Uncle Ted looks at me with an expression I can't make out.

A lot of fun, huh?

"I guess." I shrug.

I hope that's the only way you ever have to shoot and kill a man. The other way is a lot less fun.

"You've killed a man?" I try to ask casually, but it kind of comes out in a squeak. Not my most macho moment, but give me a break, I wasn't ready for this.

Quite a few, yes.

What did Uncle Ted *do* before he retired? I wonder what sort of professions call for killing men. Or more precisely, "quite a few" men. Was he a soldier? A *hit man*?

Let's talk about something else. Why do you like these games so much?

I'm happy to move on. "I don't think the shooting games are all that—and that's the truth. It's more something to do with my friends when we hang out. What I really like is what are called escape-the-room games."

Tell me about them.

Sure, why not? "They're kind of puzzles, where you're stuck in a room and have to figure a way out."
Great-Uncle Ted's eyes survey the space around him.

There's only one way to escape this room.

"Well, I don't agree," I say eagerly, standing up to look around. "There are all sorts of exits, if you look carefully. Not just the door. There's that window. You could tie your sheets together and climb down there, or maybe there's an air-conditioning duct—"

TAP TAP TAP.

My brilliant analysis is interrupted by the sound of my great-uncle's pencil tapping loudly on the pad to get my attention.

I was actually referring to dying, Ted. Try to keep up.

I sit down, deflated. "I guess I didn't think of that," I say honestly, "because you seem so alive."

Great-Uncle Ted does his best to roll his eyes.

Don't bother sucking up to a dying man, Ted. You any good at these room games?

"Never seen a game I couldn't solve or beat. I'm always the top scorer—that means I've solved them quicker than anyone else. I guess that makes me the best," I say, before realizing how obnoxious it sounds. "That sounds like bragging. Sorry."

You ever heard of Dizzy Dean?

Okay, that's a little random. But old people do that some-times. The name does sound kind of familiar, but I can't place it. I shake my head.

One of the best pitchers in the history of baseball.
When you go home, look up what he said about bragging.

Great-Uncle Ted settles back onto his pillow. He's clearly tired.

I stare out the window, watching the headlights of the traffic below making patterns on the ceiling. "Yeah. That's about the one thing I am good at," I say softly, almost to myself. I hear scratching, and he's up and writing more.

Don't ever sell yourself short, Ted. Your mother says you're very smart.

I nod my head and laugh. "Yeah, I know, I just don't 'apply myself.' She's always saying that. Lila's the smart one."

Lila is my big sister, the bane of my existence. Lila the straight-A student, Lila the president of the student body. Lila, who got the highest Board scores in La Purisma High's history. Lila, who gave the most beautifully written senior address at her graduation, currently crushing it in her freshman year at Harvard. I mean, seriously. Why even try to compete with that?

Your mother told me you're smarter than your sister. You just don't know it.

Oh, snap! I hope there's a burn unit at Harvard, because Lila just got *smoked*. Big-time!

I'm starting to like Great-Uncle Ted. But I feel bad. We've been talking about me the whole time I've been here. Well, except for the part about him killing a lot of people. I'm pretty sure I don't want to hear more about that.

"So I guess you knew my mom when she was a little kid," I begin. "What was she like?"

Amanda was a pain in the a

He stops and his eye drifts up to my face and back down to his pad.

Amanda was a pain in the a̶ behind, if you'll excuse my French.

I can't believe I thought this was going to be boring. This is *great*! "Seriously? How so?" It takes all the self-control I can muster to get this out without cracking up.

He writes for a long time, then hands the pad to me.

When she was nine, she had this thing where no matter what you would ask her she'd say, "That's for me to know and you to find out."
Like you'd ask her, "What flavor ice cream do you want?"
"That's for me to know and you to find out."
"What movie do you want to see?"
"That's for me to know and you to find out!"
"Do I have lung cancer?"
"That's for me to know and you to find out!"

I choke at that last one.

Great-Uncle Ted waves his hand wearily.

I made that last one up. But she did say it all the time. She
thought it was cute. It stopped being cute after the first day.
Then it was annoying as heck.

Great-Uncle Ted pauses.

But she was always smart. And I'm very proud of her.

Great-Uncle Ted was the one who paid for Mom to come to California from Hawaii and go to nursing school. She's been working here at La Purisma General Hospital for as long as I can remember.

Great-Uncle Ted looks up from the paper, and his wise, half-lidded eyes meet mine. He scrawls on the page and holds up the pad.

Please tell me about the games you play. How you solve
these puzzles.

Wait. Is a real, live adult person actually asking me *details* about the games I play? This is unheard of.

So I go on and on, explaining how the games work, how at first nothing seems to make sense. But then, as I put my mind to it, a little click goes off in my head and the pieces begin to fit. It's an awesome feeling when it all comes together and you get it right.

Great-Uncle Ted seems genuinely interested, especially when I tell him about a particularly tricky puzzle, where if you look carefully at what appears to be a bunch of random drinking glasses on a tray, you realize they actually resemble the hands of a clock set to a particular time. Which is one of the main clues to solving that game.

"You know, maybe if they let me, I can come back tomorrow with my laptop and show you some," I'm saying, when I see that his head has fallen back onto the bed and his eyes are closed. "Great-Uncle Ted! Are you all right?" I gasp. "Should I get Mom?"

He wearily reaches for the pad and writes carefully.

I'm just tired. But I'm happy to see you again, Ted.

"I—I'm so glad I could talk to you too, sir," I say, feeling my breathing slow down again.

I feel so much better about everything now. You are ready.

Huh? What does that mean?

"That's good, sir."

The old man looks up at me. The energy is clearly draining out of him.

You must promise me one thing.

"I know, sir. I promise I'll work harder in school, and I'll never tell Mom you thought she was a pain in the behind—"

I think he'll laugh at this, but instead, he gathers his strength and writes furiously across the pad.

No! Listen to me! You must promise me

He's writing slower now, forcing the words out of the pen.

"Yes, sir?"

Great-Uncle Ted falls back and throws the pad at me.

THE BOX IS ONLY THE BEGINNING. KEEP LOOKING
FOR THE ANSWERS. ALWAYS GO FOR BROKE!
PROMISE ME!

With great effort, he tugs on my sleeve. I lean toward him. He pulls me down until my ear is close to his face. I can just make out the word he is saying.

"Promise!" the old man croaks. He releases my sleeve. He looks peaceful now, like a weight has been lifted off his shoulders.

As my great-uncle falls asleep, I hear my own voice, sounding far away, whispering, "I promise."

CHAPTER 2

IT'S ALL IN THE GAME

"Well, for someone who didn't want to see his great-uncle again, you certainly spent enough time in there," my mom says as we're driving home from the hospital.

When I backed quietly out of his room, my mom was having a whispered conversation with the two ICU nurses on duty. She looked worried.

I start to answer her, when a car cuts her off.

"Darn it," she mutters. Living with my mom is like being trapped inside a PG-13 movie when it's shown on TV and they dub in ridiculous words over the cursing. I once saw her close the trunk of the car on her finger, and she screamed, "Gracious!" I was pretty sure this was the first time since like 1913 a grown-up had ever used the word "gracious" when anyone else would have screamed a curse word. When I asked if it hurt, she said, "It hurts like heck."

Luckily, we don't live that far from the hospital, so the trip is short.

My dad is waiting at the door with a look of concern on his face. "So how's the old guy doing?" he asks as my mother walks into the house.

"They said he's resting comfortably, if you really want to know," Mom says.

I should probably explain here that this is something of a sore subject with my parents. Great-Uncle Ted has pretty much kept to himself all these years, never once coming to the house or seeing my dad or me or my sister. But Mom has always visited him, bringing him meals, keeping him company. Sometimes, when I was really little, she used to bring me with her. Even though he wouldn't even come to my parents' wedding, Mom still wanted to name me after him. Considering how little Great-Uncle Ted seemed to like him, my dad wasn't too thrilled, but still, I'm named Ted, so I guess my mom won out.

"Well, that's good, right?" asks Dad.

My mom looks at him and shakes her head. "Artie, you know as well as I do that when an ICU nurse says someone is 'resting comfortably,' what it really means is 'It's just a matter of time.'"

My dad comes over and puts his arms around her. She rests her head on his shoulder. My dad may not do everything right, but I'll give him this: he gives great hug.

"I'm sorry, sweetheart," Mom says to him. "I didn't even ask. How did your dinner with what's-his-name go?"

"Graham. Just fine. He's a very . . . impressive guy."

As if having my great-uncle in the hospital weren't enough, my dad has a new boss. The chairman of the English department of the college where Dad works retired this year. Everyone thought Dad would get the job, but instead they brought in this fancy guy from New York to take over.

So Dad didn't get the big promotion he was expecting, which hasn't helped the mood in the house.

This being summer, Lila should be home to help defuse all the tension, but Lila being Lila, she of course got something called a fellowship, which means she gets to stay at Harvard and assist some graduate student in their research.

When Dad told me Lila was going to be a fellow this summer, I tried to get him to say "She's a smart fellow, she felt smart" five times fast, but he didn't think it was funny.

Anyhow, Dad met his new boss tonight.

"He said he looks forward to working with me," Dad says.

"That sounds good," my mom says.

My dad squeezes her. "Mandy, you know as well as I do that when your new chairman says he looks forward to working with you, what it really means is it's just a matter of time."

They both laugh, and then Mom sighs. "I'll be in the laundry room if anyone needs me."

Dad and I exchange relieved glances. This is a good thing. Mom loves folding laundry. It calms her down. It seems to make her happy to see all those dirty, messy things become a pile of warm, neat, clean goodness.

Sometimes I wonder if this is some secret Japanese thing, like folding origami.

Of course, Mom isn't technically Japanese, she's from Hawaii. So probably not.

With any luck, she'll feel better after she's done a few dozen socks and pairs of underwear.

"I think we're all a little stressed out right now," says my dad, king of understatement.

I know what's coming next. Dad calls out to the laundry room: "Do you know where—"

"Under the newspapers on the kitchen table," my mom's voice comes back.

He doesn't even have to finish the sentence.

In times of crisis, we all turn to different things for comfort.

Like how little kids have a favorite stuffed animal or pillow. And maybe some kids still have one now, even though they're big—like a dinosaur puppet named Gerald that they got when they were two but that they still take out now and then and rub on their face and it— Anyway, maybe they still do. I'm not going to judge them.

Grown-ups are no different. Only with them, it's books. Some of them turn to the Bible. Or if you're Jewish, the Torah.

My dad has a different Holy Book. The Purely Provence catalog.

Now, I would agree that it's a little weird, what with him being an English professor and everything, but I swear to you, he spends more time looking at the Purely Provence catalog than at any book in his library.

Instead of stories, it has page after page of beautifully photographed rooms in the South of France. My dad calls it a lifestyle. I think he wants to live inside that catalog, in a world where he eats breakfast in a spotless kitchen filled with old furniture. It's just that (as my mother helpfully likes to point out) "that stuff would look ridiculous in a Southern California house built in 1985."

For example, his favorite thing in the world:

"Honey, a French farmhouse table is only three thousand dollars!"

I suggest that there are only two things wrong with us owning that:

1) We're not French.
2) We don't live in a farmhouse.

Besides. For that kind of money, you could probably get a pretty nice *new*-looking table.

"It *is* new," he tells me. "They make it look old on purpose. They drag chains across it so it looks old and beaten-up—it gives it character. It's called 'distressed' wood."

"They're not even real homes," my mom calls from the other room, knowing that he's mooning over his "darn catalog," as she says. "They're just made-up. You know it's a fantasy."

"But look," Dad says, sighing like a teenage girl looking at a pop star. "There are no piles of newspapers and students' papers and unpaid bills anywhere. It's all so clean."

I suggest that the reason might be because if you live in a French farmhouse, you don't get newspapers and bills.

"That's the whole point," Dad says.

I don't know how to answer that.

He really loves that catalog.

"You know, you've been wanting that table for years," I say. "Why don't you just buy it already."

"It's not that simple," Dad says. "Right now, it's either buy that table or send your sister to Harvard."

He sighs and goes back to drooling on his catalog.

"I think I'll go to my room," I say, needing to get away from French farmhouses.

"Good idea. I know you're dying to finish that book you've been so engrossed in," Dad teases. He thinks it's hilarious to say this when he knows I'm going upstairs to play a game on the computer.

"*The Brothers Karamazov,* right, Ted?"

This is our standing joke. Apparently *The Brothers Karamazov* is some big, difficult Russian novel that no kid would read (or even pronounce). Except Lila, of course. She read it when she was twelve. So that makes it funny. Ha ha.

"You bet, Dad. I'm just getting to the good part."

"Which part is that?"

I want to say, "The part where the hero's sister, Lilavich, gets eaten by wild bears," but I somehow know tonight isn't the night for it.

I head upstairs.

I look down at Great-Uncle Ted's pad.

Your mother told me you're smarter than your sister. You just don't know it.

Heh heh. Well, that's one to hold on to for later.

As I walk down the hallway, I catch a glimpse of myself in the mirror. It's funny how my features match my mom's more than my dad's.

Sure, I've got a bigger nose, but then, what do you expect? My mom's nose is practically nonexistent. She calls it the "Asian no-bridge thing" and complains that her glasses always slip down. But other than the nose, I got the Asian side, all right. Lila didn't, with her bushy hair and slightly upturned eyes. People always think she's Hispanic, or maybe Italian. Not me.

There is no doubt about my Japanese ancestry. My mom loves to tell this story of when I was little and napping in a stroller and our family was in Chinatown. An old Asian woman passed by and peered down at me. She looked at Lila, then at my Jewish dad, then gripped Mom's arm, leaned in, and chuckled, "Asian blood is *strong* in that one!" I love the fact that Mom always seems kind of proud when she says that last line.

I walk into my room, step over the piles of gaming magazines on the floor, and head to my laptop.

Bzzzt!

I pull out my phone and fall into the chair by my bed. It's from Caleb. Again.

Caleb Grant has been my best friend since first grade. When you've been friends that long, you pretty much know everything about each other. For example, I know that right about now, Caleb would normally be totally lost in drawing superheroes, but today is different. He's completely clueless about my great-uncle and all I've been through. He just wants to talk.

I don't feel like talking just yet. Caleb will understand. He's good about those things.

So what's up?

Sorry about not talking. I'm gonna play a game then we can talk I text back.

Which one?

Caleb always likes to play along. At least until he gives up. I check my favorite game site, slapfivegames.com. There's only one new room escape game, but I'm stoked because it's by one of the best designers, Brainwaiver, from Japan.

It seems like the best escape games come from Japan for some reason. It makes me proud.

This one looks simple enough—*The Sad Room,* it's called.

I send the link to Caleb and click on the Start button. The game loads in.

Like pretty much every game of this type, the goal is simple: escape the room, using items you find as you investigate the space.

This one opens, and I click around the screen and see a bed, a desk, a couch, and a door. There's a potted plant by the couch. This is how you always start, just clicking things at random.

Hanging on the wall above the bed are three paintings. The painting on the left shows a strange design. The middle painting is a landscape with flowers. The third painting is of a skull. I zoom in for a closer look and see that someone has scrawled "Beware" on it.

I move on to the desk. It has a glass of water on it, and a lamp. But the lamp doesn't work, which I know means either it's hiding a secret or I'll have to figure out how to fix it later. There are three drawers in the desk. Two are locked; the third contains a book. Most of the pages are torn out—only two are left. One has a hand-drawn diagram of a circle connected in some way to a pulley, which I know will clue me in to something I'll build or operate later. Sometimes I'll even just have to find another picture of this same drawing somewhere. Pretty typical.

Moving on to the bed, I click the blankets, the headboard, the pillow, until something moves—I find a crumpled piece of paper under the pillow with some sort of obscured diagram.

I could go on and on through the whole game, but nobody's interested in every step. It's more fun to play than to hear about, right?

This one is kind of tricky, though. I find a key under a part of the rug (don't ask how I knew what part—it involved holding up a piece of paper from under the couch to a mirror, and trust me, it was a little more complicated than that, but I'm giving you a break here). The key doesn't fit anything in the room, though, so—

Bzzzt!

Yup, exactly on cue, a text from Caleb.

OK. Officially stuck. Going to the WT.

Loser. Hitting the walkthrough page already? A little brainpower, that's all this needs. Oh, in case you don't know what a walkthrough is, it's like this:

See, if you get stuck and want to wimp out, like Caleb usually does at some point, you click on this link and it takes you to a screen that walks you through the game step by step.

Some kids do it so they can brag about finishing the game. Other kids have just gone crazy and can't figure it out.

It's like cheating to me.

As I've said, I don't need no stinkin' walkthroughs.

I click on the desk for like the millionth time, and this time a new angle pops up and I can get to the underside of a drawer. I click, and it opens to reveal a key, which opens a box that has a phone book in it.

Until now, this game hasn't been all that challenging. This should have been the final step, but the game designer is cleverer than most.

I click on the phone book, assuming it will open and turn to a page with a phone number circled. Then, typically, you'd put the series of numbers (the phone number) into the combination lock on the box on the couch and get the key to the front door and that would be that. I'd win the game.

The problem is that the phone book won't open. It just sits there.

I'm telling you, no matter how I click on it, it won't move.

Think, I say to myself. It says *Springfield, Mass.* on the cover. Is it an anagram? It has to mean something.

Wait a minute. I look at the painting with "Beware" scrawled on it, which I haven't had to use yet.

I open a new tab and type "Beware, Springfield, Mass." into Google. Nothing significant. But numbers also come from names and addresses, so I try again, this time with "B. Ware, Springfield, Mass."

There's a B. Ware Funeral Parlor listed!

I copy down the funeral parlor's phone number and go back to the game and the combination lock. Too many numbers. Maybe just the last four numbers?

I try that. It doesn't work. Wait, of course . . .

I go back to the Google screen and check out the address: 4351 Parker Road.

Back to the game, type those numbers into the combination, and hear the sweet sound of the box clicking open. Inside the box is a key that matches one I found earlier. I pick up the other key and find that it nests in the one I just got from the box.

I drag the keys to the front door with my mouse. There's a flash of light, an open door, and I win the game—*like a boss.*

I'm vaguely aware that a phone is ringing somewhere in our house.

I look at the high scores page and note that, as always, I'm the top scorer, having finished the game faster than anyone else. I think of asking Mom if maybe I can bring the laptop to the hospital tomorrow to show Great-Uncle Ted how I solved the game. I bet he'd like that.

I glance over at the pad with Great-Uncle Ted's writing on it.

You ever heard of Dizzy Dean?
One of the best pitchers in the history of baseball.
When you go home, look up what he said about bragging.

I go back to the Google page and type in "Dizzy Dean" and "bragging." I can't help smiling when I see the quote on the screen: *"It ain't braggin' if you can do it."*

Pretty cool. Great-Uncle Ted is a pretty cool guy, all right.

Suddenly, I hear my mom make a sound I swear I've never heard before, and I know immediately that something is wrong.

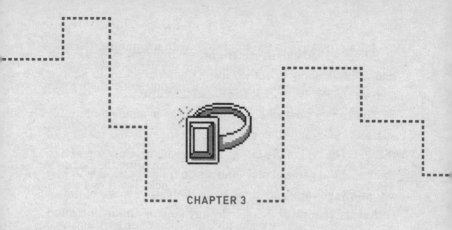

CHAPTER 3

UNCLE TED'S WILL POWER

Here are some words and phrases I have heard over the last few days that I am completely sick of:

1. Funeral
2. Departed
3. Uncle Ted's estate
4. Passed away

I guess I'm lucky. No one in my family has died since Mom's father "passed away" when I was a little boy. My dad's parents live in Brooklyn ("I think each is just trying to outlive the other. Spite is all that keeps them going," my dad likes to say, but I don't think he means it).

It's weird to think that someone I just saw could just . . . not be there all of a sudden.

Sure, I've had kids in class be absent from school and everyone will talk about how they lost a grandparent or an aunt or something, but it's always been someone else.

This time it's me who is sitting in a car, in an uncomfortable suit and tie, going to some lawyer's office for the reading of the will. The will of the one grown-up who actually seemed to think that the games I play (and am so freaking good at, if I do say so myself) are something more than just a waste of time.

At least there isn't going to be any funeral. Great-Uncle Ted specified that he wanted to be cremated and have his ashes sent back to Hawaii.

It seemed that for most of his life he didn't want to have anything to do with his family here or there. Except for Mom. Of course.

Whenever I would ask about him, all Mom would say was "He's had quite a life and deserves to be left alone in peace."

With Mom and Dad talking business up front, I take the time to phone Caleb real quick. Things have been so hectic I haven't even had a minute to call.

"Yeah?" He sounds bummed, like he always does at his dad's over the weekends.

"How's it going?"

"You know . . . the usual. Dad's acting all weird, and Gina wants to be my best friend. I hate it here."

Gina is Caleb's father's second wife.

"I don't blame you."

"How's all the stuff with your uncle?"

"On our way to meet with a lawyer about it now."

"Oh, man, good luck."

"Thanks, dude, you too. See you Monday?"

"If I survive the weekend."

It's been so unreal the last few days, any chance to talk with Caleb makes things a little more normal.

My parents are talking softly in the front seat. I hear my dad say something about how Great-Uncle Ted's ashes will be buried "in the punch bowl." This piques my interest.

Some weird Hawaiian tradition? "Umm . . . you're burying Great-Uncle Ted in a punch bowl?"

My mom laughs. "That's what they call the national cemetery in Honolulu."

"You know your Great-Uncle Ted was a hero, right?" my dad asks.

Even from the backseat, I can see my mom's ears turn an interesting shade of red.

"Uncle Ted fought in the big war. He got a medal and everything," continues Dad.

So that's what he was talking about when he said he killed a lot of men. At least, I hope it was.

I poke my mom in the arm. "Why didn't you ever tell me?"

"He never liked to talk about it. He used to say it was a long time ago and he wasn't really a hero and he just wanted to forget it."

A silence falls over the car. I look out the window and stare at what could charitably be called "the scenery." We live in the San Fernando Valley, just over the canyon from what most people think of when they think of "glamorous Los Angeles."

On *that* side of the canyon is Hollywood, Beverly Hills, Rodeo Drive.

On our side are dozens of dinky little suburban places, like La Purisma. Not much different from anywhere else, with people going about their boring lives. The only difference is that we have palm trees. Big whoop.

It's kind of like the lunch tables at our middle school. The other side of the canyon is like the cool table, and we're the kids at the other tables, near enough to see them, but we know we'll never be invited to join, if you get my drift.

So La Purisma was named after some famous mission that was here in the early days. It would be cool if it was still here, but it's long gone. Nowadays people joke that "La Purisma" is Spanish for "strip mall."

But we've left La Purisma miles back.

My dad turns the wheel sharply, and all of a sudden we're turning off into a nasty part of the Valley I've never been in before.

It seems to be made up mostly of manicure salons and gas stations.

My dad steers the car into a small, L-shaped group of buildings. I can see a karate school, a noodle shop, a dusty grocery store, and an old office building.

"Make sure you lock the doors," Mom mutters to Dad. I look out and see some sleazy-looking guys loitering near the grocery.

I wonder how many kids my age have ever been to a lawyer's office. I haven't. I've always pictured lawyers' offices looking like they do on TV or in the movies. You know, you go up in a sleek elevator in some impressive glass-sheathed towers and then you're ushered into a dark-wood-paneled room with large leather chairs and shelves filled with law books.

Yeah, well, this looks more like the back room where we get our car repaired.

We all carefully pick our way up a rickety flight of stairs and find ourselves in front of a dented door with a plastic name-plate pasted on, the kind you get at a stationery store.

Mom knocks politely. No answer.

We wait, and watch the characters wandering on the street, who look like they escaped from some reality TV show about drug addicts or drunks. My dad knocks this time, a lot louder than my mom. After a little bit, the door opens, and we find ourselves in the offices of Ben Huang, Esq. (don't ask me what "Esq." stands for. It's on the nameplate).

Mr. Huang matches his office perfectly. A large, sweaty old man, he smells of some funky aftershave—I bet he started wearing one brand in the seventies when it was popular and never changed it.

Mr. Huang is also rocking a pretty sweet diamond ring on his pinky. I am totally impressed by this until I see my dad turn to my mom, raise his eyebrows, and mouth the words "He's wearing a pinky ring," in response to which Mom puts her hand over her mouth and shakes her head. So maybe it isn't so impressive.

Mr. Huang shakes hands with the family (I know I will continue smelling that aftershave on my hand for days).

"So nice of you all to come," Mr. Huang wheezes as he settles himself into the chair behind his desk, which is littered with files and papers of all colors and sizes.

We find places to sit and he begins.

"We are gathered here for the purpose of reading the last will and testament of Takateru 'Ted' Wakabayashi. Dear Uncle was eighty-eight years of age at the time of his passing. There are a few things I need to establish before I get to the actual reading of the will itself."

Mom pulls a yellow legal pad from her purse.

"I promised the relatives back in Hawaii that I'd write down everything in the will. Let's just hope he gave something to Auntie Tomoko. Otherwise I'll never hear the end of it."

Mr. Huang looks up from his papers.

"As I call your names, please answer 'Present.' If anyone listed is not here, under the terms of Dear Uncle's will, I cannot continue."

It's creeping me out that Mr. Huang insists on saying "Dear Uncle" with the same sympathetic smile every time, but then again, it goes with the rest of the general smarminess that hangs off the old guy like his cheap aftershave.

As Mr. Huang reads our names, we all say "Present."

" 'I, Takateru 'Ted' Wakabayashi, being of sound mind and body, do hereby grant . . .'" And on and on.

I look over and see that Mom is furiously writing down all the amounts the lawyer says, like she's trying to finish a test in the last minutes before time is up.

"Auntie Tomoko will be very happy," she mutters more than a few times.

Finally, Mr. Huang puts down the paper and wipes his forehead with a grimy handkerchief. He smiles and says, "This is the end of Dear Uncle's will."

My mom begins to put her pad away when the old guy holds up his hand.

"That *was* the end of Dear Uncle's will until two days ago. I was summoned to his bedside in the hospital. There he dictated to me a codicil to the existing will. For the benefit of our youngest visitor, I will explain what a codicil is."

Right. Like I'm the only one in the room who doesn't know what a codicil is.

I look at Mom and Dad, and apparently I *am* the only one who doesn't know what a codicil is.

"A codicil is a document that adds to, rather than replaces, a previously executed will," Mr. Huang says, smiling at me like I'm a moron. "Now, a codicil may add or revoke small provisions, or . . ."

Here, Mr. Huang looks down and twists the ring on his pinky. He's clearly relishing the moment. ". . . it may completely change the majority, or all, of the gifts under the will."

"He better not have taken everything away from Auntie Tomoko. She'd kill him if he weren't already dead," Mom says grimly.

Mr. Huang smiles again, looking a little nervous. "There are only two provisions to the will as it stands."

He reads off a single piece of paper. Clearing his throat, Mr. Huang peers down onto the page and begins to read.

" 'First codicil to my last will and testament: I hereby award from my estate to Lila Gerson the sum of eighty thousand dollars, to be used to help pay for her education at Harvard University.' "

Mom gasps, and tears fill her eyes. She grips Dad's hand so hard I thought it was going to fall off. Clearly she didn't expect this.

" 'Second codicil: I leave the entire contents of my apartment on 103465 South Alta Vista Avenue in Loca Grande, with all the treasure it contains . . . to my great-nephew Ted Gerson, who is so good at solving puzzles. Search hard and you will find it.' "

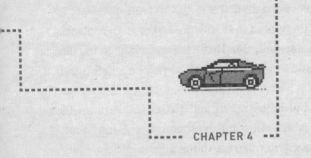

CHAPTER 4

A CHANGE IN PLANS, OR DAD'S LITTLE SURPRISE

"Just remember what your mother said," Dad warns as he pulls off the freeway at the Loca Grande exit.

"I know. . . . I know. . . ." I'm leaning my head on the window, feeling the impatience spilling over inside me, like when I'm waiting for a new game to load in.

"Just don't get your hopes up," Mom said, when she heard me on the phone discussing with Caleb what "all the treasure it contains" might mean. "My uncle had a funny idea of what treasure was. He tended to um . . . keep things. . . ."

The plan is simple. The apartment is paid up until the end of the month. That gives me a week to go through everything in the apartment and figure out what's trash and what's treasure. Caleb is going to help, and anything we find, we split.

And here's the awesome part: since my great-uncle was a war hero, it's possible he's left some souvenirs from World War II lying around!

Sure, Mom said in no uncertain terms that she's visited the apartment dozens of times and has never seen anything of value.

She's also making me bring rubber gloves and bleach, "just in case."

So what? This is going to be an epic week.

Hanging with Caleb, going through a lot of cool stuff.

Besides, what Mom and Dad think is treasure and what I think is treasure are two different things.

And my great-uncle must have had *a pretty good* reason to have given whatever it is especially to me. Obviously, there is *something* special behind that apartment door.

Caleb's dad, Gene, has already dropped him off.

My dad and Caleb's dad are both English professors at California State University La Purisma, and we basically grew up together: barbecues in the summer, trips for winter break, last-minute get-togethers on weekends.

Then, a year ago, Gene grows a ponytail and announces he's leaving Doris and Caleb and moving in with an associate professor named Gina who's like ten years younger than Caleb's mom.

This, not surprisingly, is causing a lot of problems, and Caleb is dealing with it the best he can.

Maybe it's just a coincidence, but around that time his dad moved out, Caleb started drawing a lot more pictures of guys punching each other.

If he starts drawing a new villain called Evil Dad and has some superhero kicking his butt, we'll know for sure.

Usually, Gene would stick around to shoot the breeze with Dad, but things have been a little strained between them since the divorce.

"Hey," mutters Caleb as he pushes his blond hair out of his eyes and adjusts his glasses.

He looks over at me and Dad, just standing there.

"My mom had to go meet the lawyer to get the key," I explain.

My dad clears his throat. Clearly there is something on his mind.

"Listen, I thought maybe you guys could use some help cleaning everything up. . . ."

"That's okay, Dad. But it's nice of you to offer," I quickly respond.

The last thing we need is to have my dad here while we're going through stuff.

And what if we find something awesome, like a German Luger or a samurai sword? Parents are funny about letting kids keep things like that.

"Actually, I wasn't talking about me. You know about the new head of the English department?"

"Of course. Your new boss," I say.

"Guess what? Funny thing. His daughter is going to be in your class next fall. He's eager for her to make new friends here, so I kind of invited her to help you guys."

Caleb and I exchange stricken glances. *Whaaat?*

"Dad. Please tell me you're joking."

Of course, I should have known. My dad has always been like this—springing bad news at the last possible moment, when there's nothing I can do about it. The last family vacation, just as we were entering the hotel room, he told me there was no Internet access. Two weeks. No Internet. This might even be worse.

My dad is cleaning his glasses, not looking up.

"Why didn't you tell me this before?"

Finally, he looks up. "Well, Ted, I liken it to taking the dog to the vet. You don't tell him you're taking him to the vet—he'll never get in the car. You just say you're taking him for a ride. . . ."

"And when you get there, you cut off his—"

"Ted!" my dad warns sharply.

"Glad to know you see me like the family dog," I mutter.

"It's a metaphor," my dad starts to explain, "like—"

"I know what a freaking metaphor is, Dad—like comparing spending the next three hours with some girl we've never met to spending an eternity in hell," I answer.

"This is going to be worse than PE next year, when we have to shower with the other boys," moans Caleb.

Leave it to Caleb to put things in the proper perspective.

"Look," my dad says, getting suddenly serious, "she doesn't have any friends. She's just moved here. It won't kill you to be nice."

"But—"

"Ted, at least this way she'll know some people before school starts. Her dad wants her to like it here. It's rough, moving all the way across the country and not knowing anyone."

"Dad . . . some random girl . . . I mean, I don't mind, like, meeting her, but—"

"Who says she's gonna want to spend time with two boys, anyway? Why couldn't her dad find some girls here for her to hang out with?" Caleb asks.

"Apparently there aren't any girls your age around this time of the summer. Graham really wants to get her out of the house. He says all she's been doing since they moved is sitting inside and reading books."

I let out a groan. A nerd girl. A weirdo. How did the coolest thing I was going to do all summer just turn into the most aggravating? Babysitting some snotty girl who'll probably think Caleb and I are idiots for playing computer games. Just what I need. One more person judging me.

"So it's okay, right?" asks Dad hopefully.

"Does Mom know about this?" I ask warily.

"Yes, and I know how . . . disappointed she would be if you couldn't be nice to a new member of your class."

Dad has shamelessly played the Mom card. Against which there is no defense.

The Mom card is all-powerful.

At this moment, I know that the answer has to be yes. I am defeated. By my own father. How Darth Vader.

"I guess so. How about she comes over tomorrow and helps out for a day? That would be good, right?"

"Ummm . . . I don't think that's going to work," Dad says.

There is a sound of a car pulling into the parking lot. I assume it's Mom's, but then I see it. A gleaming, sleek luxury car, the very picture of coolness. I'm not much of a car guy, but even I know this one. Lexus. Top of the line.

"The thing is . . . I kind of already said yes," Dad says sheepishly. "I guess that's them."

The doors open and a man strides over, and he and my dad shake hands. Then a girl gets out to follow him, closing the door with a soft *thunk* that somehow manages to sound expensive.

The first thing I notice is how she's dressed.

Knowing that this will probably be a hot and dirty job, Caleb and I have put on our funkiest clothes. I'm in an old pair of cutoff jeans and a T-shirt my Hawaiian relatives sent one Christmas that I would never be caught dead wearing in public, with a picture of a pig in a hula skirt on a surfboard under HANG LOOSE! (of course) written in big letters.

Caleb is wearing pajama bottoms and a T-shirt that once had a picture of Captain America on it but has been washed so many times it now looks like it says C P AIN AM I .

It takes me almost a minute to realize the girl is wearing jeans. I've never seen jeans so pressed and spotless. They look brand-new, like her pristine deck shoes.

I notice that her long blond hair isn't pulled up, even though it's going to be a sweaty day, most likely, but rather hangs down her back, held in place with a headband, like Alice in Wonderland's.

As she gets closer, I sense something else about her that I can't put my finger on, something that sets her apart from the girls in my class. Certainly she dresses differently, and wears her hair differently, and doesn't bounce around like the popular girls in my grade.

I feel bad for her for a moment, imagining her trying to fit in at a new school, and being teased for her clothes, and—

Then, as her father is about to introduce my dad to her, and she smiles exactly the right kind of smile to meet an adult, it hits me. What makes her different is that she's just *perfect*.

I can tell. This is a girl who has never said or done anything inappropriate in her entire life. And for some reason, this really, really bugs me.

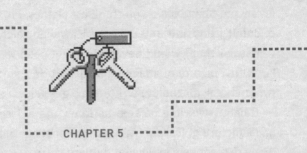

CHAPTER 5

ENTER THE ARCHERS

"Ted! Hello?"

I snap around and look at Dad. Apparently I've been standing here like an idiot while my dad was introducing me.

"Sorry about Ted, Graham. He's a little, ah, distracted, I guess, what with his great-uncle . . . you know . . . Ted, this is Graham Archer. The new head of our English department."

Graham Archer is tall and broad-shouldered. His full, golden hair shines in the sun.

Dad takes off his grubby baseball cap and mops his shining scalp with a paper towel from his grimy Dockers pocket.

I turn back to the Archers, who don't look like the same species as us.

Do they even sweat, these people?

It's kind of eerie. It's a hundred degrees out here, and it's like the two of them have some sort of force field around them, as if the Valley dust wouldn't presume to land on their per-fectly pressed polos.

The girl turns to my father. "Hello, I'm Isabel."

"Isabel Archer!"

At this, my dad breaks into a silly grin, the kind he makes when he's sure whatever he's about to say is clever.

I brace myself.

Addressing Isabel, my dad winks (yes, *winks*) and says, "You're obviously intelligent, but are you excited as well?"

I assume Graham Archer is going to punch my dad's lights out for saying something so rude, but instead, he laughs out loud.

"Very good, Arthur! I'm impressed."

"I haven't been teaching Henry James for ten years for nothing!" my dad says.

Wow. Dad always says that when he makes one of his lame "literature" jokes, the only ones who laugh are English majors. Because they have to.

Then Isabel laughs too. It's an "I am getting the grown-up reference and appreciating it while you two dweebs haven't a clue" laugh and it seems so superior that it makes the six-year-old in me want to pick up a clod of dirt and rub it into her nice pink polo shirt and see if she'd find *that* funny.

Of course, I know the twelve-year-old me isn't allowed to do things like that.

I then look down at my ridiculous outfit and realize that the twelve-year-old me is dressed similarly to the six-year-old me and I feel even more awkward.

Graham turns to me and gestures to his daughter. "Ted, this is Isabel. I think you're in the same class next year."

"So . . . uh, nice to meet you. This is my buddy Caleb."

Caleb nods at Isabel, who nods back. Graham, of course, reaches out and shakes both our hands. His grip, as I'm sure you can guess, is neither too firm nor too weak. It's perfect, like the rest of him.

My dad looks around. Rocks on his heels. Cracks his knuckles. Such a smoothie, my dad.

"So . . . we're just waiting for my wife to show up with the key. She had to get it from the lawyer. Always waiting on the wife. You know how that is, I guess—oh, I'm so sorry."

I don't know why, but Dad turns bright red. Graham Archer nods and shrugs.

"No worries. Forget about it," Graham replies, as if he means it.

"What do you know? Here she comes now!" Dad perks up like a puppy in a pet store setting eyes on its new owner. "We can beat a hasty retreat. I've still got a load of finals to grade."

"And I have plenty of boxes to unpack," Graham says, "so I'd best be going as well. Have fun, Isabel, and I'll see you around three?"

Isabel calls after her father and runs up to him as Mom's car pulls into the parking lot. It seems like she's desperately trying to get him to take her with him, to leave these two losers as soon as she can. I hear little snatches of the conversation, mostly Graham's lilting, soothing voice: "It's only a few hours. . . . Remember our deal? I promise I won't be late. . . . I know. . . ."

In the distance, my mom has parked the car, and the door flies open.

Dressed in her usual grubby change-at-work clothes, Mom

rushes toward us, waving the keys over her head like a trophy. She passes Dad and Graham, gives Dad a little kiss, and heads our way.

"Hi, guys! Sorry I'm so late! That lawyer couldn't find the keys, then I realized I needed to stop for gas, and you'll never guess who pulled up right behind me!"

Mom finally stops to take a breath. She laughs at herself, leans over and kisses me on the cheek, waves at Caleb, and for the first time turns and sees Isabel. Her eyes widen. And then her face changes in an instant, and she says those words that fill me with dread and remind me why today is different.

"Why, *hello*! Is this Graham Archer's famous daughter I've heard so much about?"

Isabel shakes my mom's hand. Lightly.

"Isabel Archer. And you must be Mrs. Gerson?" she chirps.

I can only marvel at her ability to talk to parents. This is a skill no twelve-year-olds in La Purisma possesses. Even the cool ones. Are all kids from New York City fluent in Parent?

Mom bursts into a huge smile. "I certainly must! Arthur mentioned that he invited you to join the boys today. I just didn't think you'd actually want to spend your time doing this . . . with them. . . ."

"My father was worried I'd become a recluse"—Isabel smiles—"so I agreed to do this on one condition: he buys me the complete Charles Dickens set I've been wanting."

Oh, right. She's a *reader.*

"So you're a *reader,*" my mom sighs, as if somehow this elevates Isabel to yet another realm of perfection.

"Yes, but only books for adults. I don't enjoy reading books for kids our age. Have you ever noticed how often the mother is dead? Or the father left home when the child is little? Or the hero or heroine is an orphan?"

Caleb looked up. "You know, I never noticed that."

"Yes, well, you wouldn't necessarily. But it does happen. All the time. And then at the end it always turns out the father is somebody amazing, and he comes back, or the mother is actually a secret agent off on a mission or something ridiculous like that. It would be like my mother all of a sudden coming back to life."

There is a moment of silence. None of us knows what to say. Isabel turns to my mom.

"I hate those books," she adds brightly. "That's why I like reading grown-up books better. They don't make up stuff like that. Except maybe Dickens. He always has that sort of thing. Like in *Oliver Twist*, you know?"

"Sure," I agree, having vaguely heard of *Oliver Twist*. I promise myself I'll try to read about it online as soon as I get home.

"Oh, that's right. I was so sorry to hear about your mother," my mom says, switching gears with all the finesse of Mack truck with a blown clutch. (Okay, I actually don't know squat about cars, but I heard our mechanic use that expression once when he was telling my dad a story and I've wanted to use it ever since.)

And now we know why Dad was apologizing when he mentioned wives to Mr. Archer.

"Thank you, Mrs. Gerson. That's very kind of you."

"We're *all* so glad you've come to join the boys. Aren't we, boys?"

Isabel laughs again, and it's totally not like the annoying screechy giggles of the girls in my class. No, Isabel has an even, knowing—okay, I'll say it again—*perfect* laugh. She laughs like a grown-up. It makes her even more unnerving, if possible.

If mom calls us "boys" one more time, I'm going to puke, so I try to get things back on track.

"So, *Mom,* you were saying how we'd never guess who was at the gas station?"

"Oh . . . right. It was Donna Yamada, Mr. Yamada's daughter!"

Caleb and I exchange looks.

"Ted, I've told you about Mr. Yamada a thousand times. I swear, you're as bad as your father. Mr. Yamada was one of your great-uncle's most loyal customers when he had the liquor store. He visited Uncle Ted every day at the hospital, practically."

"Riiight . . . yeah. You did tell me about him. I didn't know he had a daughter."

"That's who used to drive him there. Anyhow, he was so upset over the news. When I told her what you were doing, she asked if you found anything from the old store —you know, an ashtray or something—if her father could have it to remember Uncle Ted."

"Sure, Mom, of course," I reply. "No problem."

Mom is heading up to the door, key in hand.

"Where are you from, again, Isabel?"

"Umm . . . New York City."

"Did Ted tell you that's where his father is from? We haven't been back in ages!"

The door seems completely unwilling to budge. Or perhaps in some sadistic way it wants to prolong my agony by stubbornly refusing to open. Anything is possible in a world where I am going to spend the next few hours with this girl who clearly wants to be anywhere but where she is.

"There! Finally! I think the door must have swelled up in the heat. Ta-da!" With a final push, Mom opens the door.

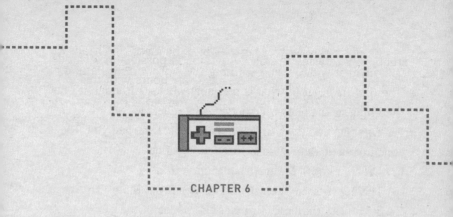

CHAPTER 6

THE GOOD, THE BAD,
AND THE JUNKY

The first thing that hits us is the smell.

It's a combination of old newsprint, cooking grease, and some sort of old-guy smell—maybe body odor mixed with liquor and cigarettes.

But that's nothing compared with the look of the place. Empty bottles are everywhere. There are bags of food on the stained couch. And I don't even want to think about what those stains are from. As a matter of fact, there are stains of all sorts of interesting colors on the floor as well. On the part of the floor that's visible, anyway. Most of the floor is covered by cartons of old magazines or grimy broken appliances from about twenty years ago that Great-Uncle Ted didn't bother to wash.

It's kind of like a Museum of Gross.

Anything too big to pile is stacked against the wall, and the boxes are all balanced precariously one on top of another. There is barely room to walk.

Mom quickly weaves her way into the mess. She heads for the nearest window and with a grunt pulls it open, letting in the first fresh air in what is probably weeks. Although it's hot and muggy, the feel of the outside is a relief.

Over her shoulder, my mom calls out, "I warned you, Ted. I *said* my uncle didn't like to throw things out."

"Yeah, I know, Mom . . . but I didn't think—"

Having thrown open two more windows, Mom turns on a large fan. As the breeze ripples the pages of the newspapers and magazines piled up on the chairs nearby, she puts her hands on her hips. She turns to Isabel.

"I'm sorry, Isabel. I guess this is a little shocking."

Isabel shrugs. "I don't know. I'm from New York City. I've smelled worse. In the subway, in used bookstores . . . I'm more worried about *that.*"

My mom follows Isabel's eyes to the old refrigerator wheezing in the corner.

"It's fine," Mom laughs. "I emptied it the night my uncle was taken to the hospital. I had a feeling he wasn't going to come back." As Mom says this, I see her face crumple, and she turns away.

"Well, you kids have fun. I have to get to work. I've left big bags for all the trash in the kitchen. If you fill those, we can get more. I think Isabel's dad is picking her up in a couple of hours?"

Isabel nods absentmindedly as she continues to take in the mounds of stuff.

"Okay, guys, I'll swing back on my lunch hour to get you two boys. I don't want you spending too much time in this heat! Good luck!"

Then my mom hops over an old toaster oven and winds

between a box crammed with old videocassettes and an unopened carton of ramen noodles covered in a layer of dust and heads for the front door.

We watch her go.

All three of us stand motionless, no one quite knowing what to do first.

In the silence we hear my mom's car start, pull out, and drive away.

Then Isabel speaks. For the first time, with no grown-ups around.

"Um . . . if it's all the same to you . . ."

I know where this is going.

"Would it be okay if I wait for my dad outside? I brought a book, and—"

"Sure, of course," I say. I don't blame her. She didn't agree to clean this dump, Caleb and I did.

Relieved, Isabel actually smiles and hightails it outside. She pulls an old chair near the door, and we see her lean it up against the wall. She carefully wipes the seat and arranges herself on it.

Meanwhile, Caleb and I get to work, picking stuff up and seeing if Great-Uncle Ted left any German Lugers or samurai swords, you know, just lying around.

A bright voice calls from outside. "So, your mother's Japanese—"

I know she's just trying to make conversation, but for some reason, this bugs me.

"Actually, she's *American*," I hear myself say, adding, "Why do people always assume that Asians are from somewhere else?"

Isabel lets out a puff of breath and clears her throat.

"Hey, man, that's a little harsh. . . . I'm sure she didn't mean—" Caleb begins.

"Obviously she's American," Isabel sniffs. "If you'd let me finish, I was saying Japanese American."

I try a lame attempt at damage control.

"I didn't mean to jump down your throat, but it's something that—"

"Believe me, I have plenty of Asian friends back in New York. That's something I don't need to be lectured on."

Before I can get into it with Miss Private School, Caleb jumps in. "So what's the plan here? Just poke through everything until we find something valuable?"

From the doorway, a blond head speaks. "What makes you think you're going to find anything valuable?" Isabel asks. "Looks like he was just an old pack rat."

Before I can stop him, Caleb answers, "Ted's great-uncle left the contents of the apartment to him. He said there was some sort of treasure buried here."

Aha! Now the blond head appears at the door. "Wow! Nobody told me that. You think it's true?" She comes in and stands next to me, surveying the debris.

I don't want to get her hopes up. "My mom doesn't know anything about it. And she's the only relative who was close to him. Who knows what the old guy thought was a treasure."

Caleb stretches, making his already scrawny body look even skinnier, if possible. "Man, this place is packed. Where do we start?"

I look around the room and instinctively take inventory. My right hand twitches like I'm clicking a mouse.

"First things first. Let's collect whatever looks like trash and put all the newspapers and magazines together," I suggest. "And then maybe see if any of the appliances still work."

"Right," Isabel answers. She kicks a box at her feet and picks it up. She heads to the nearest garbage bag.

"Whoa! Wait a minute!" Caleb yells, pushing through the garbage at his feet and peering into the box Isabel is holding.

"You were going to throw that away? You're kidding, right?"

Isabel looks down and then back at Caleb like he's lost it. "Ummm . . . is there any reason why not? It's just some old video stuff. Most likely broken. Who would want it?"

Caleb reaches gently into the box and holds something up. It's a small, rectangular gray box with a button in the shape of a cross on the left side and two red buttons on the right. A wire connects it to a larger gray box in the carton, surrounded by large plastic slabs with colorful names on them.

"Ted, look at this!"

"Wow," I whisper. "Never seen one of those in person."

"So is someone going to let me in on this, or is one of you about to call that thing 'my preciousss' and fight to the death over it?" Isabel asks with a smirk.

I give her major points for the LOTR reference but take something off her score for the smirk.

"Wow. There's something you actually know nothing about?" I say.

"Just tell me what it is already, okay?"

I can tell she's about to walk out the door again, which would be fine, but I also know I'm being a jerk.

"Sorry. It's an old Nintendo gaming system. It's like a classic. I never in a million years thought Great-Uncle Ted would be into this."

"Well, it has to be his," Caleb says, turning the remote over. "He wrote his name on it and everything."

There, plain as anything, is "Wakabayashi" written in black marker.

"You think this was his buried treasure?" Caleb says softly, going over the various games in the box.

"Maybe . . . ," I say. "He did mention something in the will about how I liked puzzles. And video games are kind of puzzles. Maybe this is all he meant."

"I don't think so."

We both look up at Isabel. She has a thoughtful expression on her face.

"You said it was *buried* treasure. This was right out in the open."

"Well, Caleb was kind of dramatizing when he said that. He actually said I've been given all the treasure this room contains, but I'd have to search for it."

"Still, we didn't have to search for it too hard. I say he was referring to something else."

"Yeah, well, you certainly would know what my great-uncle was thinking, you two being so close and all," I snap.

"Whatever. I was just trying to— Forget it."

I watch as the immaculate jeans of Isabel Archer walk back out the door into the California sunshine. I'm probably being a jerk again, but I'm not in the mood to be bossed around.

From the other side of the room, Caleb calls out: "Do you think there are any old comic books? He must have *some* old comic books, right?"

The other thing about Caleb, besides his ability to draw really well, is his dream.

His dream is to one day own a copy of Amazing Adventure #1.

What makes this particular comic book more important, than say, Detective Comics #2, #3, #4, etc.? Or any other comic book, for that matter?

It so happens that this is the comic book that features the origin story for a group of special crime fighters, the Alloys! (not that I'm so excited about this—the exclamation part is part of their name).

I should back up a second and explain what an alloy is. The only reason I know is because of something that happened to me when I was eight years old. I was the only kid in my class whose parents were of different races, and for some reason this rubbed one kid in particular, Morrie Friedman, the wrong way.

Morrie Friedman's father owned the Miracle Delicatessen in La Purisma ("If your sandwich tastes great . . . it's a Miracle!"). That day we had been discussing Passover, and the teacher asked the kids in the class who were Jewish to raise their hands, so I did.

Well, during recess, Morrie Friedman started in on me, telling me that no way should I have raised my hand since I wasn't Jewish because my mother wasn't Jewish, that I was only *half* Jewish, so I wasn't as good as he was.

I was pretty upset about all this, and told my mom, who just stroked my hair and said she was sorry. That didn't make me feel much better, but that night my dad came into my room and sat on my bed and told me about alloys.

He told me that the pure metals, like iron and nickel and zinc, aren't all that strong—they break easily, and aren't useful in their pure state. It wasn't until men began combining metals, creating bronze, that civilization moved forward. Think of the skyscrapers and bridges that never would have been built without alloys like steel. He went on to tell me that it was a scientific fact that these combined metals, or alloys, are stronger, more useful, and far more valuable than any pure metal on its own.

I'm pretty sure my genius sister would have known exactly what was going on, but I'm not Lila, so I had to ask him what that had to do with me. That's when he said that I was like an alloy, the combination of two ancient and proud cultures brought together to create something that can be stronger, better, and more useful than anyone else.

I asked him if this included Morrie Friedman, and he said, laughing, "Especially Morrie Friedman, whose father wouldn't know a good bagel if it fell on him."

I never knew if my father read this somewhere (like a book called *Things to Say to Your Half-Jewish, Half-Asian Son When Some Jerk Makes Him Feel Like Dirt*) or if he made it up himself, but I've never heard him talk this way before or since.

Of course, the comic-book Alloys! had nothing to do with being Jewish (at least, I don't think so). It was about these three scientists trying to combine certain elements together to make an unbreakable, all-powerful alloy. There's some kind of accident involving radiation (I know; there's *always* some kind of accident involving radiation in these comics—it was the 1960s, what do you want?), and each scientist is transformed into a being made of pure metal. There's Mr. Mercury, who is super fast; the Tin Man, who is super flexible; and Iron Girl, who is super strong.

Whenever I tell anyone about this, they always say,

"Wouldn't it have been funny if Iron Girl got together with Iron Man and had little Iron babies?" Guess what? I thought of that first. I already told it to Caleb, who said, "That wouldn't happen, Ted. Iron Girl is actually made of iron, but Iron Man is just a rich guy in a metal suit. He's not actually made of iron."

When it comes to the Alloys! Caleb takes everything very seriously.

At some point in every story, of course, they realize that they can't defeat the villain individually, so they combine their powers to create a super superhero, Alloy, who kicks the butt of whichever villain they ripped off from Marvel Comics that month. The whole series lasted about six issues and then disappeared. So why did Caleb want issue #1 so badly?

When his parents split, his dad gave him his comics collection from when *he* was a kid, and it had all the Amazing Adventure issues except #1. So now Caleb haunts eBay, comic-book stores, every corner of the Internet. I know it sounds stupid, but I think in some way he believes that if he finds that issue and completes the set, somehow his life will get back to the way it was, and his dad will come to his senses, stop acting so weird, leave Gina, and go back to his mom.

Mom says I psychoanalyze people too much.

I think the likelihood of Caleb's dad coming back is probably the same as the likelihood of Caleb's finding a copy of a comic that wasn't all that good to begin with, a comic that no one in his right mind would want to save. But of course I would never tell Caleb that. If he wants to look for it, why not let him?

So I say, "Hey, you never know. Knock yourself out."

Meanwhile, I know that I have to do something about the Isabel situation. And believe me, it is a situation. If my mom and dad find out that I insulted the daughter of my dad's boss and hurt her feelings, I'll never hear the end of it.

What's needed is a peace offering.

I look around the room, and it hits me like a thunderbolt. Sometimes I'm so smart I surprise myself.

"Wow, Caleb," I say loudly. "Look at *all those old books* in that *bookshelf* over there."

A head peeks around the doorframe. I smile and gesture to a large bookshelf against a wall. Isabel stares at it, transfixed.

I see the look in her eyes. "You know, if you want any books, help yourself. I don't think they're valuable or anything, but—"

Isabel has already jumped over a carton of old bags of rice and is peering at the titles excitedly. "Thanks, this is awesome. I just love looking at old collections of books. They tell you so much about a person."

Crisis averted.

"It looks like your great-uncle was into World War Two," Isabel observes as she wipes some dust off a couple of the volumes.

"Yeah, he served in the war, apparently. My dad said something when we were heading to the reading of the will, how he was a war hero. It's kind of weird, though. . . ." I let my voice trail off.

Caleb looks up. "What's weird?"

"My mom said he never wanted to talk about the war. He always seemed to act like he wanted to forget it. So—"

"Why does he have so many books about something he wanted to forget?" Isabel finishes my thought. "That is kind of funny. But they don't look like they've been opened in years."

"So why didn't he just throw them out?" I wonder.

"Take a look around," Caleb laughs. "Does it look like he ever threw *anything* out?"

He's right. If the apartment resembles anything, it looks like a setting for some crazy escape-the-room game, what with all the random junk piled up all over the place.

I'm happily surprised that for the next half hour or so, Isabel helps me separate things into piles while Caleb searches in vain for his ever-elusive Amazing Adventure #1. We even find a couple of old matchbooks with TED'S WINE & SPIRITS on them. If we don't find anything else, maybe Mr. Yamada would like those. Most of the stuff, especially the clothes and the old coffeemakers and things from the liquor store, we'll send to Goodwill.

Out the window, there's the sound of a car pulling into the driveway. Just from the hum of the well-tuned engine, I can tell it's Isabel's dad.

Isabel gets up and brushes some nonexistent dirt off her jeans. "I guess that's my father."

Caleb drops his twentieth stack of magazines. "Well, that's good. I don't know about you guys, but I need a break."

I stand up and wipe the sweat and grime off my face with my shirt. Then I remember that Isabel is right there, and that it's probably not the smoothest thing I've ever done.

I look over at Caleb, with his drenched hair and sweat-stained T-shirt, then back at Isabel.

There isn't even a hint of sweat. I'm telling you, this is *weird*.

I'm not sure how to leave things, but I manage to say, "Umm . . . well, thanks for helping out. It was a real . . . help. . . ."

"Hey! Maybe you could come by tomorrow?" Caleb adds, sounding like he means it.

Isabel looks out the window at her dad. She keeps looking as she replies, "I don't think so. We're kind of busy, you know, unpacking at the house and stuff."

I try to find some way of keeping the conversation going. "So . . . if we find anything, we'll tell you in the fall when we see you at school, okay?"

Isabel turns away.

"Maybe."

"What? So you're going to pretend you don't know us once school starts?" Caleb snorts.

"Caleb! Chill out!" I say a little more sharply than I mean to.

"It's not that," Isabel falters. "It's just that . . . well . . . my old school back east is holding a space for me. I haven't decided yet whether I want to stay here with my father and go to a new school or stay with my friend's family and go back to St. Anselm's."

Whew.

"Okay . . . well, good luck with that," I say. Lame.

"Thanks. It was a lot of fun meeting you two."

"Hey, I know! Maybe we can keep up on Instagram?" Caleb throws out as Isabel heads for the door.

"Oh, I'm not on Instagram, but thanks for asking," Isabel says, putting the last nail in the coffin. There's a deep, rich beep from the car below (even the car horn sounds expensive), and with a little wave, Isabel Archer is gone.

CHAPTER 7

THE GAME OF TED 1.0

Of course, tonight at dinner, the last thing I want to do is talk about Isabel, so that's the *only* thing my mom and dad seemed interested in.

As soon as we sit down, Mom clasps her hands and stares at me, trying far too hard not to smile.

"So . . . that Isabel girl seemed nice," she throws out.

I say a silent prayer of thanks that Lila isn't here. My life would be a living hell with my big sister hearing that I spent the day with a girl.

Dad starts. "Since her name is Isabel Archer, of course I asked if she was intelligent and excited!"

"Artie," my mom laughs.

That's it.

"Can someone please explain this reference to the moron at the table?" I ask. "I thought that Graham guy was going to deck you when you said that, but he just laughed."

"It's from *The Portrait of a Lady* by Henry James," says Dad. "Isabel Archer is the name of the main character. And when she's first introduced in the story, and gazes out onto the lawn in this English estate, she's described as 'intelligent and excited.'"

Naturally, my mom feels compelled to add, "If you had been paying attention during the last twelve years, you would know that your father always makes his students discuss that phrase when he teaches the book."

Dad, good old Dad, tries to change the subject. "So tell us! Did you find anything? Any treasures?"

"Nope. We mostly made lists of what was there. Like five huge bags of rice stacked up in a corner. Who keeps things like that?"

"Your great-uncle," sighs my mom, helping herself to the last of the salad.

"Actually, a lot of people who grew up poor tend to keep things. They're so afraid it will all be taken away at some point," Dad says, and takes a sip of lemonade. "But your great-uncle seemed to take that to extremes."

"So what time do you want me to drop you off tomorrow? Did you set a time with Caleb and Isa—"

"Actually," I say as I clear the dishes off the table, "there is no 'and.' Isabel's not coming back. As a matter of fact, she probably isn't even going to go to school here. She said they're keeping a place for her at her old school in New York, and she'll live with some family friends."

"That's too bad," Mom says, frowning in disappointment. "But I guess she needs to do what's right for her."

I deposit the dishes in the sink and head for the stairs.

"Yeah. So is it okay if I go upstairs and lie down? I'm kind of tired."

"Of course, darling," my mom calls after me. "Get some rest!"

When I get to my room, instead of hopping on the bed, I fall into my desk chair and turn on my laptop.

An escape game or two is just what I need right now. At least *they* always make sense in the end, no matter how strange or mysterious they seem when you first start them.

Life isn't so neat. Caleb's dad isn't going to magically become a good guy again, and Isabel isn't going to stick around and go to some junky old public school in the middle of boring old San Fernando Valley when she could be living in New York City and going to some cool private school.

And what do I care, anyway?

The familiar browser window opens, my doorway to an hour or two of riddles that have solutions, in a world where treasure is *always* behind the last door.

I navigate to one of my favorite pages, looking for something new to play. Blinking in the corner, with a Click Here button beckoning me, is a game I've never heard of before.

"Time to play *The Game of Ted*!" the colorful graphics proclaim.

To tell the truth, I'm not that surprised to see a game with my name on it.

I've played *Dead Ted,* about a zombie; *Ted or Alive,* about a chase after a master criminal; even *Teddy or Not* (my least favorite), a dating game for girls, for which I got endless grief at school.

I click on the button and a welcome screen appears as the

game loads in. It says in bright curling letters: "Solve the Mystery! Solve the Puzzles! Find the Treasure!"

As the bar reaches 100%, I click on the Start button and see with a jolt of pleasure that it's an escape game.

An escape game with my name on it! Awesome.

The first room opens, and—

It's an apartment.

Crammed with boxes.

I move my mouse and notice my hand trembling slightly.

It can't be.

Yet there it is. In the corner, stacked up under a sheet, are bags of rice. And when I click over into another part of the room, the screen reveals a shelf of World War II books.

I rub my eyes. This can't be happening.

The game is clearly set in my great-uncle's apartment.

Now I'm actually shaking. This is much too weird. I get up from my desk, thinking hard. Caleb certainly could have drawn it—he can draw anything. But he knows nothing about game design. Besides, making these things take days ... weeks, even.

For a second I consider Isabel. She's smart enough, that's for sure. But she seems to hate computers. Is it all an act?

Unlikely. It doesn't matter anyway. I've never played an escape game that I couldn't beat.

I just need to approach it like any other game: as a set of problems to be solved. So what if it looks like my great-uncle's apartment? It's just another game, and I'm going to beat it.

I hold my breath and press the Start button.

As I'm clicking around the screen, the view changes angles, as if I'm walking through the actual apartment.

I think back to all the rooms I've visited in the games I've played. The bedrooms, living rooms, garages, laboratories I've been trapped in—even a mummy's crypt in one corny game I played once when I was bored.

I click under the rice bags and a coin appears and lands in my inventory. I keep clicking away, finding more and more clues, when a thought strikes me.

What if this isn't just a game?

What if these clues are actually *in* the apartment?

I push my chair back so violently it tips over, and I end up on the floor in a heap. The crash is loud enough to attract attention, and I hear footsteps coming up the stairs.

"Ted? Are you okay?" Mom's voice. Concerned.

"Yeah, Mom!" I yell, a little too loudly and cheerfully. "Must have slipped!"

"Are you sure?" Her footsteps are outside the door now. She pauses as she turns the knob.

I lunge for the keyboard and minimize the window just as she opens the door. She peers in to find me sprawled across the chair, scrambling to my feet.

"Teddy, you're exhausted. I *told* your father it was too much work for three kids! I'm going online and finding people who clean out houses."

"Don't! Mom, please! I want to do this!"

Mom leans her head to one side and holds my face in her hands. I know it's stupid, but I kind of love when she does this.

"Ted Gerson. Since when are you so into lifting boxes and cleaning up filthy old apartments? You don't even pick up your underwear."

She's right. I have to think of something convincing.

"It's not that girl, is it?" Mom says, smiling.

Oh, for crying out loud.

"Would you just drop that! She's not even coming back, remember?"

"So what's the appeal of cleaning out all the junk of some relative you barely knew?"

I sit on the bed. My laptop glows behind my mom, beckoning me.

"The thing is . . . he left that stuff to me. I just know there's more there than it seems."

Mom sits down next to me and rests her head on my shoulder.

"Teddy . . . I knew him as well as anyone. He was a wonderful man, but a little strange. He probably thought all those old newspapers and things *were* a treasure of some kind."

"Maybe so, but Caleb agrees with me. There might be stuff we could put on eBay or something. I could save up for college."

"Okay. Just promise me you won't work too hard."

"It's kind of nice, Mom. I didn't know him, but I'm getting to know him after he's gone, through his stuff. We'll just poke around a little more and see if anything's there."

"I'll make you a deal," Mom says, rising and going to the door. "You have till the end of the week. Then I call Goodwill and they can cart whatever they want away. Sound fair?"

"Perfect." I give her what I hope looks like an "I love you so much, my understanding mother" smile while she leaves the room, and wait until I hear the click of the door and her footsteps heading downstairs before opening the screen again.

Still there.

I look over my inventory list.

I start putting the pieces where I know they have to go, and just like other games, one set of clues leads to others, and I know I'll be able to solve this in a matter of seconds.

And then something happens.

Or rather, it doesn't.

I *know* I have to put the books in a bookcase in a certain sequence. But no matter how many ways I try it, no matter how many times I put them in, nothing happens.

I've played enough of these games to know exactly what to do.

But somehow, it isn't working.

I look at the clock. It's two in the morning. I've been playing the game for five hours! It feels like minutes. And I still haven't solved it.

My eyes keep drifting to the corner of the screen where the yellow button marked Walkthrough taunts me.

Just press me, it coos. *All your questions will be answered.*

It's a point of pride. Ted Gerson has never, in hundreds of these games, had to use a walkthrough.

I know I'm missing something. But as the minutes tick by, I start to make the grim realization that to learn what I need to know, history has to be made.

Gritting my teeth, I press the Walkthrough button.

The screen changes, and there it is: a numbered set of steps, taking me through the game.

I skip over most of the steps, which are (as I knew they would be) exactly what I've already done, and stop when I get to the bookshelf. In the walkthrough, it's full of books. But in *my* game, there's a space in the shelf.

There was a book here in the walkthrough. With a green cover.

A glitch? The one and only time I give in and use a walk-through, and the freaking thing doesn't even work?

I don't finish the walkthrough. No point. I close the laptop in disgust.

CHAPTER 8

AN INTELLIGENT
AND EXCITED RETURN

"I *told* you I was leaving in five minutes." Dad's fingers are drumming on the steering wheel.

I jump into the passenger seat, simultaneously trying not to choke to death on a major bite of toast and texting Caleb to let him know we're on our way.

I barely have enough time to slam the car door before Dad pulls out of the driveway.

"You know I have to get to the office. The 405 gets totally blocked, especially on hot days," Dad says, easing into traffic. As usual, it's slow going, even though it's already after ten.

"Well, you're not going to like this, but—"

"I'm *not* going to stop for breakfast."

"Sorry, Dad. Caleb's dad stranded him, so we've got to swing by and pick him up."

"*What?* Oh . . . okay . . ." My dad's face sets into a hard expression. I think he's a little fed up with his friend, but he won't say so in front of me.

As Dad turns off the freeway and heads toward Caleb's house, I see something that fills me with happiness. "A doughnut store!"

"I guess I could use some more coffee," sighs Dad, slowing down at the entrance.

A little while later, goodies in hand, we swing into Caleb's driveway.

"Doughnuts! Awesome!" Caleb declares as he slides into the backseat behind me. He reaches for the bag and peers in. "Chocolate cream! My favorite!" He leans back against the seat, eyes closed, mouth full of doughnut, then smears some of the chocolate icing on his upper lip. He pushes his glasses down his nose and says in his best (in other words, worst) English accent, "My eternal gratitude, good sir. You are a gentleman and a scholar. And now, to the apartment, I say!"

Even Dad has to smile.

Seeing Caleb in such a silly mood is so great. And thus the gauntlet has been thrown. I look into the now-empty bag and see the powdered sugar that has settled at the bottom. I pour the bag on my head, dusting my hair white. "Now, now, no need to hurry, Jeeves. This whippersnapper needs to learn to slow down!" I croak.

I am a riot.

Caleb cracks up as Dad shakes his head in disgust. "All I know is you're cleaning all that mess off the seats," he says as he pulls into the dusty parking lot.

We pile out of the car, Caleb with his chocolate mustache and me with powdered sugar in my hair.

Which wouldn't be embarrassing in the least if a certain

young woman in spotless khaki pants and a perfect button-down weren't waiting for us by the steps leading to the apartment.

"Isabel!" Dad says. "We weren't expecting to see you today!"

"So it seems," says Isabel, trying her best not to look at me and Caleb.

I quickly shake the white stuff from my hair. Out of the corner of my eye, I see Caleb frantically wiping his upper lip with the bottom of his T-shirt, leaving a lovely brown stain. Somehow, even though I know it's just chocolate, it's gross. I silently point this out to Caleb, who hurriedly tucks his shirt into his pants.

Dad, master of small talk, brings up exactly the thing I wish he wouldn't. "Ted mentioned last night that you're going back to your old school in the fall—"

Isabel shoots me a look. It's the first time she's even glanced my way, and it isn't the cheerful greeting I hoped for.

"I'm so glad your son has figured that out for me. To be honest, I haven't decided yet."

I'm not sure if being discussed in the third person while standing right here is worse than being ignored. I decide it is.

"That's not exactly what I said. I said you're *probably* going back. Sorry if I misunderstood you. Oh, and good morning."

Isabel smiles and shrugs. "No worries. Just wanted to clear it up. And good morning to you too."

Dad looks at his watch and sighs. "Terrific. Now I'm never going to get a space on campus." He makes a small bow. "I hope you don't mind my saying that I think it's wonderful you're named after a character in a Henry James novel!"

"It was my mother's idea, actually," Isabel says in a soft voice.

Clueless, Dad continues, "Your mom sounds like she's— I mean, was . . . I mean—"

Isabel lets my dad off the hook. "Yes, I consider it a gift."

"As well you should!" my dad calls as he heads back to the car. He gets in and drives off.

I stand there trying to decide whether to ask Isabel why she came back.

Maybe it's better to just leave it be.

Caleb has other ideas. "Thought you were outta here."

"My father kind of strongly suggested I come back and help you. He thought I was being rude."

"You weren't being rude!" Caleb yelps. "I just assumed that was your personality!"

I can definitely do better than that.

"It's great you're here!" I say brightly. "I mean, it'll be great to have an extra pair of lips."

Isabel stares at me.

"What?" I ask.

"You just said it's great to have an extra pair of lips," Isabel says, trying to keep a straight face.

"I did not! I said 'an extra pair of hands.'"

"Dude," Caleb chuckles, "you totally said 'an extra pair of lips.'"

"Will you two excuse me?" I ask. "I'm going to go upstairs to the second-floor balcony and throw myself to my death."

"Is he always this dramatic?" I hear Isabel ask as I'm heading away.

"Not usually. That was pretty lame, right? I mean, if you threw yourself off a second-floor balcony, you wouldn't die anyway. Maybe break a few bones . . ."

"Are you two coming up or what?" I yell.

"You *do* have the key, right?" Isabel says as they climb up behind me.

"Of course I have the key. I did say 'the key,' right? Or did I say 'the lips'?" I mutter, opening the door.

And I see my great-uncle's apartment again, looking just the way it did in the game I played last night.

The game.

"Ted! What's up?" Caleb asks as I stand there, mouth open, not moving.

I must have fallen asleep. Dreamed the game up. Sure. I *was* exhausted. . . .

"My dad's coming back in a few hours," Isabel says. "Shouldn't we get to work?"

I am standing, frozen, still staring at the corner of the room, as if something is going to jump out of the refrigerator.

"Ted, you're weirding us out," Caleb says.

I would have seen it yesterday, right? Then again, I didn't move all the bags out of the way yesterday. Maybe . . . *It's easy,* I tell myself. *I'll just move the last bag, and there won't be a coin taped to the bag, and then I'll know I was dreaming.*

Caleb and Isabel watch as I slowly move bags of rice out of the way until I get to the one leaning against the wall.

I feel my chest tighten.

The bag has a logo printed on it, under the words *Tokyo Fine Rice.* A small circular logo with a carp in it. But this logo has something else. A coin is taped over it.

A small silver coin with a sheaf of wheat, a shield, and the word *Italia* on it.

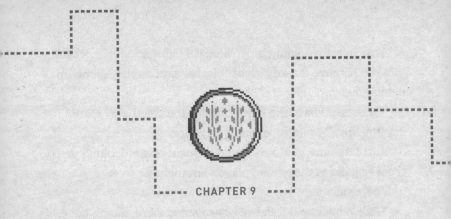

CHAPTER 9

JUST WALKING THROUGH

I take the coin off the bag and move into the center of the room.

"Wow! That's kind of random," Isabel remarks.

"Weird . . . but I guess old guys do weird things, huh, Ted?" Caleb adds, trying to snap me out of it.

"I wouldn't necessarily call it weird," I answer, heading for the old desk. It's covered in clutter, everything from old broken watches and coffee cans filled with pennies to dried-up soy sauce containers.

"Let's just imagine," I begin, "that this is a game. You know, something my great-uncle set up. There's always something in the desk, right, Caleb?"

I push the chair out of the way and pull at the first drawer. It's locked, as it's supposed to be. And I know what I'll find under the second drawer. I pull it out and feel underneath.

There's a second coin taped there. I hold it up and show the others. This one is a dull silver color, with a double-sided ax on it and the words *Etat Français*.

Isabel's eyes widen. "How did you—"

Caleb nods. "Ted just knows these things. But, Ted, you really think that . . . ?"

I walk to the opposite corner of the room. "And where there's a rug, there's usually—"

I reach under a tatty shag rug covering the stained floor.

Both Isabel and Caleb can see a third coin. "Whoa," Caleb breathes. I look at Isabel, expecting her to be impressed at my brilliance.

Isabel's cheeks are reddening. For the first time, there's a crack in her composure. "But how did he—"

"Ted is the best there is at these kinds of games," Caleb says, his eyes glued to me as I head into the bathroom.

"What kind of games?"

"Escape-the-room games. You have to figure out how to get out of a locked room by collecting items hidden around the place. If his uncle made something like that, Ted will figure it out."

I flush the toilet.

I emerge with a fourth coin.

"Oh, gross," Isabel says, making a face.

"What? All I did was flush so that the water would empty the tank behind the bowl, and then reach in and see if anything was there," I tell them, holding up the fourth coin. "And it was."

"That is disgusting," Isabel says. "I hope you washed your hands."

I put the last coin next to the other three. Each is from a

different country, and the last one has a large eagle on its back, with a swastika above it.

"These are from World War Two, aren't they?" asks Isabel.

"I think so," I say, clearing the debris from the desk.

"Maybe they're rare coins!" suggests Caleb excitedly. "Maybe this is the treasure we're looking for!"

"C'mon, Caleb. If he set the room up like a game, would that really be the end of it?" With that, I pick up the last newspaper on the desk. There are four neat flat, rounded grooves carved in the desktop underneath, just big enough to put the coins in. Caleb's eyes get wide as he sidles closer to see what I'm doing.

Carefully, I place the coins in the graves. I have to make this look convincing. Like I'm doing it for the first time. So I do it wrong on purpose. Austria . . . France . . . Germany . . . Italy.

"Why are you putting them like that?" demands Isabel. Clearly she gets a little snippy when she doesn't know something.

"I just noticed these grooves in the desk," I lie, peering intently at the desktop. "See how the coins fit?"

"So he's trying alphabetical order," Caleb says, peering over my shoulder.

Nothing happens.

"I'll try another combination at random," I say.

This time I do the right combination: Italy . . . France . . . Austria . . . Germany . . .

I put the last coin in. There's a soft *click* and the top of the desk releases, on a hinge. I lift it up. Underneath is a small chrome lamp.

"Cool," says Caleb, his eyes bright with excitement.

Isabel backs away. She holds her arms tightly across her chest, looking back and forth between me and Caleb.

"Okay, you've had your fun. I guess you had a real blast thinking this one up."

"What are you talking about?" I ask.

"This whole thing," Isabel continues. "You know, acting strange . . . and then the whole trick with the coins. How long did it take you to rig that? I've got to hand it to you, you had me going for a while."

I roll my eyes. Two can play at this game. "Why the heck would we plan to prank you when you *told* us you weren't coming back? That makes no sense."

Isabel sits looking at the floor for what feels like forever. Then her arms relax.

"I . . . guess that's true . . . ," she says in a small voice.

"Hey, I was freaked out too, if that helps any," Caleb chimes in.

Isabel looks at me searchingly. "So . . . if you didn't plan all this . . . how did you know about the coins?"

Now is the time to tell them about the game. Normally, I'd tell Caleb in a heartbeat. But Isabel . . . well, I don't know her. What if she doesn't believe me? What if she thinks I'm crazy? Tells my parents? Yeah, she's the type who would. Better to keep it to myself for now.

"Like I said, Great-Uncle Ted even mentioned puzzles in the will. I know it sounds crazy, but I woke up this morning and I just wondered if—"

"—your great-uncle set up the room like a puzzle to be solved!" Caleb finishes my thought, his voice rising.

"I dunno . . . I just started looking at the room the way I

look at the games I play on the computer, and started thinking about what it would be like if it *was* a game, and—"

"You mean you were able to figure out where the coins were, and where they were supposed to go and everything, just because you play a lot of these games?" Isabel says breathlessly.

"Yep. Ted really is like a genius at these games. He hasn't lost one yet."

"Wow," Isabel says.

I decide I like the look on her face. Not admiration, exactly. Not yet. No, it's more like the kind of look you get when you watch a clip of a dog opening a refrigerator on YouTube. Like you can't actually believe a creature that dumb is doing something that smart.

Like I said, not exactly admiration, but I'll take what I can get.

I hold up the chrome light.

"No bulb." I turn to Caleb. Why not make him look smart too, right?

"Probably a bulb somewhere in a locked drawer or something?" He starts pulling drawers open.

"Maybe . . ." I squint. I pretend to look around the room, knowing full well where the bulb is and how to get it. The hard part is making it look convincing. "But I just got one of the coins from a drawer."

Caleb stops and fills in the rest of my thought. "And they never repeat the same gag twice within five actions."

I look around the room, hands on hips. Finally, I let my gaze settle on the calendar tacked to the wall. The image up top is titled *The Beauty of Hawaii.*

"That's kind of strange," I muse out loud.

Caleb shrugs. "So what? It's a calendar. Lots of people have calendars."

Isabel approaches it. "It's from 1986! Why keep a calendar from 1986?"

"That's what I was wondering." I nod.

"And not a speck of dust on it! June eighteenth is circled in red, and in the circle are the letters 'NG,'" Isabel reports. She looks at me like I will know what that means.

Like I'm smart.

It's a great feeling, I decide.

Caleb starts guessing. "'NG' could mean a lot of things, I guess. . . . No good, need gas . . . or just the initials of someone he was meeting."

"Yeah . . . but if it *was* some kind of clue, it would refer to something in the room," I hint, trying hard not to blurt out what the answer is.

"The calendar's hung right next to the sink. Maybe something in the kitchen? Nut grater?" Isabel starts going through the cupboards, pulling out gadgets. She even checks under the drawers.

All of a sudden, she looks up, alarm written on her face. "Oh, no! I just realized something! What if whatever we're looking for was in the fridge! Your mother threw everything out!"

"Yikes! That's right!" Caleb looks panicked.

Isabel's eyes narrow at me. "Wait a minute. How come you don't seem disappointed?"

"It's just that I don't think he'd leave it in the fridge. He'd have to have set up the game a long time ago, so it can't be perishable. We're ignoring the most important part of this. It's a calendar. From 1986. There has to be something else in this room from 1986."

Caleb and Isabel look around the chaos of the apartment.

"Half the stuff here could be from 1986," Caleb moans.

"Yeah . . . but it would have to be marked from 1986 for us to find it, right?" Isabel answers, scanning the room. Suddenly, her eyes light up.

"Magazines and newspapers! You think?"

She looks at me for approval. This is far more fun than I ever expected. I smile. I have to admit, Isabel is pretty good at this.

A look of hopelessness fills her face. "It would take weeks to go through all these. . . ."

Caleb catches me smirking. "He's already figured it out. I know that expression."

"Well . . . ," I say slowly. "Most of this stuff is kind of random. When we were going through everything yesterday, I noticed only one group of magazines that was carefully in order." I oh-so-casually shift my glance to a tower of yellow.

" 'NG.' *National Geographic*," Caleb groans. "Of course. It's so obvious."

"You *actually* think your great-uncle went to all this trouble?" Isabel asks skeptically.

"Only one way to find out," I say, putting my finger on the spines of the magazines. "1984 . . . '85 . . . '86 . . . January, February . . . June! Here it is."

The two others crowd around me as I pull it out. There's a beautiful orchid on the cover, along with the legend *This Issue: The Flowers of Hawaii.*

Isabel laughs. It's not her grown-up laugh either. It's more like she's a kid, just like us. "Wow. You'll make a believer of me yet."

Caleb grabs for the magazine. "Let me guess! June eighteenth was circled. So try page eighteen."

I pull it away from him and thumb through the issue to the right page. There in ink, in the margin, is written "9554."

Caleb looks back at the calendar and smiles. He maneuvers his way over to it and carefully removes it from the wall. Behind it is a small safe. With four numbered wheels.

He enters the code into the wheels and the door swings open.

"Uncle T, you made this too easy. Even I knew that one," crows Caleb. He reaches in and pulls out a bulb and a scrap of paper. Examining the paper, Caleb looks annoyed. "It's blank."

"Bring them here," I instruct Caleb. Carefully, I plug the lamp into the wall and screw the bulb in. It glows with a faint purple light.

"I should have known," Caleb groans.

"What is it?" Isabel asks, looking down as I hold the paper under the light.

Like magic, a series of numbers appears.

"UV light," Caleb answers. "You see it in games all the time. The ink only shows up under ultraviolet light. That's like the easiest thing in the world and I missed it."

"'475, 570, 400, 510, 650,'" I read off. "It's a series of some kind. . . ."

"What has three numbers?" Isabel asks. "It's not a date. Could be a serial number or something? Maybe on one of these old radios?"

"I got it!" Caleb says proudly. "You move the hands of that

clock on the wall to all these times, in sequence. That's so old. It's like in practically every other game!"

Oh, poor, sad deluded Caleb.

I break it to him gently. "Only one problem. There isn't any time that's 475 . . . or 570."

Isabel peers closely at the page. "Turn it over," she suggests. "There!" She points. "There's something else written on the back!" Unlike Caleb, Isabel doesn't seem to miss a thing.

"I *never* remember to look on the back," mutters Caleb, shaking his head. He reads out what's typed on the back. "'540.45 DDS.'"

"That one's easy," Isabel chirps. "It's referring to a science book." Both Caleb and I stare at Isabel openmouthed.

I know from Google that it's a book, and even know which one it is. But how does *she* know?

"Maybe," I say, trying not to sound too impressed.

"How the heck are you so sure about that?" marvels Caleb.

"It's the Dewey decimal system," says Isabel, peering down at the bookshelf. "'540' refers to the sciences. My guess is there's some science book here somewhere that might have the—"

"You know the Dewey decimal system numbers by heart?" I ask incredulously.

Isabel looks at me like I'm the weird one. "Of course. Anyone who spends enough time in a library, you just learn stuff, you know?"

We cross to the grimy bookshelf against the wall on the far side of the apartment. It's immediately clear which book it is. Unlike the others, it isn't covered in dust. It's sitting by itself, on its side. Isabel picks it up and reads the title out loud:

"*'Ultraviolet and Visible Spectroscopy: Chemical Applications* by C. N. R. Rao.'"

She looks up at us. "One page is dog-eared."

Isabel turns to the page and reports, "It's a chart." She reads from the bottom: "'The visible spectrum, as divided by wavelength.' Yep, the numbers seem to be similar to what's here." She looks up at me quizzically. "But how do we use them?"

"Whoa, slow down," Caleb says, peering at the book over her shoulder. "What exactly do the numbers correspond to?"

"The colors in the visible spectrum. Each number seems to represent a different color."

Something clicks with Caleb. "Yeah, there was something like this in a game called *Escape the Lab*. Remember?"

I nod. "You set up glasses in such a way that the colored liquids in them corresponded to the order in the note."

Caleb looks around. "The only problem is that there are no test tubes . . . or bottles . . . or prisms . . . or anything I can see that would make different colors."

Isabel puts the book down and does a quick search. "Nope, nothing."

"So glad you agree," Caleb says.

"I was just making sure," Isabel retorts.

Time to change the subject.

"Guys! Guys! Who says it has to be liquid? Or even light? Maybe it just refers to the order of the colors."

I reach down and pull off some books that are stacked on their sides. There behind them on the shelf is a series of books with different-colored jackets.

My heart starts to beat a little faster. This is where the walk-through let me down.

Where *is* that last book?

I kneel down, and the others join me.

"Caleb, read off the numbers on the paper. Isabel, find the corresponding color, and we'll see what happens. . . . What's the first number?"

Caleb goes to the desk and peers at the paper under the light.

"475," he reports.

"475 nanometers . . . that's blue!" Isabel calls out excitedly.

I pull out the colored books and replace the blue-covered book first.

"570."

"That's yellow!"

"400."

"Violet!"

I feel my hands go damp. I know what's coming next.

"510."

"Green!"

I search the bookcase, just like I did the night before in the game. As I know only too well, there is no green book.

"Uh, guys . . . there's no green book," I sigh, sitting back on my heels. So the walkthrough really was accurate. No book. Now what?

There's silence in the room. Then, unexpectedly, laughter.

Isabel is laughing. But this time, it's her annoying, grown-up, "I know something you don't know" laugh. "Oh my gosh! Who would have thought?"

"What?" I ask irritably.

"Remember yesterday, when you said I could take home any book I liked?"

"Yeah . . ." The truth begins to dawn on me.

"You don't mean . . . ," Caleb says.

Isabel goes to her backpack and fishes around. She pulls out something and holds it in front of her.

"Shakespeare's sonnets. I always wanted a nice copy, so I took it home."

It's covered in a beautiful green jacket. So that's it.

Caleb takes the book and riffles through it. "So after you read these, you can tell us if they're any good."

I'm still trying to figure out how the game knew the book wasn't in the room, so I'm only half listening to the following conversation: "They're amazing. Some of the greatest poems ever written."

"Wait . . . you've actually read all these?"

Isabel nods. "That's nothing. There was a guy at my school who memorized them."

"Whoa." Caleb whistles. "That's some punishment. What did he do? Set fire to the girls' bathroom or something?"

"It wasn't a punishment," Isabel says simply. "He wanted to do it. It was fun."

That last sentence hangs in the air, refusing to go anywhere, like a fart in an elevator.

Finally, Caleb, master of knowing exactly what not to say, pipes up. "Ted can burp the entire alphabet." This is said with exactly the right mixture of pride and awe that Caleb must think will make any New York City private-school girl gasp in admiration.

But somehow, amazingly, Isabel looks less than impressed.

I realize it's time for me to take back control of the situation.

Carefully, I place the green book next to the others. "What's the last number?" I ask, eyeing the remaining volumes.

"650," Caleb says, his voice hardly above a whisper.

"That's red," Isabel adds, her voice trembling with excitement.

"Here goes nothing," I say as I slide the final book into place.

CHAPTER 10

NOT JUST A GAME

There is a creaking noise, and I jump back as the entire bookshelf seems to close in on itself.

It takes a moment for me to realize it's actually hinged in the middle, and some catch has been released.

Holding my breath, I gently push against the center books, and the whole thing pivots, pulling back and revealing a small compartment.

In the center is a wooden chest. I'm about to reach in, when—

"I don't think you wanna do that."

I turn and see Caleb crouched down next to me. He puts his hand on my shoulder. "You have no idea what could happen. It could be booby-trapped. You said your great-uncle was weird."

"But he *wanted* Ted to find it," Isabel says. "Why would he do anything to hurt him?"

"Maybe this wasn't for Ted," Caleb says. "What if someone *else* was looking for it?"

"Then they would have had to get this far." Isabel is getting exasperated.

"Besides, who else would be looking for this?" I ask.

"He might have had enemies," Caleb says.

"You read too many comic books," sniffs Isabel.

I turn back to the little compartment. "Look, I'm the one he left this stuff to. Clearly this was a test to see if I could solve the puzzles. And I did. So—"

"Don't you mean *we* did?" Isabel asks, hands on hips.

Oh, how I hate the hands on hips. Luckily, Caleb has my back. He stares at Isabel incredulously. "You . . . you think Ted couldn't have solved this without your help?"

I look back at her, trying my best not to look cocky. Not sure I succeed.

"I am kind of good at this," I say simply.

"Yeah, I guess so," Isabel admits.

Will wonders never cease?

"So reach in, already."

I put my hand in and feel something hard and smooth. The top of a box. I put my other hand in and gently retrieve it. I carefully bring it over to the window, where there's more light.

It's a wooden box, the kind you might keep jewelry in, but slightly bigger. Hinged in the back, it's secured with a single inlaid lock, with the keyhole showing in the front. On the top is a beautiful hand-carved scene of a tropical beach at sunset. A woman in a grass skirt and lei is resting against a palm tree.

Isabel leans in and takes a deep breath, a small smile forming on her face. "What kind of wood is that? It smells so rich."

I can't resist. "I'm sorry, did I hear right? Is there actually something else you don't know?"

"I wish you would quit that. I already asked you about stuff I don't know. I don't know a *lot* of things," Isabel snaps. "And when people ask me about things I *do* know, I'm nice enough to tell them, as opposed to being a snot rag about it."

I ponder whether anyone has ever called me a snot rag before. I decide they haven't.

And let's face it, I *was* being a snot rag.

"Sorry. I think it's called Koa wood. It's native to Hawaii. My mom has a jewelry box she got there, and it has the same smell."

"So the key's got to be around here somewhere, right?" Caleb starts rushing around the room and pulling at the curtains.

I shake my head. "The key's hidden somewhere else."

"But that can't be the end of the game!" Caleb protests. "And what makes you so sure?"

"Well . . . one of the last things my great-uncle told me before he died was 'The box is only the beginning.' This is where this part of the game ends. Finding the box."

Turning the box over, I let out a small gasp. "And here's our next clue."

Taped under the box is a cigarette lighter. I take it off.

It's an old silver lighter, with a medallion of some kind on the front. The medallion is a six-sided shield, with a hand holding a torch inside it. Scratched into the box where the lighter was attached is a number: 1405.

"I bet you have to hold the box under the UV light!" Isabel pipes up, looking like she's the only one in class who's figured out the answer to a particularly hard question.

"You only use those things *once* in a game. Don't you know anything?" Caleb scoffs.

"Maybe his great-uncle didn't spend all his time playing games like some people. It's worth a shot," grouses Isabel, folding her arms and glaring at Caleb.

I hold the box under the lamp. Nothing.

"See?" crows Caleb.

Snot rag #2.

"Wait, Caleb. It wasn't a total waste of time," I say, trying to make Isabel feel a little better. "Look at the way the number is carved into the surface. It's just hacked in there. Like someone was in a hurry. After all these preparations. It's weird."

"I told you. He had enemies," Caleb says darkly.

"Maybe . . . Right now, we've got to figure out what 1405 refers to."

"It could be a date in a book," Isabel muses, looking over at the shelves. Then, seeing Caleb's look, she immediately adds, "But he wouldn't use books twice. Would he?"

"I don't think so," I say.

"I still say it's got to do with the clock. He was in the military, wasn't he?" asks Caleb.

"They use the twenty-four-hour clock, right?"

"Which would make it 2:05 p.m.," I remark, walking over to the wall clock in the kitchen.

"You watch. He'll enter the time, and a compartment on the back will open, and there will be the key." Caleb smiles at Isabel.

I slowly take the clock off the wall. There's a battery compartment in the back. I carefully set the time. I know from years of playing these games that the trick is to turn the hands to two o'clock and continue to turn it a full twelve hours. *Then* it will be 14:05.

I adjust the minute hand so that it's on the line right after the five-minute mark and listen for the click.

No click.

I turn the clock over and open the battery compartment. Nothing but a pair of old batteries. Not even a note. I shrug. "Sorry, Caleb. No key."

"I don't mean to sound stupid or anything, but could the key just be inside the lighter?" Isabel asks, shifting it in her hand.

I laugh and run over to her side. Sometimes you *can* outsmart yourself.

"Oh, yeah!"

Isabel gives me a look that says *Like I need your approval* and hands the lighter over to me.

"You do it. He was your great-uncle."

I slowly pull the lighter out of its case.

Nothing. Empty.

We stand in silence, contemplating the box and the lighter.

I close my eyes and try to concentrate. It's hard, feeling Isabel looking at me, expecting me to have the answer.

A loud buzzing noise makes us all jump. I realize my phone is vibrating. I pull it out of my pocket and answer.

"Hey, Mom. What's up?" I turn away from the others and take the call into the kitchen.

A few minutes later, I come back and tell the others the news. "Okay, guys, there's been a little change of plan. Apparently the only day the Goodwill people can come before the end of the week is tomorrow. So that means we've got to have this place all ready for them to cart stuff out of here by the time we leave."

"That's impossible! It's noon already!" protests Caleb.

"Then I guess we better get back to work," Isabel says briskly.

"You think we can get this stuff organized in one afternoon?" Caleb asks doubtfully.

" 'The prospect of being hanged focuses the mind wonderfully,' " quips Isabel.

Caleb and I stare at her.

"What? You don't know that quote? It's Samuel Johnson. We used to say it all the time at St. Anselm's the night before a big test if we hadn't studied."

"We just say 'I'm screwed,' " says Caleb, bless him.

As we get out bags and start to throw things in, I wonder about what kinds of friends Isabel has back east, who quote people I've never even heard of.

"What is it again? 'The prospect of being hanged . . . ,' " I begin.

" '—focuses the mind wonderfully,' " Isabel finishes.

"I have to use that one on my dad," I laugh. "He'll love it."

"I think he knows it," Isabel said.

"Yeah, but he doesn't know *I* know it," I add, raising my eyebrows.

The next two hours are a blur of activity as we move stacks of magazines, take what few clothes remain in the closet and fold them, put books in boxes, and neatly pile up all the things that might be of value to someone at Goodwill.

I leave out the box with the old video games, and Isabel's eyes light up when she sees a volume of *Great Short Fiction from the* New Yorker.

"Would it be okay if I took this?" she asks me.

"Sure. Knock yourself out." I check my watch. Mom should be here any minute. I go over to the now-clean desk, with only the Koa wood box sitting on it.

"1405. I guess I'll ask my mom if she knows what it might mean."

"Sure," agrees Caleb. "She knew him better than anybody."

"No!"

We turn to look at Isabel. There's a look of surprise on her face, as if she didn't mean to sound quite so vehement.

"Why not?" I ask.

Isabel's brows knit in concentration. She traces her finger over the box in my hands as she works through her thoughts. "It's just that . . . I think your great-uncle wanted *you* to figure this out. On your own."

"Well, he's already blown that. We've helped him," Caleb says.

"No, we haven't," Isabel persists. "I mean, it's like you said. You let us guess some of the clues, but you knew the answers already, didn't you?"

Isabel looks at me full in the face. I'm glad I don't have to lie to her.

After all, I did know the clues in advance. I just don't have to explain how. "Yeah. These things kind of jump out at you after a while, you know?"

"No, I don't, and neither does Caleb," Isabel laughs. "Don't you see? Your great-uncle knew you had some sort of gift."

"Well, I don't know about that," I begin, feeling my ears getting warm.

"She's right, Ted. You never have to use a walkthrough ever. That's unreal. You just know where the clues are. It's like some sort of spider sense," Caleb adds, turning to Isabel. "He's awesome."

Aw, shucks.

I don't want to hear Isabel's reaction to that. "I just probably spend too much time playing on the computer. That's what my mom says, anyway."

"Whatever. All I know is when I walked into this room, all I saw was a bunch of junk and garbage. You saw patterns and clues that I bet your mom wouldn't have seen in a million years," Isabel says. "Here's what I say: wait at least until tomorrow. We'll all think about that number and see if we can't figure it out."

"We probably should take the box, right?" says Caleb anxiously. "But what about your mom?"

"Yeah. I'm pretty sure she's never seen it before or she would have wanted it," I say, turning it over in my hands. "She'll ask all sorts of questions. Better not tell her yet."

"Stick it in an old bag and put something on top of it," Isabel suggests. "She'll just figure it's some junk you think is interesting."

"Good idea," I agree. I look around and see an old shopping bag from a long-closed grocery store that presently holds an entire year's worth of *Bass Fishing* magazines and dump them out. Isabel wads up some old newspaper and puts it on the bottom, and I place the box inside. Caleb carefully places the box with the video games on top of it.

"This could be the most valuable thing in the whole apartment," he says.

I shrug and cover the top with more newspaper. I then stuff the lighter in my pocket.

We hear the old car pulling up and my mom calling for us to come down. Her eyes crinkle as soon as she sees Isabel. "I didn't know you were coming back! How nice! Did you find anything worth keeping?"

"Just a few books," Isabel says, holding out what she's taken.

"Books!" exclaims Mom, giving me an approving look. "You really are a *reader*!"

Kill me now.

"Yes. Yes, I am," says Isabel, sounding as if my mom hasn't said the stupidest thing possible.

"And you've got something too, I see!" Mom continues, turning to me, pointing to the shopping bag. "What's that?"

"Some old magazines," I lie.

Luckily, my mom isn't paying attention. She seems to not want to spend any more time at her uncle's apartment than is absolutely necessary.

The deep hum of the Archermobile can be heard from up the block, and after he parks it, Graham bounds out, as lively and well groomed as a champion golden retriever.

"I'll see you guys tomorrow morning, when the Goodwill people are here," Isabel calls over her shoulder, trying to intercept him. But Graham is too quick for her.

"That's what I like to hear!" Graham beams happily, then turns to my mom. "She needed a little convincing to come back, but I felt—"

"Father. Let's go." Isabel, for the first time, actually looks uncomfortable.

"Righto. We're off! Great seeing you again, Amanda!"

As they pull out, I can see Isabel sitting, arms crossed, her mouth set in a tight line.

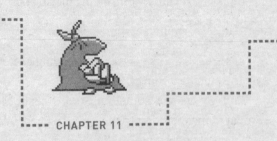

CHAPTER 11

ENEMIES AND FRIENDS

At dinner tonight, all the talk is again about Isabel. And St. Anselm's, her old school.

"Lila called today!" exclaims Dad. "She says there are a bunch of kids at Harvard from St. Anselm's. Apparently it's one of the finest private schools in New York."

"Well, if *Lila* is impressed . . . ," I snort.

"Yeah, she kept going on about how all these celebrities send their kids there, and how all these other famous people actually went there . . . fashion designers, actors, novelists. . . . Not only that, but half the people who write for the *New Yorker* are school parents: authors, artists, you name it."

"I wonder why Graham is sending her to La Purisma," my mom muses. "I mean, it's not exactly—"

"Hey! La Purisma is a great school!"

"Since when do *you* like your school?" asks Mom pointedly. "I seem to remember someone describing it as a waste of time," she adds, wiping her chin.

"Maybe Ted is getting his priorities straight this summer," my dad says, smiling at me.

"Yeah, maybe I am," I respond, gazing at my dad with what I hope looks like admiration and maturity.

"I see!" Mom regards me with a weird grin on her face I swear I've never seen before. "Speaking of your priorities, Isabel seems like a very nice girl."

OMG.

"For crying out loud, Mom!" I say. "Can we give this a rest!"

"All right, I'll change the subject," says Dad agreeably.

"Thank you," I say gratefully.

"Aren't you going to thank me for inviting Isabel to help out? It sounds like that extra pair of hands really made a difference."

"Thanks for changing the subject, *Dad*," I answer. "Yes, having an extra person was great. Especially when Mom called and said the Goodwill people are coming in the morning."

"Don't tell me you got everything packed up this afternoon?" Mom asks incredulously.

"Well," I say, trying to sound casual, " 'the prospect of being hanged focuses the mind wonderfully.' "

Dad's eyes pop open. "I am impressed. Nice quote."

"I don't play computer games *all the time*," I say modestly.

Dad nods appreciatively. "So do you know who said it?"

"What?" I answer.

"I just wondered if you know who said the original quote."

Darn! I should remember this.

"That's okay," Dad says gently. "It was Samuel Johnson. But

it's great that you know it. Did you learn that from Isabel?" he adds, as if somehow this is going to make it better.

"If he did, that's fine," says Mom, beginning to clear away the dishes.

I get up to help. Anything to get away from this conversation.

Dad, ever the professor, calls after me, "Oh, and you can tell her when you see her, the actual quote is 'Depend upon it, sir, when a man knows he is to be hanged in a fortnight, it concentrates his mind wonderfully.'"

My mom turns, remembering something. "By the way, did you find anything for Mr. Yamada?"

"Mr. Who?"

"Mr. Yamada!" Mom says, her teeth set in frustration. "The man who used to visit Uncle Ted every day? His daughter wanted you to find something from the store?"

"Ohhh . . . right . . . his old customer . . ." The matchbooks! I was so focused on the game, I totally forgot to take them!

"Was there anything in that shopping bag?" Mom asks.

"Nah, it's just magazines, like I said," I answer quickly. "I'm sorry, Mom. But we put aside some matchbooks for him. When the Goodwill guys come, we can get them."

"I hope so. She really sounded like he wanted you to bring him something."

I wipe my hands. "I'm totally beat. I think I'll head upstairs to bed."

"I'm sure you are. I can't remember the last time you did so much hard work."

Mom kisses me on the forehead. "Yuck. Take a shower first. You stink."

Dad has been reading and gets up and stretches. As I walk by, he gives me a quick hug.

"You look dead, kid. No computer games tonight, huh?"

"Nope. I need to be up in the morning to leave with Mom. She's meeting the Goodwill people with us at nine sharp."

"Sounds good. Sweet dreams."

I slump into my room and fall face-first onto my bed. My eyes wander over to the shopping bag I oh-so-carefully hid in my closet, holding the box that will not open.

Without even thinking, I grab my laptop, turn it on, and find my way to the gaming site I bookmarked.

A small shiver goes up my back as I watch the welcome screen for *The Game of Ted* appear.

There it is. Again. For real.

I reach into my pocket and fish out the lighter. I place it on the desk and rub it.

For luck.

I log on and once more play through the game.

This time, all the books are there. Just as I remember from the walkthrough, the game ends with the discovery of the box and the lighter.

But now something is blinking in the corner. A new box has appeared.

"Coming Soon! *The Game of Ted 1.2*!" it announces.

I click on the link, but nothing happens.

Coming soon? But how soon? And what will it be?

■ ■ ■

I am still turning all this over in my mind as Mom and I pull into the apartment complex the next morning.

Caleb and Isabel are already here. She's reading and he's sketching. Both look up with relief when they see me.

"We were supposed to find a memento for your great-uncle's old friend Mr. Yamada," Isabel starts.

"How did you know that?" I ask, amazed.

"I was there when your mom said it, remember?" Isabel says impatiently. "I meant to look for something nicer than just some old matchbooks, but I guess with all the other . . . things . . . going on, it slipped my mind. I'm so sorry, Mrs. Gerson."

Mom regards Isabel with a mixture of awe and adoration. "You are the most *thoughtful* young lady I think I have ever met. That is *so* nice of you, Isabel!"

"She even remembered his name!" I mutter to Caleb. "How does she do that?"

"I'm telling you, man, superpowers," cracks Caleb as he shuts his sketchbook and stands up.

A giant truck with GOODWILL printed on the side pulls up to the apartment entrance.

Two men get out of the cab and lumber toward us.

"Hi!" my mom says, extending her hand. "I'm Amanda Gerson. We talked on the phone?"

"You didn't talk to me. I just drive and pick up the stuff. You talked to Mrs. Harris. We're looking for a Mr. Waka . . . Waba . . . Wabakay . . ."

"Wakabayashi. That was my uncle."

"Okay, lady, we're good to go. So where's the stuff at?"

My mom points upstairs. The littler guy squints.

"There ain't no pianos or stuff like that up there, right? 'Cause we don't take pianos down no stairs."

Mom assures them there are no pianos.

"And everything's in boxes or bags, right? We don't take nothing loose," he adds.

"Everything's either in cartons or bags, or set aside to be dumped," I pipe up. "We made sure of that."

"Shall we, gentlemen?" my mom says, and gestures to the stairs.

The two men follow her up the stairs. Caleb, Isabel, and I take up the rear.

Mom puts the key in the lock and opens the door. The big man peers in.

"What th—"

He beckons to his buddy, who takes a quick look, turns around, and heads back down the stairs.

As he passes us, he shakes his head. "You shouldn't waste people's time like this, you know?"

We scramble up the stairs and look into the apartment.

Mom is in the middle of the room, trying to talk to the big man, her eyes wide. "I'm sure there's been some misunderstanding. I'm so sorry. . . ."

"Well, when you figure it out, you call Mrs. Harris," he says as he storms off.

It's total chaos. The place is a shambles.

Every bag has been ripped open; the furniture is cut to shreds, the newspapers strewn all over the place. The drawers in the desk have been pulled out and broken.

Someone has been searching for something. Something they want very badly.

My mom is shaking, she's so mad. "Is this what you call clean?" she fumes. "I took time off from work, brought those men here, and this is what—"

"*Mom!*" I yell. "Are you *serious*? Do you think this is how we left the place?"

"Mrs. Gerson," Isabel says calmly. "There has been a break-in. We need to call the police."

My mom sits down. She looks around the room. "I'm sorry. . . . I just . . . Of course . . ."

She takes out her phone and dials 911. As she waits, almost to herself, she murmurs, "Who would do such a thing?"

"Enemies," Caleb declares grimly.

CHAPTER 12

MY FATHER IS ALWAYS COLD

"If anything of value turns out to be missing, you'll need to go down to the division office and make a report."

"Oh, I don't think that's going to be necessary," my mom says. "And thanks so much for your time."

"No problem. That's what we're here for." The young police officer grins as he strides out the front door, tipping his hat as he goes. I wonder if he practices striding around in those boots in front of a mirror at home. He's really good at it.

"They didn't even send a detective," mutters Caleb.

"I think they only do that if something of real value was stolen," my mom says gently.

Isabel speaks up. "Maybe someone just assumed he had money, so they broke in looking for it."

"Well, that's certainly what that nice officer thought . . . or that some kids saw you working here and decided to trash the place after you left," my mom continues, sitting on a box of ramen. "He said they see it all the time. Bored kids . . . summer . . . out of school, nothing to do . . ."

I've been quiet ever since Mom opened the door to find the disaster inside. I can feel my brain going a mile a minute. I didn't even say anything as we waited for the police, while Mom went on and on about how she should have never let us do this alone, it was too dangerous, blah blah blah.

"One thing, Mom," I finally say.

"Yes, Ted?"

"There was no break-in. The door wasn't forced, or left open or anything."

"You probably forgot to lock it last night," Mom answers.

"That couldn't be it," says Isabel.

"And why not, dear?" asks my mom. "We all make mistakes, even Ted. No one's perfect." She smiles at me, which only makes it worse.

"But you unlocked the door when we came in. Which proves it was locked in the first place," counters Isabel.

"That's right!" I say.

Caleb throws down his pencil in frustration. "So how did they get in?"

"Maybe the lawyer had an extra key. Or someone in his office copied the one he had." I'm thinking through the options like I do when playing a game. "Or one of the other tenants has a key. . . . Of course, the landlord also has one. . . ."

"Or maybe . . . ," Mom begins, weaving her way over to one of the windows. She reaches down and gently opens it.

"Unlocked!" she calls back to us.

I slump against the torn couch.

"I can't believe we didn't check the windows. How dumb can you get?"

"It's not your fault, honey," my mom says consolingly. "I'm the one who opened it. It's not right to expect you to think of everything. Don't worry. I'm calling a company to come and clean all this up."

I'm sitting at our family dining table with Isabel and Caleb, drinking lemonade. Caleb has his sketchbook open, idly doodling, while Isabel has been flipping absentmindedly through the pages of the Purely Provence catalog. "So . . . who likes the Purely P?" she asks.

"That would be my dad," I admit. "He's really into it."

"Wow!" She's come to page 385. "Looks like your father likes this."

"Yeah," I say, "he's totally in love with it."

"That's so funny," she says. "We have this table."

Of course.

I figure, why not make a joke out of it. "My dad is gonna die when he hears this," I say. "Do you think he can come visit it sometime?"

"It's in storage," Isabel says, being little Miss Literal as usual. "We didn't think it went with California, you know?"

Oh, snap.

My turn. "That's cool," I say. "I always wondered who actually bought copies of French farmhouse tables."

"Oh, no. Ours isn't a copy, ours is the original," Isabel says, and then laughs that grown-up laugh that is just so irritating.

"Oh?" says Caleb skeptically. "How did your table end up in the Purely Provence catalog? Did someone just happen by your house one day and see it and say, like, 'Can we borrow your table?' "

Isabel doesn't even look up. It's like this is the most fascinating photograph she's ever seen.

"Not exactly. The man who owns the company went to Harvard with my father. He's always loved that table." Then she adds casually, "Like your dad, Ted, I guess."

Game, set, and match—Isabel Archer.

"I've never actually seen it in the catalog. They did a really nice job." Then she closes it with a loud bang and stares at me in irritation.

"What's up, Isabel?" I ask.

Isabel sighs. "We're kind of stuck, aren't we? We still don't know what 1405 refers to."

"*We?* You're sticking around after today?"

"Of course!" she laughs. "I certainly want to be there when you open the box!"

"*If* we open the box," Caleb moans.

"I have a feeling Ted's going to figure this out," Isabel says simply. Her gaze is suddenly so strong and direct I have to look away.

"Thanks for the vote of confidence. But all we have to go on is this," I mutter, pulling out the lighter.

"Uncle Ted's lighter. You didn't tell me you found that." My mom has come in with a tray of drinks and cheese puffs.

"Sorry, Mom." I shrug. "But with all the excitement, I guess it slipped my mind."

Mom reaches out and takes the lighter from me. She rubs it and smiles.

"You can have it if you want," I suggest. "You know, as a way of remembering him."

My mom's face hardens. "This lighter helped kill him. He

must have smoked three packs a day, each cigarette lit with this thing. I never want to see it again."

Then she brightens. "You know who probably would like it? Mr. Yamada! You never did get those matchbooks, did you? I'm going to call his daughter."

We watch her leave the room, then turn to each other.

"Isn't that the guy who she said was your great-uncle's most loyal customer?" asks Caleb, his voice rising with excitement.

"And she said he visited him every day in the hospital, right?" adds Isabel, nodding.

I grin. "Yep, he's the guy. If anyone knows what 1405 means, I bet it's him." I call into the kitchen, "Mom, do you think it would be all right if Caleb and Isabel came with me to give Mr. Yamada the lighter? They'd like to meet him too."

Mom sticks her head out the door. "I'm sure that would be fine, but let me check with his daughter first."

I hear my mom chattering on and on with Mr. Yamada's daughter. It's all arranged. Mr. Yamada would be delighted to meet me and my friends. He has no grandchildren and always loves being around young people.

Mom comes into the room with a strange expression on her face.

"What's up?" I ask. "I thought I heard you say it would be fine."

"Yes . . . ," my mom begins. "But when I offered to come too and say hello, she said he would prefer to meet with you kids alone. Isn't that odd?"

Isabel puts down her lemonade and takes a cheese puff. "Perhaps you remind him too much of your uncle, and meeting you would be too painful?"

"Maybe . . . ," Mom muses.

"Or maybe he's just a cranky old guy who just does weird things," Caleb suggests.

"We'll let you know," I promise.

Mom laughs. "It's all right. I've got a few errands to run near their neighborhood. We made plans for me to drop you off at two, and then I'll swing by an hour later. Will that be okay with your schedule, Isabel?"

"Just fine, Mrs. Gerson," Isabel replies, taking another cheese puff. "Father isn't free to pick me up until four anyway."

Isabel never calls her dad "Dad." It's always "Father." She's so weird.

As we head out, I nudge Caleb. "Look at my fingers." They're covered in cheese-puff dust.

"So what?" says Caleb, holding up his own orange fingers. Then I nudge him to look at Isabel's.

Spotless.

"B-but—I saw her eat them," Caleb sputters. "How can anyone eat cheese puffs without leaving telltale cheese-puff dust?"

"It can't be done, dude. It's like she's not human," I say darkly.

■ ■ ■

The Yamada home is all the way on the other side of Laurel Canyon, in Gardena.

"We're almost there," Mom announces. "There's one thing you should know about Mr. Yamada. His daughter told me he was in Amache, and ever since then he's cold no matter how hot the weather is. So his room isn't air-conditioned, and don't be put off by the fact that he's wearing a sweater."

"I'm sorry, but what is Amache?" asks Isabel.

"They still don't teach much about the camps in school, do they?"

"You mean the internment camps?" Isabel asks. "Of course. We read *Farewell to Manzanar.* It was incredible what this country did to their own people."

"Yes, well, Amache was the camp in Colorado, and Mr. Yamada has never recovered from the winters there," Mom says quietly. "That's why he's always cold. Always. Even in the middle of summer."

As Mom turns onto a quiet street shaded with palm trees, Isabel looks at us.

"What?" demands Caleb.

"You really should read *Farewell to Manzanar.* I mean, it's like your history, Ted. I thought all schools taught it."

"Maybe we're getting it this year," I guess. "You know, Purisma isn't some fancy private school."

"I would have thought you'd have read it anyway. Over a hundred thousand American citizens put into camps during World War Two just because their parents came from Japan." Isabel leans forward. "Was your family interned, Mrs. Gerson?"

"No, only the most powerful and influential, about two thousand out of the more than one hundred and fifty thousand Japanese Americans in Hawaii were interned. The rest of us were spared, but only because there were so many of us," Mom says simply. "They were such a big part of the workforce that removing them would have ruined the economy, especially since there was so much recovery to do after Pearl Harbor. People on the mainland lost their homes, their businesses, everything. Most people in Hawaii . . . didn't."

My mom spots an open space a few houses down from where Mr. Yamada lives with his daughter and eases the car over to the curb. We kids get out and walk toward the big house on the corner, and she waits to make sure we get in okay.

As we approach the entrance, I hear the thrum of an expensive car rumbling behind us, kind of like the Archermobile. I quickly turn to see that it isn't Mr. Archer at all. It isn't even the same make of car.

This one is a cool black Jaguar XJ6 sedan, gleaming in the California sunlight, driven by a man with a narrow face and a thatch of neatly trimmed gray hair. He passes us just as we find ourselves at the door to the Yamada house, ringing the bell.

The front garden is like something in a park, with a pond in the middle. Swimming lazily in the water are bright orange-and-white fish, swirling and circling, just like in a koi pond you'd find in Japan.

Mr. Yamada's daughter opens the door and greets us with a big smile.

"Hello, hello, hello!" she sings. "I'm Donna Yamada. My dad will be right with you! Come in! Come in!"

Everything about Donna Yamada is big. She's got this large face with huge eyes and a round nose. I glance at Caleb and know that he is dying to draw her. He wouldn't have to exaggerate anything. She already looks like a cartoon character.

"I'm so glad you made it," Donna booms. "I hope the traffic wasn't too bad!"

"No traffic at all, Ms. Yamada," I reply. "I guess we came at the right time."

Donna leans forward and looks at me, beaming. It's like coming face to face with a giant Macy's Thanksgiving Day Parade balloon. Unnerving.

"You have to be Ted. I can see your great-uncle in you."

I want to say something along the lines that duh, I'm Ted, seeing as I'm the only one here who looks remotely Asian. But Donna is so nice (and hovering dangerously over me), I can't imagine saying anything mean to her.

As she ushers us in, Donna points. "You see that plaque?" She glances at me. "As I'm sure Ted knows, those two Japanese characters"—she turns to Isabel and makes pointed eye contact—"or kanji, spell out *Yama* and *Da*. Our name! *Yama* means 'mountain,' and *da* means 'rice paddy.' 'Rice paddy beside the mountain.' *Yama-da!*" Donna says, wide-eyed and slowly.

"You wouldn't by any chance . . . be an elementary school teacher, would you?" I ask.

Donna's face brightens even more, if possible. "As a matter of fact, I am! Very good, Ted! I teach third grade at Gardena Elementary!"

Donna motions for us to follow her. She picks up a tray of glasses of ice water she set up in the kitchen. "My dad may not show it, but he is very excited that you're here. Don't be put off by him, okay? He's kind of formal.

"Take these," she says, motioning to the glasses. "You'll need them."

She leads us down a hallway to the back of the house. She opens a door, which leads to a small greenhouse attached to the back of the garage. As soon as she opens the door, the heat envelops us like a blanket. I see Caleb's bangs go limp against his forehead. His glasses fog up and my shirt immediately starts clinging to my chest and back like a damp towel.

Only the eternally cool Isabel looks unchanged.

CHAPTER 13

THE MAN WHO MAKES TREES

There is a man with his back to us, wearing a heavy wool sweater buttoned all the way up. He's clearly involved in something that's more important to him than a group of kids. Without turning around, he greets us.

"Thank you so much for this visit," Mr. Yamada says in a formal tone I've only heard in movies.

Then he turns, and I see there's a smile on his face.

Unlike his daughter, he's small and compact. I guess you could say he's elegant, in a way. Donna must have gotten her size from her mother's side of the family.

His eyes crinkle into small lines as he smiles wider, and he bows to us.

For once, I'm glad Isabel knows how to talk to grown-ups so well. While I stand there awkwardly, Isabel starts simply. "Thank you so much for seeing us." She makes this ridiculous formal little bow, which makes Mr. Yamada laugh out loud.

"I am guessing *you* are not Ted's grand-nephew?" he jokes.

I step forward. "That would be me."

"A great pleasure to meet you." Mr. Yamada leans forward and examines my face for a moment. "Yes, I see . . . your uncle in you."

"And I'm Caleb Grant, um . . . a friend of Ted's," Caleb adds, as if he needs to explain his reason for being here. He bows too.

"And this lovely young lady is?" asks Mr. Yamada, turning to Isabel.

"Isabel Archer, sir. Is that a bonsai?" On a worktable behind Mr. Yamada is a small dish holding a perfect miniature tree, with a series of metal tools and wires next to it.

His face lights up. "You know bonsai, Miss Archer?"

Isabel approaches the tiny tree and propping her elbows on the table, rests her head on her hands. "A little. I know that it's a Japanese art of pruning and twisting trees so that they grow in a special way."

Mr. Yamada motions Caleb and me over to join Isabel.

"It is that . . . and it is *not* that. Those are the techniques by which one turns an ordinary tree or a cutting into bonsai. But bonsai is much more."

Mr. Yamada looks at the tree and slowly picks up a pair of beautiful silver scissors. He leans in and with great delibera-tion snips a tiny leaf from one branch.

"For the lover of bonsai, it is a symbol of something which brings us closer to nature, and to perfection itself, although we may never achieve it," Mr. Yamada continues, looking lovingly at his little tree. "This is what is meant by the expression 'heaven and earth in one container.'"

Right now, it feels like all the sweat in heaven and earth from one container has been absorbed in my shorts.

He points to the tree. "Tradition holds that three basic virtues are necessary to create a bonsai: *shin-zen-bi*, standing for truth, goodness, and beauty." He turns and looks at me. "Your great-uncle possessed these virtues as well."

I nod, not sure what to say.

"So my great-uncle was into this stuff?" I ask.

Mr. Yamada laughs, and I swear his whole body shakes.

"Ted? Bonsai? He used to tease me about my love for these things. He found it all very silly. Your great-uncle was a very practical man."

"Can you tell me anything else about him?" I ask.

"He talked very little about his past before opening his shop. At one point I saw that some scientific journals had been delivered and asked about them," Mr. Yamada remembers. "It seemed he was a scientist of some kind after the war."

"Yes," Isabel interjects, "we saw some of those journals at his apartment when we were cleaning it up. And lots of books."

"Very odd, your great-uncle quitting his well-regarded and well-paid profession like that, wouldn't you say?" asks Mr. Yamada, watching us.

Then he stops, turning to his tree.

Snip!

At this point, I would sell Caleb to the circus for another glass of ice water.

"Then again, as you get older, you tend to cut away those things that are not necessary. Like this tree, I suppose." Mr.

Yamada studies his little tree for a moment more. "Part of bonsai is to cut away everything that is not essential, leaving only the essence, the pure truth of the object. Perhaps your great-uncle was doing some pruning of his own."

"Maybe," I say, but then I remember the stacks of rice bags and futons and newspapers piled up in the apartment. "I'm not sure how good my great-uncle was at pruning things out of his life."

"Yes, well . . . he was a good man, and did not deserve to go the way he did."

I pull the lighter out of my pocket with a damp hand and hold it up. Time to get this show on the road.

"We found this when we were cleaning his apartment. We thought maybe you would want it, to remember him by." Mr. Yamada's eyes widen at the sight of the lighter. He seems genuinely surprised.

"You—you found it?"

"Yes," I say, looking at him, thrown by his reaction. Why is he so surprised? "Is there something wrong?"

"No, not at all." Mr. Yamada pulls himself together and is once again the model of composure. "It's only that I haven't seen it in some time. . . ."

"I'm sure he would have wanted you to have it," I continue.

Mr. Yamada reaches out and closes my hand around the lighter. It's something of a shock to feel the coldness of his hands, even in this oven of a room. What did those winters in the camp as a child do to him?

"No, he would have wanted *you* to have it," Mr. Yamada says gently. He stares at it for a moment. "You do know the significance of that figure, I hope?"

"No, actually, we were hoping you would be able to help us with that," Caleb says.

"That's the symbol for the Nisei brigade—the all–Japanese American unit that served bravely in World War Two," Mr. Yamada says proudly. "Your great-uncle was in it, and served throughout the entire campaign."

"What was the number of the unit?" Isabel asks suddenly, catching my eye.

"There was the 100th Battalion and the 442nd Regiment. You should learn about their history," Mr. Yamada replies, turning to me. "People thought of us as dirty Japs after Pearl Harbor, and thought some of us could be spies. That's why they started the internment camps. They said if there *were* any spies, the camps couldn't do any harm. But when the call went out for volunteers to fight in Honolulu, they were looking for fifteen hundred men. *Ten thousand* showed up. Those were some of the finest soldiers in the army."

And Great-Uncle Ted was one of them! Awesome!

"Did he ever talk about that time?"

"I'd ask him, but he'd always wave me away, telling me it was a long time ago and he wanted to just forget about the whole thing."

"Did he ever show you any souvenirs from the war?" Isabel asks, holding her glass to her forehead. "Like a wooden box, maybe?"

"I don't remember any wooden box," Mr. Yamada says quickly. "The only thing I remember seeing that he brought back from the war was a Colt .45 automatic, which he always kept behind the counter."

"For protection against robbers?" Caleb guesses.

"Maybe," Mr. Yamada muses. "His store was in an area in downtown LA called Little Tokyo. Back then it was . . . less safe."

I think back to the ransacked apartment. I look over at Caleb and know what he's thinking. "Was he afraid of something?"

"Maybe. He would never say."

"Did you ever visit him at his apartment?"

"I didn't even know where he lived," Mr. Yamada protests. "One day his shop was there, and then the next thing I knew, it was closed and no one knew where he had disappeared to. I was very sad, as he had the best selection of sake—rice wine," he said, bowing slightly to Isabel, "that anyone had in the area. Also, he was such fun to talk to."

"But you visited him in the hospital, didn't you?" asks Isabel.

"Yes, it's a funny thing. One of the parents in my daughter's third-grade class was a nurse on his floor. She mentioned that there was an old Japanese man on the floor and happened to mention the name. My daughter remembered it and told me. I was so happy to have been able to see him before he passed."

I feel the need to ask one more question. "What kinds of things would my great-uncle talk to you about when you would visit him?"

Mr. Yamada looks puzzled.

"Well . . . he was in a lot of pain. But sometimes he actually would talk of the war. And he would joke about how his luck had finally caught up with him."

"What did he mean by that?"

"I guess he'd had some close calls, and lost more than a few friends. And he'd been able to live a long, healthy life up to that point. But being put on the thirteenth floor, he felt, was an omen."

"So he was superstitious?" asks Isabel.

"I think he just felt it was one more sign that he wasn't going to get better. Soon after, they moved him into the ICU, and I never saw him again."

Mr. Yamada turns back to his little tree.

Caleb coughs. He looks like he's having trouble breathing.

"I gotta get out of here," he whispers to me. "I think I'm allergic to something."

"Well, thank you very much for your time, Mr. Yamada," I say.

Donna meets us in the hallway, where the cold air is like a welcome slap in the face. I'm so grateful she has paper towels for us, which Caleb and I happily use to dry our faces and sopping-wet hair.

Isabel, on the other hand . . .

"You're a very . . . dry . . . girl," Donna remarks.

"Thank you," Isabel answers with a small smile. "I get my sense of humor from my father's side of the family. I think it's kind of a New England thing—"

"Actually, I was referring to the fact that you don't sweat much," says Donna.

"Oh . . . right. . . . I guess that's an East Coast thing too . . . ," Isabel says quickly.

Yeah, right. An East Coast thing. I think of my uncle Morty, back in Brooklyn. If the temperature goes above seventy, sweat stains the size of grapefruits sprout under each armpit. We head outside to wait for my mom.

"Well, other than finding out that sitting in a sauna makes

you lose about ten pounds of water weight, I don't know what we learned in there," Caleb grouses.

"I thought all that stuff about bonsai trees was fascinating," says Isabel.

"Wait a minute," I say.

"What?" asks Isabel.

"He said my great-uncle thought it was a bad omen that he was on the thirteenth floor, right?"

"Yeah, so what?" says Caleb.

"La Purisma General Hospital doesn't have a thirteenth floor."

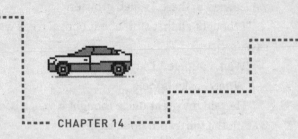

CHAPTER 14

NO ANSWERS,
BUT MORE QUESTIONS

"What are you saying?" asks Isabel. "It only has twelve floors?"

"No," I answer. "It has sixteen floors."

Caleb looks at me like I'm from another planet. "Dude, I don't know how to tell you this, but if it has sixteen floors . . . it's gotta have a thirteenth floor."

Before I can say anything, Isabel breaks in. "I stayed at a hotel where they skipped from the twelfth floor right to the fourteenth floor. No one wanted to stay on the thirteenth floor because it was bad luck. Is that what you mean?"

"Exactly. Lots of hospitals don't have thirteenth floors. My dad teases my mom about it all the time. 'All those rational scientists, believing in superstition.' Of course, it's really for the patients."

"So why would Mr. Yamada say that about your great-uncle?" says Isabel.

"Maybe what he meant was that your great-uncle would have been on the thirteenth floor if there was one," Caleb suggests.

"Which means he would have been on the—"

"Fourteenth floor!" we all say at the same time.

I take out the lighter and turn it over. 1405.

"So you think that was his room number?" says Caleb slowly.

"Only one way to find out," I say.

At this point Donna bounces out and joins us.

"Your mother called," she announces. "She should be here any minute."

"Thank you for all your help," I say, trying my best to sound like Isabel in her "talking to grown-ups" mode.

"It was my pleasure, Ted," Donna answers. "It isn't often we get visitors. It makes me feel so good to hear Dad talking with people."

"He doesn't have friends?" asks Isabel.

"Most of them have moved away to live nearer their children . . . or died . . . ," Donna responds. I notice that her smile is pasted in place, but her eyes have turned sad.

Then her cheerful demeanor returns.

"That's why it was so nice when he could visit your great-uncle. It gave him something to do, somewhere to go. And just talking about him seems to, I don't know, *revive* my father somehow."

"I'm glad," I say.

"It's so funny . . . he hasn't spoken of Ted since his passing, and here he is today, having two whole conversations about him."

"There was someone else asking questions about Ted's great-uncle?" Isabel asks.

"Right before you came, actually. I thought you knew him."

"Why would you think that we knew him?" I ask.

"It was that man who's writing an article about your great-uncle for the paper in Hawaii. He said he had gotten my dad's name from your mother, so I assumed he'd talked to you already."

My mind is spinning. I'm a terrible liar, but I still manage to say, "Oh, right. He must have talked to my parents when we were at Great-Uncle Ted's apartment cleaning up."

"Well, he was very respectful and seemed to take a great interest in talking with my dad. That unit your great-uncle served in during the war was quite important, you know. Those men were real heroes." Donna squints and looks up the street.

"Oh, here's your mom now. I'll just say hello!"

My mom pulls up, and she's apologizing before she's turned the engine off. Donna will hear nothing of it, offers her water and cookies, and the two carry on like old friends.

I turn to Isabel and Caleb, who have the same expression on their faces.

"So what do you think?"

"Did your mom tell you about this reporter?" Caleb asks.

I shake my head. "Not a peep."

Isabel frowns. "From what Mr. Yamada said, this regiment was very important, so why wouldn't they do an article on your great-uncle?"

"We need to find out what he did in the war. Maybe this guy knows?" I say.

On the way home, Mom eyes us in the rearview. "So was Mr. Yamada nice?"

"He's a very interesting man," Isabel pipes up. "He's quite knowledgeable about bonsai."

"I've always wanted to learn about that," sighs my mom, "and ikebana—flower arranging."

"I know!" Isabel says, somehow not making it sound obnoxious. Well, not *too* obnoxious.

"It's was just so hard, with the kids . . . and the work at the hospital . . ."

"Speaking of the hospital," I say, "do you happen to remember where Great-Uncle Ted was before they moved him to the ICU?"

"You mean his floor? He was on fourteen, sweetheart, where Pearl is the floor nurse."

"Do you remember what his room number was?" I ask, trying to sound as casual as possible.

"I don't know. Who remembers those things?" Mom answers.

Isabel looks at me, opens her eyes wide, and nods at my mom.

She wants me to ask her something else . . . but I'm not sure what. She keeps looking at me as we drive along in silence. I get nothing.

Finally, she says loudly to me, "Wasn't that a *nice* chat we had with Donna before your mom came?"

"Yeah, I guess so," I reply.

Isabel slumps down in her seat in frustration. Clearly I'm missing something.

"We also learned a little bit about his war service," says Isabel. "Apparently he was in a very famous army unit."

"Oh, yes, that's right. I forget the number. The Nisei brigade, he used to call them. He'd get invited to reunions all the time, but he never wanted to go," Mom says.

Finally, it sinks in. Duh.

"Oh, Mom. Did some guy from a newspaper in Hawaii call and ask questions about Great-Uncle Ted?"

"A newspaper? What are you talking about?" My mom sounds genuinely confused.

"Before we came, this guy had been at Mr. Yamada's and—"

"Wait a minute! The gosh darn traffic is just terrible here. I'm going to pull off and take the side road."

I know enough not to talk to my mother when she's changing her driving plans. This requires the utmost concentration and focus. I turn to Isabel, who mouths the words "thank you" as sarcastically as one can mouth words.

As we pull onto a local road, Mom returns to the land of the talkable.

"What were you asking? A newspaper?"

"A man came and talked to Mr. Yamada and said he'd gotten his name from you."

"That's strange," my mom says. "No one's asked me about him. No one's called."

Her mood changes as we pull up to Caleb's house. "First stop!" she trills. Caleb hops out.

"Text me or phone me later," he calls back to me. I nod.

Next, we drop Isabel off at her house. It's in Treemont Oaks, the part of La Purisma Caleb and I simply call "The Rich Place." We glide down a tree-lined street of large, immaculate houses and pull into a wide gravel drive beside the Archer-mobile, sunlight sparkling on its pristine exterior.

"I'll let you know anything I find out," I promise Isabel.

As she walks toward the house, I realize I don't have her cell number.

"Hey!" I yell after her.

"917-555-6554," she says, without even turning around.

And with that, she walks into the imposing house.

On the drive home, I turn things over in my head. What's the deal with this man who says he found Mr. Yamada by asking my mom?

For some reason, I think about Isabel as I watch the palm trees swaying over Ventura Boulevard, looking ridiculous next to the minimalls filled with sad-looking fast-food joints, discount jewelers, and chain stores.

Not a bookstore in sight. What does Isabel see when she looks at this dumpy little place?

As we turn onto our street, I notice a familiar-looking car. A black Jaguar XJ6 sedan, driven by a man with a narrow face and a thatch of gray hair.

And it's pulling out of our driveway.

CHAPTER 15

I LEARN THAT NO VISITORS MEANS NO VISITORS

We enter the house to find Dad calmly sitting at the dining room table, looking at (what else?) the Purely Provence catalog.

"Someone was here looking for you, Ted," he says pleasantly. "You just missed him."

I try to sound casual. "Yeah, I saw the car pull out. Who was it?"

"He said he's from the *Honolulu Star-Advertiser* and he's writing an article about the division Uncle Ted was in."

Mom turns to me in triumph. "That must have been the man who visited Mr. Yamada!"

"He wanted to talk to me? Why not Mom? She was his niece."

"He told me he needed something dramatic to end his article, so he was hoping he'd get a good quote, and the nurses at the ICU said Uncle Ted had spent a lot of time with you near the end, so . . ." My dad's voice trails off.

I sit down at the table and find myself rubbing the back of my neck, the way I do when I'm trying to solve a particularly hard clue in a game.

"It just doesn't make sense," I say, thinking out loud. "He doesn't need to talk to me in person. He could have called, or emailed. Why did he fly all the way over here from Hawaii?"

Dad shrugs. "He said something about coming to LA to do research at the Japanese American National Museum. He was interviewing people who knew Ted, like Mr. Yamada, and thought as long as he was in the area . . ."

"Okay, but why not call ahead? Weird."

Mom rejoins us. "He was probably just driving by and remembered we lived near here."

"You can ask him yourself," my dad says. "He's coming back tomorrow. I told him you and Mom would be here in the morning."

"That's cool," I say. "Yeah, I just wish I had something to tell him."

"For heaven's sake!" Mom is going through her purse.

She's amazing. Even when I hear her and Dad argue and she gets mad, the most I've ever heard her say is "Darn it, Artie!"

"What's wrong, honey?" my dad asks. "Don't tell me. You left your wallet at the Japanese market?"

"Not this time. No, I left the book I was reading at the hospital. Darn! I was just getting to the good part."

My father mutters something under his breath. This has been a long-standing source of irritation to him. The wife of an English professor only reads books that patients leave behind in the hospital. And of course, these are inevitably the kind of books you buy at a hospital gift shop or an airport.

You know—the kind whose covers show guys with their shirts open to their navels and women swooning in their arms? They have titles like *Crime of Passion* (if it's romantic) or *A Passion for Crime* (if it's a mystery), and most have the author's name in big raised letters with the words "*New York Times* Bestselling Author!" (Dad always grumbles, "That's a sure sign it's great literature.")

Mom hits my dad playfully. "Stop it, Artie. This one is pretty good. Part of it takes place in Japan, remember? I told you about it three times already."

My dad shrugs.

"I don't know why I bother. You never listen. I think you're afraid you might like it."

"Would it make me cry?" my dad says.

"Shut up," my mom answers. "Not everything has to be Henry James."

This is another joke in the family. It's also a bone of contention that Mom hasn't ever tried to read any of the works of an author her husband has taught for ten years.

"I'll make you a deal," Dad tries once more. "I'll read this masterpiece if you read just fifty pages of *The Portrait of a Lady*."

"I'll think about it," my mom laughs. "But now I won't even get a chance to finish it until Monday."

I have a brainstorm.

"I can go get it for you," I offer.

"That's so sweet, honey, but it's not necessary."

"No, really. It's at the desk, right? I don't mind. I need the exercise anyway."

Ever since I turned twelve, I've been allowed to bike back and forth to the hospital. It's all local roads, and I've done it plenty of times. Like I've met my mom for lunch, or biked to the hospital after school to hang out and do homework and head home with her after her shift ends.

"Well . . ."

I can tell Mom *really* wants to finish the book.

"This is ridiculous," mutters my dad. "I can tell you how it's going to end. Devon, or her adorable son or daughter, will melt Erik-with-a-K's heart and he will learn to love again."

"That would be lovely, Ted. I appreciate it so much," my mom says, kissing me on the top of the head.

It feels good to get on my bike and move around after being in that stifling greenhouse.

Still, I keep coming back to the way Mr. Yamada's face lit up with surprise when he saw the lighter. It's as if he knew it had been hidden.

How much did Great-Uncle Ted tell him?

I pull into the hospital parking lot in record time.

On the first floor, I greet Ronnie the security guard, who looks surprised to see me. Ronnie seems to carry much of his considerable weight in his butt and has the face of a basset hound, but he doesn't miss anything.

"Your mom's not on today," Ronnie says, scanning the call sheet.

"She left a book here, so I offered to get it for her." I smile.

"Just sign in and head up, man." Ronnie watches as I sign the book that keeps a record of every visitor, where they go, and how long they stay.

I finish and head up to the tenth floor. As I get out of the elevator, the operating room nurses are all clustered around a box of gourmet chocolates probably sent by a grateful patient.

Connie, a small woman with a head of tight curls, spots me and calls out, "I should have known! What? Amanda found out about this candy and sent you to take some?"

All the ladies laugh, and I feel my face turn red. "I'm, uh . . . just here to get a book she left at the end of her shift."

"Oh my gosh! She left her book!" cries Rowena. "She sent you to get it? That woman sure loves her books!"

"No, actually, I offered," I say. "Do you know where she left it?"

Rowena pulls something out of a drawer in the nurses' station.

"I've got it right here." As I reach for it, she pulls it back and turns it over.

"Wait, I have to see what makes this so amazing," she announces, reading aloud from the back cover. "'*Love's Savage Kiss*—a tale of love and revenge spanning three generations, from the streets of war-torn Japan to days of free love in San Francisco to the high-tech world of today's Seattle . . . this story will touch your very soul with its searing portrayal of forbidden passion and illicit romance!'"

The room erupts in laughter and Rowena raises her eyebrows. "I'm not sure if I can trust you with this, Teddy. You promise you aren't going to read this yourself?"

Why do people think this is funny?

Another round of giggles, and I assure Rowena I'll give it directly to my mom. Rowena hands me the book and then pulls me into a hug. "You know I'm just playing. You're growing up so fast, Teddy! You're as big as your mom now!"

I endure this torture and wave goodbye to the other nurses. They all call after me as I step onto the elevator.

I get on and, once the doors close, punch the button for the fourteenth floor.

One look and I can see the nurse on duty is Pearl. My heart sinks. I've only met her once before, at some Christmas party or other, and still remember that I've rarely seen such a scary-looking woman. Her face seems to be made entirely out of sharp angles, from her forehead down to the beak of her nose, which leads to the tiny line of a mouth, then to the jutting chin, which looks like something cut out of sheet metal, or maybe concrete.

She's busy entering information into a computer when I approach the desk.

"May I help you?" she asks crisply, without looking up.

"Hi, I'm Ted Gerson."

Pearl keeps at her work. Clearly she's waiting for me to continue.

"My mom's Amanda Gerson. She worked with you, and used to—"

"Yes, I know. I was sorry to hear about your uncle."

"My great-uncle. At any rate, I believe he was in room 1405."

Pearl looks up at me, like a vulture sizing up its prey. "Yes, that's right. Is there something I can help you with? I have to get back to these reports."

"I think he may have left something there. Would it be possible to check?"

A bony hand appears from under the desk. It waves me off like a fly.

"Anything found in the rooms is brought to the lost and found." Pearl's laser beams cut through me again. "I would have thought you'd know that."

I push on. "Yes, but it wasn't there, and it's something quite small. They might have missed it."

Pearl folds her arms. "First of all, it's impossible that the cleaning crew missed anything. They removed all your great-uncle's possessions when they moved him to the ICU last week. Secondly, the present patient, Mrs. Krausz, has expressly forbidden any visitors . . . even her immediate family."

I think for a moment.

"Was she here when my great-uncle was in the room?"

"Yes, she was," Pearl says briskly, in a tone that suggests that the conversation is over as far as she is concerned.

"In that case—"

"I have already told you she has requested no visitors. She is recovering from spinal surgery and has great anxiety about infection. Please respect her wishes. If you have any other questions about anything your uncle may have left behind, please address them to the nurses on the ICU floor, or, as I told you at the beginning of this conversation, the lost and found."

Pearl goes back to her computer. Behind her, I see a bank of video monitors, each one showing the patient in the rooms on her floor. If anyone went in unannounced, Pearl would know about it in seconds. And Ronnie would be called, or one of the orderlies, and that would be that. So slipping in is out of the question.

"Those monitors are state-of-the-art," Pearl says proudly. "We've been given a grant to test them out. Saves so much time, being able to watch all the patients without leaving the station."

"I guess it would," I say, and turn to go.

As I'm about to leave, Pearl says something under her breath.

"Excuse me?" I ask.

"I don't know why you people keep coming here like this, taking up my time."

"You people?" I'm getting confused.

"Just this morning, one of your relatives came in asking about room 1405. I told him about Mrs. Krausz and he got quite unpleasant."

My relatives?

"I'm so sorry. . . . I didn't know that. I wonder which one of my relatives it was. What did he look like?"

"He wasn't Asian, which was kind of funny. But he said he knew your uncle through your father's side, and I explained that first of all, only blood relatives could visit, and second of all—"

"Yes." I nod. "The lost and found."

Pearl smiles. Somehow, this makes her face look even more unpleasant.

"Exactly. So you can understand my impatience."

"Absolutely," I say. "I would feel the same way."

I back away as Pearl calls out to me. "Regards to your mother." She notices the book in my hands.

"Oh, are you reading *Love's Savage Kiss*? It's one of my favorites! I'm such a sucker for romance!"

I wait until the elevator doors close before I allow a look of amazement to come to my face. The image of Pearl reading romance novels is almost funny enough to erase the shivers I got at the thought of someone else asking about the room. And lying about how he got there.

And I have a pretty good idea who that someone is.

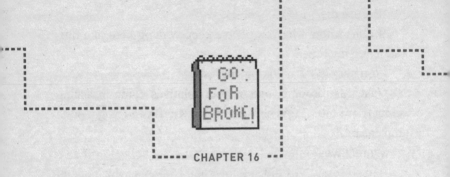

GO·
FoR
BROKE!

CHAPTER 16

UNEXPECTED GUESTS

The doors open and I go to sign out at the desk, where Ronnie is looking off through the glass partition, watching a rerun of some *CSI* show on the television in the waiting room.

"The husband killed her, I figured it out," he says as I write in the time I'm checking out. "I always figure it out," Ronnie adds. "I shoulda gone into forensics. I got like a gift. I don't miss nothing."

"Cool," I reply. Then something occurs to me. Whoever visited the fourteenth floor and talked to Pearl had to have signed in.

Ronnie seems to be intent on his show. At the same time, he's making the kind of conversation with me that non-Asian people think is small talk with kids who are even part Asian.

"You see that kung fu movie on Classic Film Channel last night?"

"Kung fu's Chinese, not Japanese."

"I just thought you might be into martial arts films."

Word to the wise: we are all so over this.

"Sure, Ronnie," I say as I turn my head to look at the sign-in sheet on his clipboard. I reach over and quietly start flipping through the pages, looking back through the times . . . I get as far as noon when a large hand slaps down on the board.

"What do you think you're doing?" Ronnie demands.

I should have known. Like the big man said, he misses nothing.

I'm good at a lot of things, but lying to large men with guns and loud voices isn't one of them.

"Teddy, you know that's not allowed. What were you looking for, anyway?"

"I, uh . . . Someone who said he knew my great-uncle was visiting, and I just was curious when he was here."

"Oh yeah?" Ronnie asks, picking up the clipboard. "What's his name? I can check it for you."

"It's not important. I—I was just kind of wondering," I stammer, backing away.

"Yeah, that's what I thought," chuckles Ronnie.

I turn to go.

"Hey! You forgot your book!" Ronnie glances at it. "*Love's Savage Kiss,* huh? This any good?"

My humiliation is complete as Ronnie scans the back cover. "Nice reading, kid."

"I *told* you. It's for my mom. She left it here."

"Riiight. You did. My mistake." Ronnie grins as I turn and walk toward the elevator, which I take down to the parking garage.

As I bike away from La Purisma General, a dozen thoughts are tumbling through my mind, one after the other. I need to think this out.

I steer my bike over to the curb and pull out my cell. My mom answers on the second ring. "What's up, honey? Trouble finding the book?"

"Nah, I got it. Listen, we're not having dinner for like an hour, right?"

"Maybe a little longer. I've been in the garden. Why?"

"I thought I'd stop at Caleb's and hang out."

"I don't know, Ted. You sure you can keep it to an hour?"

"I promise."

"All right, then. Say hello to Doris for me."

"I will. Thanks, Mom!"

I click off and head over to La Veranda Boulevard. Caleb's is between the hospital and our house, so it works out perfectly.

His mom's car isn't in the driveway. She's most likely at the gym, which is pretty much where she's been living since Caleb's dad left. The front door is unlocked, so I sprint upstairs.

As I expect, he's hunched over his drawing table, finishing up yet another perfectly sculpted superhero beating the pants off some other superhero.

And yes, the guy being punched has a ponytail.

Way to work out those issues, Caleb!

He pushes the paper away and looks up at me.

"So," I launch in right away. "Remember when Donna Yamada told us that some man had visited her father and asked all sorts of questions about Great-Uncle Ted?"

"Yeah. That was kind of creepy," says Caleb.

"The same guy came to my house while we were gone. He's

coming back tomorrow. My dad says he's from some news-paper in Hawaii and he's writing a story about that unit my great-uncle served in."

Caleb puts down his pen. "And he came all the way here? How important was your great-uncle anyway?"

"That's what I said. But you haven't heard the weirdest part. I think he was at the hospital, asking about room 1405."

"Wait. Before you go any further, shouldn't we tell *her* about this?"

"Tell who?" I ask, already knowing the answer.

"I just think Isabel might, I dunno, find this interesting, don't you?"

"Yeah, probably."

I sit on his bed and we stare at each other.

"So . . . call her," he says.

"*You* call her," I answer.

"It's your news," Caleb says, sounding logical for the first time in his life.

I hate him.

"Yeah, but it's your house, so it's your phone," I suggest.

"So what? Use your cell."

He has me there. So now I have to call a girl. So what? So it's weird. Don't ask me why, it just is.

"I'll call," I say slowly, "but . . . it has to be on speakerphone, and you have to talk too."

"Deal!" Caleb says happily.

I dial Isabel's number, and she picks up.

"So . . . what're you doing?" I ask, feeling like this is how phone conversations probably start with girls. Since this is a first, I'm kind of winging it.

"Um . . . reading. You?"

"Just hanging out here with Caleb."

"Hi!" Caleb yells at the phone.

"Am I on speakerphone? I hate that," the disembodied voice of Isabel says.

"Sorry. It's just that I wanted to tell you about what happened today at the hospital, and—"

"You went to the *hospital*? I want to know everything!"

So I tell them. When I get to the part about how impossible it is to get into the room, there's a sigh at the other end of the phone. Clearly Super Detective Ted has disappointed Isabel.

"I guess that's that," Caleb says, flopping down on his bed.

"That's *what*?" Isabel says. "Something's in that room. Don't you think, Ted?"

"Yeah, but how do I find out what?"

"We could create a diversion!" Caleb suggests. "Like Isabel could pretend to be sick to lure the nurse out of the station, and then you could sneak in and—"

I cut him off. "Three things already wrong with that plan. One, no one gets into the hospital without signing in with the security guard, and he won't let us in unless we're visiting someone. Two, even if Pearl isn't the on-duty nurse, it might be someone just as bad. They won't just jump from behind the desk. These are trained professionals. And three, this Mrs. Krausz lady already said she doesn't want any visitors. So if I just walk in there, she'll call security and that will be that. And I'll have to explain it to my mom, and—"

I sit in the seat by Caleb's desk, weighed down with the impossibility of the task in front of me.

For a moment the three of us are silent, lost in our own thoughts.

Then there's a chuckle from the other end of the phone. That low, grown-up laugh I've grown to loathe.

"What? What is it?" I blurt out.

"I'm sorry, this sounds exactly like one of those games you say you play all the time. It just *seems* impossible until you find the answer." Isabel's voice turns serious. "I think you should sleep on it. I bet you'll have something in the morning."

I look at the phone. "I wouldn't count on it. I don't think you understand. There is no way I'm walking into that room."

"I have a feeling you will," Isabel says. "You'll figure it out. Your great-uncle wouldn't have set up that clue if you couldn't, and you're really smart. You just don't know how smart."

Somehow she makes me feel like the dumbest *and* the smartest kid in the world at the same time.

"As they say in Italian, *A tutto c'è rimedio, fuorché alla morte*."

For the first time since we started the call, Caleb speaks to Isabel with annoyance.

"And for those of us who don't speak Italian?"

"Oh, sorry," Isabel says. "It means 'Only for death is there no solution.'"

"Who knows these things?" Caleb asks me.

"I read it in a book," Isabel says evenly. "I remember stuff."

I check my watch.

"I gotta go. I promise I'll call or text you guys tomorrow if I think of anything," I say.

■ ■ ■

Mom is profuse in her thanks when I hand over the book.

"Another masterpiece," my dad grumbles as we sit down to dinner.

I rush through my food and excuse myself.

"Are you feeling okay?" asks my mom.

"I'm just beat. I think I need to go to bed early," I explain.

I get to my room, kick the door shut, and flick open my trusty laptop. I pull it onto the bed and try to sort out all that's happened today.

The man who says he's writing the article on my great-uncle . . . the impossibility of getting into room 1405. It *is* impossible, isn't it?

My eyes fall on the pad still on my desk with my great-uncle's last message:

THE BOX IS ONLY THE BEGINNING. KEEP LOOKING FOR THE ANSWERS. ALWAYS GO FOR BROKE! PROMISE ME!

The *box*. I start the browser and go to the gaming site I visited before.

There, as somehow I knew it would be, is a title card:

"The Game of Ted 1.2: The Hospital Room Heist."

CHAPTER 17

IT'S HOW YOU PLAY THE GAME

The rules have changed.

This time, it's not a game where you escape from a room, but one where you have to find a way in.

There's the entrance to the hospital. I click, and there's Ronnie, or at least a picture of him. I click on the sign-in book and nothing happens. Clearly this is the wrong way.

I click back and it leads me outside. I try again. I try clicking around the floor. Am I supposed to throw something to distract Ronnie, like Caleb said?

Nothing is on the floor; nothing moves.

A dead end.

I stare at the screen.

Like Isabel said, these games always have solutions. I just have to think of this as any other game.

But it doesn't feel like a game. This time I know it's real. And eventually I'll have to actually follow it up in real life.

Isn't that what my great-uncle made me promise with what was almost his dying breath?

Shoulders dropping, I catch sight of myself in the mirror. There they are. My mother's eyes.

That's it!

I wanted to smack myself in the head.

Of course. It's so simple. And it just might work.

I return to the game and play through the moves. I find myself clicking up to the door of 1405 and going through. There is something on a table, a small black rectangle. I click on it, and the game ends.

That's it? But I didn't see the object properly!

Since when don't these games tell you what you've won? It doesn't feel like it's over at all.

Still, I have enough experience to know that whatever the black shape is, it contains the key. It's possibly magnetic, and attached to the metal railings under the bed. I've seen these boxes plenty of times.

I begin the game again and play through it. This is a lot different from just finding a bunch of clues. This is breaking a whole lot of rules, and if I don't want to get caught, I have to have every step down perfectly.

Then a chill settles on me.

I click until I come to the screen showing the nurses' station. I click on the clock on the desk. It says 11:45. At night.

With a sinking feeling, I realize immediately what the game is telling me.

I have to go back to the hospital. Tonight.

Slowly, I get up from my chair and lie on my bed, going over the plan in my mind.

Almost immediately, I get up, go to my laptop, and play through the game over and over again.

If I'm going to do this, it will have to be perfect.

I'll have only so much time to accomplish the goal, and any mistake could mean disaster.

Mom could get fired. I could get arrested.

I wipe the sweat that has beaded on my forehead and check my watch for the hundredth time.

It's eleven o'clock.

I've said my good nights, so as far as my parents know, I'll be in my room until morning.

As quietly as I possibly can, I turn the knob on my bedroom door and creep down the hallway toward the stairs.

Tomorrow is a workday, so my mom went to bed at ten-thirty. Dad is also in bed, reading. He'll probably go to the bathroom before going to sleep, but that will be at eleven-thirty.

I silently thank the gods that my dad is a creature of habit, and make my way down to the ground floor. There's a moon out, and light shines into the darkened house as I move into the kitchen. There, as I knew it would be, is my mother's purse hanging off a chair. I reach inside and gingerly pull out her lanyard with her ID and pass card on it.

Next stop is the laundry room. I reach onto a shelf and feel around.

Yes! It's here! I take out what I've come for and stick it into my knapsack. I check my watch and see that I've wasted valuable time. I race outside and find my bike and helmet.

When I get there, La Purisma General looms in front of me, lit up from inside. It reminds me of the last time I visited it at night, when my great-uncle, pulling at my sleeve, made me promise something, I still don't know what.

I find a clump of bushes near the entrance of the emergency room and carefully hide my bike and helmet under it.

I hold my breath and take off my knapsack.

This will be the trickiest part.

If I get away with this, I'll have no trouble inside.

Carefully, I unpack my knapsack and silently promise to never again make fun of my mother's neat-freak behavior. She hates to clean the house and get her clothes dirty, so one day she came up with the brilliant idea to bring a few pairs of scrubs home from the OR to wear when she dusts. I pull out the green drawstring pants and top.

There's also the incredibly lucky fact that my mom is so small.

I can hear Rowena's voice in my ears: *"You're as big as your mom now!"*

I pull on the scrubs and reach into the pocket. There, as I knew there would be, are a face mask and cap that my mom uses to keep dust out of her hair and cleaning fumes out of her nose.

Now dressed, I carefully hang her ID tag around my neck, stow my knapsack with my bike, and head briskly toward the hospital.

Time to go for broke!

I avoid the lights, staying in the shadows as I creep past the front entrance, where I would have to walk by Ronnie or whoever is on duty tonight.

With our similarly shaped eyes, and everything else covered in the oversized scrubs, I look enough like my mother to pass through, but they all know her and will want to talk. Which will give it all away.

I get beyond the entrance and reach an area flooded with light and activity. The entrance to the emergency room is always busy, even in a small hospital like La Purisma. Someone always has a sick kid, or is feeling chest pains or whatever.

Tonight, an ambulance is sitting at the door, lights flashing.

I move quickly through the throng of aides, EMTs, and other staff. No one even looks up as I stride as purposefully as I can toward the elevator.

I look to my right, and just like in the game, there's a row of clipboards with paperwork to be filled out. I grab one and proceed to look busy as I wait for the elevator.

The door opens, and I get on. I see that the elevator is empty, and hit the button for the fourteenth floor.

If someone were in here with me, I'd have had to get off on the OR floor, or else they'd be curious why a nurse in scrubs and a mask was going anywhere else.

And the last thing I want to do is arouse curiosity.

I can feel my heart pounding under the flimsy green scrubs. The door opens on the tenth floor, and my stomach tightens in a knot. A gurney pushes in, and—

Oh no!

I note with alarm that it's accompanied by Clarisse and Crystal, Mom's friends from the ICU. What are they doing on this shift? If they see me, it's all over!

NoNoNoNo!

The two of them are, for the time being, bent over the gurney, concerned with securing IV drips and straps.

I slide into the corner of the elevator and turn my back to

them, writing furiously on the clipboard in my hands. I know they'll be getting off on the eleventh floor, where the recovery rooms are located.

One floor. The doors close and the car slowly, agonizingly, begins its ascent. It feels like hours.

"You're doing just fine, Mr. Ramirez," Clarisse is cooing to the patient as he moans and shifts.

The elevator slowly settles, and the doors open. Clarisse and Crystal push the gurney out, and once again, I'm alone. I slump against the wall, catching my breath.

This is insane.

When the doors open onto the darkened halls of the four-teenth floor, I see the nurses' station and the glow from the dozen monitors. Pearl is indeed still on duty. No wonder she was in such a bad mood.

A double shift. Nurses hate those.

I backtrack and head in the opposite direction. There is no way I'm going to walk by Pearl, even in scrubs, but the game figured all that out.

Slowly, I count the doors as I walk. Three . . . four . . . five. The fifth door. This should be the one.

Checking to make sure no one is in the hall, I quickly open the unmarked door. I slip in and shut it behind me.

I pull the light cord and find myself exactly where I need to be.

Now it's only a matter of keeping cool and doing everything according to the game.

In front of me, attached to the wall, is a metal box with a big pipe coming out of it. I reach into my pocket and take out a small screwdriver. I pry the hinged cover of the box open and peer inside.

There they are.

Dozens of switches, each one numbered. The circuit breakers for the floor. I have to do this just right.

I count down the breakers from the top. Seventeenth down. The one that controls the new monitors at Pearl's desk.

If I hit the wrong breaker, the lights in someone's room could lose power, or worse, some machine keeping someone alive.

I know the building has generators, but breakers have to be reset, and who knows what a few precious minutes could do if I make the wrong choice?

I locate the seventeenth breaker (having counted down three times, just to make sure) and retrieve a second object from my pocket.

My great-uncle's lighter.

I open it, flick it on, and hold it up to the switch and grimace as the smell of melting plastic hits my nose.

Then, quickly, I push the melted breaker to the off position and turn the light off.

I hear raised voices outside, and wait until some footsteps run past the door before I quietly open it and flatten myself against the wall in the darkened hallway.

I see a large maintenance man with a shaved head, a friend of my mom's named Gabriel, marching swiftly through the double doors to the nurses' station.

Gabriel is the one they always call when anything needs fixing.

I creep around to the doors to the nurses' station and allow myself a quick look through the windows in the door.

I note with satisfaction that the monitors for all the rooms have gone blank.

I put my ear up to the door and listen.

"This has to be fixed *now*. It cannot wait until morning." Pearl is lecturing Gabriel, who is fiddling with the knobs on one of the monitors.

"I dunno, Pearl. I been telling them ever since they put in this system that these monitors were putting too great a load on the circuits."

"It hasn't been a problem for months. Isn't there just some . . . switch that has to be reset or something? I need these monitors."

Gabriel looks down at the desk and indicates all the alarm buttons. "You got all that, right? I mean, if anything goes wrong, you'll know it."

Pearl isn't having it. "This is not just about their vitals. I need to see what's going on in those rooms."

Gabriel holds up his hands. "Okay, got it."

I duck down as the doors open.

Gabriel strides right past me and heads toward the closet where the breakers are.

I hear him muttering, "Before those monitors were put in, you'd just go from room to room instead of sittin' there on your lazy—"

"What was that?" Pearl calls after him, her voice rising. "When did *you* come in? I've been here since nine this morning! You watch yourself about who's calling who lazy!"

"Simmer down!" Gabriel yells back, smiling to himself. Clearly he enjoys getting a rise out of Pearl.

There's a pause, and I hear a low whistle and "I'll be—"

Gabriel's head sticks out of the closet. "You should come and see this."

Pearl's lips are squeezed tight. "You know I can't leave my station."

"The breaker looks like it burned up. Never seen anything like it. I *told* them it wouldn't hold that load."

"So what do we do now?" Pearl is sounding more and more annoyed.

"I got replacements downstairs in the supply closet. I gotta take the whole thing off and put a new one in. That's a job."

Pearl smiles. And it isn't pretty. "Then you'd better get started. I want these monitors back, and I want them back tonight."

Grumbling, Gabriel heads off to the elevators.

As soon as he's out of sight, I let out my breath and walk slowly back to where Gabriel left the cart he was pushing when the monitors went down.

Another reason this had to be done at night, I realize. During the night there's only one nurse at this station. If there were two, one would go from room to room checking the patients while Gabriel made the repairs. With one, Pearl couldn't risk being away from the desk, where she could monitor the machines for all her patients. With the video off, all she has are the ones monitoring their vital signs, which will show her if something's wrong.

I take Gabriel's cart and push it slowly in front of me and make a U-turn. There's a back entrance to the hallway with the rooms. I turn the corner and come to the double doors marked NO ENTRY—VISITORS MUST SIGN IN AT DESK and push.

The hallway is empty. There are never any visitors at this time of night.

Steadying myself, I walk slowly, counting the numbers . . . 1411 . . . 1409 . . .

I know that with the repair I probably have about fifteen minutes, max, to check out the room. Unless Mrs. Krausz is awake.

I have to trust she won't ring the call bell, summon Pearl, and end the game once and for all.

I reach room 1405. I knock quietly. No answer. Slowly, I open the door, and—

"Time for my medicine already?"

A chunky woman is sitting up in the bed, reading. *Love's Savage Kiss,* of all things.

She looks at me with saucerlike eyes above a bulbous nose and wide mouth permanently set in a resigned smile.

"I'm sorry, Mrs. Krausz, I didn't know you were awake."

"Please. I can't sleep in these places. Do I know you? I don't remember seeing you before, darling." Mrs. Krausz speaks with the rich, round tones I associate with my father's relatives back east in Brooklyn.

"I'm . . . new . . . ," I say, glad for once that my voice hasn't changed yet. "How are you feeling?" I ask, trying to sound as nurselike as I can.

"You're not a nurse, are you, dear?" asks Mrs. Krausz, smiling again.

"No, I'm . . . an orderly . . ."

Mrs. Krausz laughs. "You look a little young, darling. What's the real story?"

I decide that honesty is the best policy.

I'm about to remove my mask and then hesitate. "Would it be all right for me to take this off? I know you're afraid of germs, and—"

Mrs. Krausz puts her hands to her forehead and laughs again. "Is that what they told you?"

"Yes, that you wouldn't see visitors because of your fear of germs. Not even your immediate family was allowed in."

Another burst of laughter. "That's hilarious. That must have been my son Nathan, telling the nurse something to make himself feel better. The truth is, I can't stand all those sad faces. Who needs them? I'd rather be alone. Make yourself comfortable, darling."

I take off the mask and the cap.

Mrs. Krausz stares at me. "So how old are you, sweetheart, if you don't mind my asking?"

"I'm twelve," I confess. Normally, having a complete stranger call me "sweetheart" and "darling" would be weird, but somehow when old Jewish ladies do it, it seems perfectly natural. I begin to scan the room, looking for anything black and rectangular.

Mrs. Krausz looks at me with worried eyes. "At this hour, he's at the hospital?"

Funny, she reminds me of some of the old Jewish ladies on my dad's side of the family: they also talk about you in the third person even though you're standing right there. And they talk like Yoda, too.

I tell you, I get this every Thanksgiving.

"And you have a name?"

"Um . . . Ted. My mom's a nurse here at the hospital."

"So, Ted, you're looking for your mother? Are you lost?"

I glance at the empty bed next to Mrs. Krausz. Clearly no one has been here since my great-uncle was moved.

"Actually, I was trying to find something my great-uncle might have left here. Ted Wakabayashi?"

Mrs. Krausz made a face. "The Japanese gentleman? I'm

sorry to say, I know he was your uncle, he should rest in peace, but he wasn't a very friendly man."

"It's all right. I didn't know him very well."

I reach confidently under his old bed, where the railings are. No magnetic box. I feel all the way around. Nothing.

As Mrs. Krausz goes on and on about her family, which ones she likes and which ones should drop dead, I search the windowsills, the drapes, the closet, the bathroom. It doesn't seem to faze her in the slightest that she's having a conversation with a strange twelve-year-old close to midnight while he does a top-to-bottom search of her room.

"You find what you're looking for, sweetheart?"

"No," I say glumly, and sit on the bed near her.

Mrs. Krausz pats my hand. "That's too bad."

She peers at my name tag. "Oh, your father's not—"

"No, I'm half."

"So the other half, if I may ask?"

"My dad's Jewish," I admit. Uh-oh. I know what's coming.

Her face lights up like a Christmas tree, or more accurately, like a menorah.

"I knew it! Did your mother convert?"

"No . . . we're not really—"

"You should come to services at our temple. We have so many Asian Jewish families."

Huh. It occurs to me that maybe it would be nice to meet some other Asian Jewish kids. "That sounds nice."

"Temple Beth Shalom in Tarzana."

I get up to go. It won't be long before the monitors are back on. "It was very nice to meet you, Mrs. Krausz. And I'll be sure to tell my parents about Temple Beth Shalom."

Just as I'm about to open the door, Mrs. Krausz calls after me.

"Listen, before you go . . . maybe you can get this to work. When your uncle was here, he always insisted on choosing the channels. Then he left, and nobody seems to be able to get this to work right. Could you look at it?"

She is holding up a remote control. A rectangular black remote control.

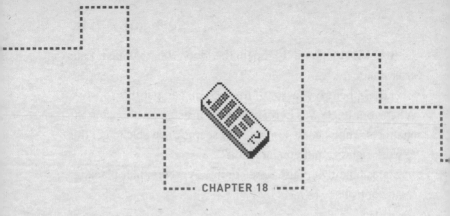

CHAPTER 18

SURPRISE VISITORS

I take the remote from Mrs. Krausz's proffering hand.

I try to sound casual, but I can hear the shake of excitement in my voice.

"M-maybe the batteries need replacing."

Mrs. Krausz makes a face. "That's funny. I remember your uncle changing them when he got here. He said he always did that. So thoughtful, he was."

So he opened the back.

It's in here.

I notice my hands shaking as I fumble for the latch that holds the battery compartment.

Slowly, I open it and peer inside.

Nothing.

No key.

I pry the batteries out. He must have put it behind them.

The only thing there is a small folded piece of paper. I take it and stuff it into my pocket. I reassemble the remote and throw it down on the bed in frustration.

No key.

Has someone else gotten here first and taken it?

Mrs. Krausz peers over with a worried look. "Don't be so concerned, darling. It's only a remote. If you can't fix it, you can't fix it. They're bringing me a new one in the morning anyway."

A whirring noise from down the corridor snaps me out of my daze. That would be Gabriel, putting in the new breaker with his electric screwdriver.

The monitors will be up and running in less than a minute.

"I'm afraid I have to go now, Mrs. Krausz. My mother . . . It was very nice meeting you."

On impulse, I pick up the remote.

"You wouldn't mind my taking this with me, would you? As kind of a keepsake of my great-uncle."

She laughs. "Of course not, darling. Take it and be well. As I said, for me, it never works." Mrs. Yoda grabs my face and kisses me roughly on the cheek. Definitely like one of Dad's aunts back in Brooklyn.

"Go safely, sweetheart. And promise you'll come visit again!"

"I'll try," I say. "As soon as I can."

"Such a nice boy," Mrs. Krausz murmurs as I leave.

I slip out the door and see the shadowy figure of Gabriel kneeling down by the closet, putting his tools away.

"How's it look now?" he yells to Pearl at the desk.

"They're back!" she crows. Even from where I am, I can see

through the double doors the glow of the room monitors lighting up Pearl's angular face.

Not a moment too soon.

I turn and see that I am directly by the staircase leading down to the ER. At least the game hasn't failed me in this.

I snap on the surgical mask and cap and sprint the thirteen flights down the now-silent stairs. I push open the door and stride purposefully through the emergency room.

As I walk by the aides and doctors, no one gives me a second glance. Those who look up just see another small Asian nurse in scrubs. Nothing new in this hospital.

And I'm out!

Panting with relief, I peel off the scrubs and stow them and the ID in my backpack.

I strap on my helmet and head out the driveway. The tires wobble as I fight to get control of my bike and my emotions. I steady myself, hit a downward slope, and begin to coast as the cool, breezy California night clears my mind.

I pull into the driveway and park my bike in the garage, leaning against the back door. Once more, I check my watch. Twelve-thirty. No chance my parents will be up.

I carefully open the door and push through the small entry leading to the kitchen. It's still and dark. Not a sound can be heard through the house. The adrenaline that has been carrying me through the last hour drains out with each step up the stairs. I lie down on my bed, too tired to do anything but sleep.

All of a sudden, I sit straight up and take the folded paper out of my pocket. I turn on my desk light. Carefully, I unfold it and see only this, neatly printed out:

コナミ

Japanese? It looks like something I've seen before, but fatigue catches up with me, and before I know it, my eyes close and my head drops.

■ ■ ■

"Ted!" someone is yelling from downstairs.

I groggily sit up and focus. I stumble downstairs and join Mom, who's standing with a tall, narrow-faced man with short gray hair.

"Ted, there's someone here to see us. Mr.—"

"Clark Kent, with the *Honolulu Star-Advertiser*." He hands me his card.

"I thought you worked for the *Daily Planet*," I crack.

Mr. Kent smiles a thin smile. "I get that a lot."

Mom sits down on the couch and folds her arms. "I'm afraid you can't stay too long. I have to go grocery shopping before I go to the hospital."

"That's all right!" Mr. Kent says. "This shouldn't take long. May I?" He indicates a chair at the dining room table and sits down. As he takes out a pad and pencil, I study Clark Kent for a moment.

He has deep-set eyes, and graying eyebrows that slope down as well, making him look weary and older than he probably is. His narrow features and neat haircut remind me of an anchorman from one of those cable news network shows my dad watches.

"Do you want to talk to Mom first? She knew Great-Uncle Ted the best. This is about him, isn't it?" I say.

Mr. Kent turns to Mom and smiles.

"This article isn't just about your uncle. I'm trying to get as much information as I can about all the brave men who fought so valiantly in the Nisei brigade."

Mr. Kent looks back at me and taps his pad with his pencil. "What I am most interested in—um . . . what our readers would be most interested in, I should say—are your uncle's . . . er, your great-uncle's last words."

"I only really talked to him once, and that was a day before he died."

A worried look comes over his face. "Oh, I see . . . so you don't know?"

"Don't know what?" I ask.

Mr. Kent coughs and reads from his notebook. "Shortly after seeing you, he fell into a coma from which he never awoke." Mr. Kent looks up and regards me with an easy smile. "Which means, I guess, that you *would* have heard his last words."

I stand up. "I really don't feel like talking about this."

My mom comes over and puts her arm around me. "That's fine, Ted. I don't mean to be rude, Mr. Kent, but I do have to get going anyway, so—"

"I'm really sorry. I'm not used to talking to young people. Please accept my apologies."

Now I don't know what to think. He seems like a nice enough guy.

I feel myself softening. "All I can tell you about my great-uncle is that he didn't really *say* anything. He couldn't speak, so he wrote everything down on a pad of paper."

Mr. Kent starts writing furiously. He tries to sound casual. "And this pad of paper—do you still have it, by any chance?"

I don't think Mr. Kent needs to know what's on that pad.

"Uh, no . . . I'm not sure where it is . . . ," I say quickly.

Mr. Kent looks up with surprise. "Are you saying you lost it?"

My mom steps in. "He didn't think it was all that important. He's twelve, Mr. Kent. I think he's been through enough, don't you?"

"I mean, I didn't know he was going to die, you know?" I can hear the edge creeping into my voice.

"I see," says Mr. Kent, fumbling to gather his things. He stuffs the notebook and pencil into his bag, gets to his feet, and smiles at me. "Of course. But if you do happen to remember his last words, or whatever he wrote on that pad, it might be a great way to end my article. If you could call me, I'd really appreciate it. My number's on that card."

I nod. Mr. Kent heads for the door. My mom goes to let him out.

At the doorway, Mr. Kent turns. "Thank you for your time, Mrs. Gerson. I'm so sorry I upset you, Ted. I'm trying to honor these men, and your great-uncle was one of them. That's all I want."

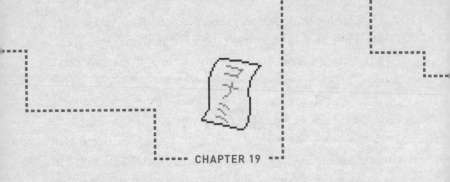

CHAPTER 19

THE GAMES OF UNCLE PETER

"Who do you think he really is?"

Caleb is in our living room, looking at the card. I called him as soon as Mr. Kent left, and he biked right over.

After Caleb was a wuss and wouldn't call Isabel (even though I called her last time), I got her on the phone and she had her dad drive her over.

"I called the *Honolulu Star-Advertiser*, and of course they've never heard of anyone named Clark Kent," Isabel says importantly.

"You called *the newspaper*? That's pretty— Wow." I cannot imagine doing that in a million years.

Caleb snorts. "I could have told you that. I knew he was a phony from the beginning."

"Then why didn't you say so?" Isabel responds, sitting on the couch. She folds her arms and glares at Caleb.

I decide now is the time to give them the news. "Guys, there's more. You aren't gonna believe this. I got into room 1405."

"Whaaat?" Caleb's eyes widen and, in spite of himself, he sits down on the couch next to Isabel.

"But you said that was impossible!" Isabel exclaims.

"Well, maybe not *impossible*," I reply, trying not to sound too smug.

"Details, details!" Caleb demands.

"I just started thinking of how I would manage this if it were a computer game, you know?" I begin.

I tell them everything, from "borrowing" my mom's stuff all the way until I came back home.

"So all I ended up with was this note," I finish, showing them the small folded piece of paper in my hand.

"You're amazing!" marvels Caleb.

Isabel is gazing at me with a dazed expression. I can't believe how impressed she looks.

"You really did this," Isabel says. "That's . . . that's . . ."

Oh, what a feeling. When Miss Know-It-All is so awestruck she's at a loss for words.

"That's the *stupidest,* most *irresponsible* thing I've ever heard!"

I have to admit I wasn't expecting this.

"But—" I try.

"But *nothing.* What if you'd been caught? Impersonating your mother, stealing her ID, damaging hospital property? Not only could you have gotten arrested, but your mother could have been fired as well!" Isabel is pacing now, shaking her head.

"But he *wasn't* caught," argues Caleb.

Isabel is still fuming. "That was just luck! I mean, do whatever you want, but to put your mom's job in jeopardy like
that . . ."

"It wasn't just luck," I say firmly. "I knew exactly what I
was doing, and the plan worked. I got in the room and got the
remote."

"How did you know?" demands Isabel. "To gamble your
mother's job—"

Okay. That does it. It's time to let them know.

I go to my room and return with my laptop.

"I think you need to see this."

"What is it?" asks Isabel.

"I was planning to show Caleb, but I want you to see it too."

An uncomfortable silence settles over us as the laptop
boots up.

Finally, I make my confession.

"It's . . . the truth. The truth about how I figured out about
Great-Uncle Ted's apartment. And getting into the hospital.
You both think I'm some sort of genius or something, but I'm
not. I lied to you. Both of you. I didn't solve those puzzles on
my own. I . . . had help."

"What kind of help?" Caleb asks incredulously.

I take a breath and say, "I know it's going to sound crazy . . .
but there's a game of my life online."

Isabel and Caleb stare at me for a long moment. Finally,
Caleb speaks.

"Right, Ted . . . and there's also a magical land where uni-
corns barf rainbows."

"Look, I don't expect you to believe me," I insist. "But that's
how I was able to figure out the patterns in Great-Uncle Ted's

apartment. And all the other stuff. I just let you think it was me being smart."

Isabel looks concerned. "Ted, that's silly. You mean there was a game that was *like* your life—"

"No!" I'm shouting now. "It *is* my life. That's how I solved it. It wasn't me. I can't pretend it was anymore."

I type "www.thegameofted.com" in the browser window and press the Enter button, then turn away.

I don't want to see my friends' faces when they're confronted with the truth.

Isabel and Caleb lean in and peer at the screen.

"This is pretty unbelievable," Caleb says in a low voice.

"I never thought something like this existed," agrees Isabel. "Never."

"See? What did I tell you?" I cry.

Caleb and Isabel burst out laughing.

"You really had me going there, dude," says Caleb.

I turn and look at the screen.

What I see is: a happy elderly couple waving at the camera, holding playing cards, surrounded by a frame of little hearts. Underneath is a quote: "Tom Mortimer and Barb Everdell— 'We met through TED! It was the best thing we ever did!'"

Underneath them is a banner announcing: "The game of TED—Terrific Elder Dating! Finally, a place for singles in the prime of their lives!"

Then, in a blinking square in the corner: "Come to the American Legion Hall on Ventura Boulevard every Wednesday for Game Night! We have all your favorites! Bingo, canasta, mah-jongg! Meet eligible singles 65 and up in a fun, no-pressure atmosphere."

"Thanks for showing us this. Looks like fun," Isabel remarks.

"*And* no-pressure!" Caleb adds.

"Too bad there's that age limit thing . . . ," Isabel manages to get out before breaking into another spasm of giggles.

I stare at the screen in shock. "Must have typed in the address wrong," I say.

There's one sure way to call up the page.

I pull up the history menu on my browser and note with satisfaction the address from the night before. Bingo!

The Game of Ted. Confidently, I click on the link, and the home page loads in.

There are Tom and Barb, waving happily back at me.

I sit, frozen in place, staring at the image, willing it to change to the mysterious game that got me so far when I needed it, and is now making me look like an idiot in front of two people doing their best not to laugh in my face.

"Maybe you fell asleep and just *thought* you played the game. It was your unconscious mind working out the puzzles," Isabel suggests.

"That makes sense, man," Caleb says. "Either that or you were getting your advice from Tom and Barb."

"You guys think I'm crazy!" I yell.

"We don't think you're crazy," Isabel says, in that voice that you use when you think you might be talking to a crazy person.

"It's just that it should be there if you said it was, shouldn't it?" asks Caleb.

"I guess that's true," I admit.

Now what? *Was* I dreaming? I close the laptop (bye, Tom and Barb) and stare at it. Great.

At least Isabel isn't mad anymore.

Now she just thinks I'm nuts.

"So . . . um . . . where's the key?" she asks gently.

"I told you. All that was there was this paper."

I show them the three symbols.

"Those look so familiar," Caleb says.

"Yeah, I know. I think I've seen them somewhere too," I answer, grateful that we're talking about something else. "But I can't remember where."

"It's Japanese. It is possible it came with the remote? You said it was a Sony. That's a Japanese company, right?" reasons Isabel.

"I don't think so," I say firmly. "Mrs. Krausz said Great-Uncle Ted was always fiddling with the remote, so it would have fallen out then, and she said it hasn't worked right since he left. He definitely put something in there. But why this paper?"

There is the sound of a door opening behind us.

My mom pushes her way in, holding two bags of groceries. Caleb and I get up to help her.

"Mom! What are you doing here?" I ask as I place the bags on the kitchen table.

"I live here, remember?"

Ho ho. Mom humor, level one.

"I *told* you I was going shopping before work. Just like your father—you *never* listen. Why, hello, Isabel!"

My mom's tone turns from irritated to honey-sweet in a nanosecond as she sees the third person in her living room.

"Hello, Mrs. Gerson. It's always so good to see you," says Isabel.

As my mom begins to put away the food, I casually pick up the piece of paper.

"Mom, there's something I found when I was going through Great-Uncle Ted's things that I wanted to ask you about."

"As soon as I get this stuff sorted, Teddy," Mom answers from inside the fridge.

Caleb and Isabel exchange grins as I stand by, handing my mom items as she calls for them. Finally, satisfied with the arrangement of her foodstuffs, Mom stands up, smiles, and turns to her oh-so-helpful son.

"Now, what did you find? Photos?" She turns to Isabel. "I hope he hasn't shown you any pictures of me from the seventies. It was a bad decade for hair and fashion. I even had a perm, for gosh sake!"

Isabel assures her I've done no such thing.

I hold out the paper. Mom looks and sighs.

"Oh, Teddy, why do you have to embarrass me in front of your friends? You know I don't read Japanese."

"So it *is* Japanese."

"Of course it is." My mom turns to Isabel. "Uncle Ted was always trying to get me to learn it when I was a kid, but it seemed so hard, and I never had any need for it, really. The only thing he taught me that I remember is if you get a mosquito bite on your leg at the beach, you should rub sand on it."

"I'm sorry?" Isabel says pleasantly, obviously thinking Mom is speaking gibberish.

My mom laughs. "It's a mnemonic. You know, a way of remembering something? That's how to remember how to count the first five numbers in Japanese. If you get a mosquito bite on your knee, it itches, and if you rub sand on it, the itch goes away. So . . . ichi ni san shi go . . . 'itchy knee sand, she go.' Get it?"

"Itchy knee sand, she go," Isabel repeats, nodding. "That's pretty cool."

"I only wish I'd learned more," Mom groans. "My brother Peter picked up more Japanese than I did. But that was at least partially because of all those video games he played."

Without warning, Caleb jumps to his feet. "Is the stuff from your great-uncle's apartment in your room?" he asks.

"Yes, but—" I reply, looking after Caleb as he dashes upstairs.

A moment later, he returns with a white cardboard box. It's the one we filled with the old video game cartridges and controllers from the store.

"We were wondering about these," Caleb asks, bringing them over to my mom.

Her eyes light up when she sees them.

"Oh my gosh! Those were your uncle Peter's! He'd die if he knew you had them!"

"That explains why 'Wakabayashi' is written on them in marker," I jump in. "They weren't Great-Uncle Ted's—Uncle Peter's last name is also Wakabayashi." Mom peers into the box. "But in all these years . . . you never mentioned Uncle Peter played video games," I say. "As a matter of fact, you never want me to talk to him about them."

Mom looks up at me. "It's . . . a sore subject. I remember when Uncle Ted took those away from him. That summer, Peter was a little older than you and worked part-time at the liquor store, helping out in the back, stocking the shelves. He even hooked this up to the TV Uncle Ted had in the storeroom.

Uncle Ted got sick and tired of watching Peter doing nothing but playing these games, so he confiscated them. Peter stopped playing games right after that."

"Uncle Peter is my mom's brother," I explain to Isabel. "He's a really successful software engineer."

"Then it makes sense he was an early gamer," Caleb adds.

"See?" I say. "He played computer games all the time when he was my age. Now look at him."

"He also had a 4.0 grade point average and took apart and rebuilt a 1975 Mustang without a manual," my mom answers. "After what happened between him and Uncle Ted, maybe you can understand why I haven't been so fond of your spending so much time with your games."

"There has to be more to the story with Uncle Peter and Great-Uncle Ted," I press. "Adults confiscate games all the time. No reason for a family feud."

Mom sighs and sits down on the couch. We all sit across from her.

"I guess I can tell you," she begins. "But your uncle Peter is still embarrassed by it."

She looks out the window.

"You see, Uncle Ted hired Peter for the summer when he was fourteen. Peter was told to watch the store, but he was so busy playing one of his games that some local kids came in and walked off with a couple of six-packs of beer without him seeing it. Ted sent Peter back to Hawaii the next day. Mom and Dad were so furious with him they let Uncle Ted confiscate his games, the consoles, and the controllers. Peter felt so guilty he never played video games again. He apologized over and over, but Uncle Ted wouldn't hear it. My folks tried to talk to him, but for some weird reason he made a huge deal out of it. He said he'd put his trust in Peter, and Peter betrayed that trust."

I see Isabel jerk her head in Mom's direction.

Picking up on the clue, I reach out and pat her hand. She continues. "Peter really tried to make it up to him, but somehow, once he broke that bond, Uncle Ted wouldn't budge."

"So that was the big story between Peter and Great-Uncle Ted?" I ask incredulously. "For the rest of his life, he wouldn't talk to him because of *that*?"

"Yes. He had Peter pegged as a disappointment from then on. I guess my brother has spent most of his life trying to prove him wrong." Smiling at the memory, Mom adds, "Not only that, but Uncle Ted threw out all of Peter's comic books too! They'd probably be worth a fortune today."

A sad silence filled the room.

Caleb looks like someone stabbed him in the heart. "That is so *harsh*," he's finally able to utter. He turns green, and I know he's convinced himself that his precious Amazing Adventure #1 was in that pile of comic books.

Hearing Caleb's voice brings me back to the present. I look down at the box at his feet.

"So what made you get those out?" I ask him.

Caleb pulls one of the boxes of games out and holds it up. "I knew I'd seen those symbols before."

On the box, above the title, is the name of the company.

コナミ KONAMI

I pick up an old controller from the box and push the buttons. I then begin pressing them in a certain sequence, again and again.

"Of course." I feel like a world-class moron for not realizing it sooner.

Caleb meets my gaze, and the thunderbolt hits him as well. "You think?" he says in amazement.

We continue to stare at each other in shock.

"Mom," I say as casually as I can, "you said Great-Uncle Ted was sick of watching Peter play his video games?"

"It wasn't that, really. It was more his not paying attention to the store that caused all the trouble. Actually, if I remember, when Peter first brought the games in, Uncle Ted was quite interested in learning about them. Peter said he used to ask him all sorts of questions."

"So it was just—Uncle Peter was playing them too much. . . ." The words are tumbling out of my mouth. I can feel my body tensing up as I push the same sequence of buttons on the keypad again and again.

"Yes, dear. Everything in moderation, right?" Mom glances at Isabel with a smile.

"Um, Mom . . . don't you have to get to the hospital?" I ask without looking at her.

My mom glances at her watch and gives a start. "Oh my gosh! With all this reminiscing, I completely lost track of the time!" She leaps up, gives me a quick kiss on the cheek, and heads out.

"See? He can be so thoughtful when he wants to be!" she calls over her shoulder to Isabel.

As soon as the door closes, I exchange high fives with Caleb.

"The Konami Code!" I whoop.

"The Konami Code! That *has* to be it!" Caleb says, excitement rising in his voice.

Isabel has had enough. "Could someone enlighten me as to what the Konami Code is?"

"To anyone who plays games, the Konami code is, well, the worst-kept secret there ever was," I explain. "Game developers always need to be able to play through the levels to do bug fixes and smooth out the playability. Early on, the Konami company used a series of button pushes to give unlimited lives and power to the player. It got leaked and became legendary in the gaming world."

I reach in and began to line up the various game controllers that are in the box.

"Ever since then," Caleb continues, "it's been used on over three hundred games. Sometimes it gives you eternal life in the game, or unlimited power. Stuff like that."

"Up up, down down, left right, left right, B, A," we chant in unison.

"*That's* the Konami Code," Caleb says excitedly as I begin entering the code into a small red controller. "You enter it into almost any game controller over the last twenty years and it will unlock extra powers or levels."

"So you think—" Isabel starts to say.

But we aren't listening. We're busy pressing the buttons on all the controllers.

"It has to be here," I say. But I enter the sequence into the last controller with no obvious effect.

"Maybe you have to put the code into the controllers in a certain order," suggests Caleb.

"It's worth a try," I answer.

As we laboriously try various combinations of controllers, Isabel sighs, reaches into her bag, and pulls out a large book.

"You could help, you know," I say with annoyance.

"I am," Isabel shoots back, not looking up from her reading.

"How? By reading about the Konami Code?" snipes Caleb.

Isabel snaps the book shut and looks up at us. "In case you were wondering, I was reading about your great-uncle."

She holds up the book. It's titled *Go for Broke: A History of the Japanese American 100th Infantry Battalion and the 442nd Regimental Combat Team.*

"Where did you find that?" I ask.

"In the library," Isabel answers. "They have all sorts of books there. You should visit sometime."

I decide to ignore that jab, and go on. "So did you learn anything?"

"Remember the four coins we found? Do you remember what countries they were from?"

"Let's see . . . ," says Caleb, "Um . . . France, Germany . . . Italy, I think . . ."

"And Austria," Isabel finishes for him. "Those were the four primary countries where the 442nd fought. That's why he picked them."

I'm only half listening. I'm looking at the cover of the book. It's a photo of a young Japanese American soldier holding several men wearing Nazi uniforms prisoner at gunpoint. I wonder if my great-uncle was anywhere near where that picture was taken, and what he saw in the war.

"So why is it called *Go for Broke*?" I ask.

"Apparently that was the motto of the regiment," Isabel explains. "It was a Hawaiian expression originally, and they brought it with them."

Caleb looks down at the remote in his hand and throws it down in disgust.

"Well, if it isn't here, he had to put it *somewhere*."

All of a sudden, I can feel the hairs on the back of my neck tingle.

Always, it's something right in front of my nose.

Like a sleepwalker, I get up, turn around abruptly, and leave the room.

I head upstairs, rummage around in my room, and then back into the kitchen.

"Guys, I think this is it."

Isabel and Caleb follow my voice into the kitchen and find me staring at the black rectangular object I've gotten from my knapsack, now on the kitchen counter.

It looks like any other cable remote, with a round Select button surrounded by arrows on the top, bottom, left, and right, to navigate on-screen menus. And, I note with satisfaction, there are even buttons marked *A, B, C,* and *D.*

Holding my breath, I slowly press the buttons in sequence.

Up. Up. Down. Down. Left. Right. Left. Right. B. A.

There's a clicking noise, and the entire back of the remote falls away.

I turn the remote around, and there, nested in the wires and circuit board, is a small gold key.

CHAPTER 20

ONE KEY LEADS TO ANOTHER

I pick up the key, turn, and press it into Isabel's hand.

"Why are you doing this?" she asks. "Shouldn't you be the one to open it?"

"I don't know," I say softly. "I think it should be you."

I go to get the wooden box from my bedroom, leaving Caleb and Isabel alone.

As I return, I hear Caleb say, "This book sounds pretty cool." He's flipping through *Go for Broke*.

"Those guys were amazing," Isabel remarks. "According to this book, they were the most decorated unit in United States military history."

"Hmm," Caleb says.

"That means they won more medals than—" Isabel starts.

"I know what 'most decorated' means!" Caleb says, glaring at her.

I put the box on the kitchen counter.

"This is it!" Caleb says.

Isabel slowly puts the gold key into the lock. She pauses as it fits in snugly. Then, her hand trembling a little, she turns the key. We hear a click.

I lift the lid, and we take out the items one by one.

All that's inside are an old paperback and a two small black notebooks.

Caleb makes a face. "This is it?" he says again, but meaning something totally different.

Isabel looks crushed. "I *knew* you should have opened it."

"That wouldn't have made any difference," I say.

"No jewels," Caleb moans.

"No gold coins," Isabel sighs.

"Who knows? Maybe it's another puzzle." I shrug.

I pick up one of the notebooks. It has formulas and scientific information jotted down in a strong hand, written in what looks like fountain pen.

Isabel picks up the book and reads the title: *"The Maltese Falcon."*

"I've heard of that!" Caleb says. "They made a really famous movie about it during the war!"

"Maybe it was his favorite book," I say.

Isabel opens the musty paperback. "So it's, what? A detective story or something?"

"I guess so. My dad always goes on and on about it, like it's the best one ever," says Caleb.

I reach behind the box and pull out the pad of paper from the hospital.

"This is the last thing my great-uncle wrote," I announce, reading off the sheet:

*"THE BOX IS ONLY THE BEGINNING. KEEP LOOKING
FOR THE ANSWERS. ALWAYS GO FOR BROKE!
PROMISE ME!"*

Caleb peers at the box and taps it on all sides. "You think
there's a secret compartment somewhere?"

I examine the empty box. Why didn't the game take me this
far? Are there things I have to discover for myself?

There's nothing else in the box. No secret buttons or sliding
doors.

It's just a wooden box. Containing nothing more than two
leather-bound notebooks and a musty old paperback.

"'Keep looking for the answers,'" murmurs Isabel. "Do you
think we didn't search hard enough?"

"Give me a break!" Caleb protests. "Ted was obviously supposed to find this. All the clues led to it. He figured everything
out . . . even how to get into the hospital! What else did his
great-uncle want him to do?"

"I don't know . . . maybe read?" Isabel answers, holding up
the book.

"Hey! Maybe it's a valuable book! A collector's item or
something. You think that's the treasure he was talking about?"
Caleb asks me.

"Maybe . . . but I keep thinking we're missing something.
Something obvious . . ."

A gasp from Isabel jolts me out of my stupor.

"What's wrong?" I ask. Isabel looks like she's seen a ghost.

"Um . . . I just looked at the first chapter . . ."

"So?" Caleb says impatiently. "What's so horrible? Bad
grammar? Something misspelled?"

Isabel holds out the book so we can see the title of the first chapter: *SPADE AND ARCHER.*

"How could he know?" Isabel stares at me, her usually cool eyes wide now.

I look at the book and read a few lines. I skip ahead.

"It seems that Spade is the last name of the hero in *The Maltese Falcon,* Sam Spade. And Miles Archer is his partner."

"That is definitely weird . . . ," Caleb mutters.

"I think it's just a coincidence," I say quickly, trying to sound reasonable. "Archer is a pretty common name. I mean, your name is in that Henry James book too, right?"

"Right. And of course, Edith Wharton named her protagonist in *The Age of Innocence* Newland Archer," Isabel reasons to herself.

"Exactly!" I exclaim. "Newland Archer!" The fact that I have no idea who Edith Whateverhernameis is, let alone what *The Age of Innocence* is, doesn't matter. If it calms Isabel down, that's all that matters right now. "Plus, Uncle Ted sent me on this mission before we even met."

Isabel takes a deep breath, and the color returns to her cheeks. "I'm sorry, guys. I just wasn't expecting to see my name in that book," she says. "Serves me right for not knowing my crime fiction."

"Archer is a mutant in the X-Factor comic books," Caleb adds helpfully.

I glare at him.

"What? I'm just saying it's a common name in literature."

"Good to know," Isabel says dryly. "My name is also used for some dumb comic-book character."

"For your information, Archer isn't dumb. He can transform

at will into pure energy, and shoots photoelectric plasma bolts from his gauntlets."

"He sounds pretty cool," I admit.

Isabel riffles through the book. "And this actually looks pretty interesting. Is it okay if I borrow it? Maybe there's something here. Some sort of clue."

"Great idea!" I say. "You can read that and report to Caleb and me. And we'll each take one of these notebooks."

Caleb picks one up and opens it. It's filled with drawings. Some are detailed diagrams, with arrows pointing to various parts of the picture; others are merely sketches with notations.

"I can look through this one," he says.

I reach for the smaller book. "I guess that leaves this one for me."

I pick up the notebook by the back cover. My thumb feels the outline of something hard between the leather cover and the cardboard backing it's glued to. I press my finger against the cover and feel it again.

Isabel and Caleb are watching me. "There's something in there?" Isabel asks breathlessly.

"I'm not sure . . . ," I say distractedly, my fingers tracing the area.

"I hope it's not like a dead roach or something, 'cause that would be gross," Caleb says with a grimace.

"It would crunch if it were a roach . . . and there would be a hole where it had crawled in," Isabel replies, glancing down with fascination.

"Yeah, I guess so," says Caleb, sounding relieved.

"I bet it's a jewel of some kind!" Isabel says confidently.

"Only one way to find out," I answer simply.

I go to a drawer and get a small paring knife with a sharp edge. Carefully, I make a small slit in the leather. I put my fingers into the hole, fish around, and, looking at the others, pull something out.

Caleb's head drops to his chest in frustration.

It's another key.

I look at it. All this for another key.

And no idea what it's for.

I slap the key down onto the counter in frustration. "It seems like every time we learn something, it just takes us back to another blank page. No matter what we do."

"Plus ça change, plus c'est le meme chose." Isabel nods.

We look at her. She just stares back. "What?"

"Just once I wish we didn't have to ask you what you mean," says Caleb, shaking his head.

"Oh, right. I'm sorry. It means 'The more things change, the more things stay the same.' I guess I thought everybody knew it."

"Maybe everybody back in your fancy private school."

Thankfully, a loud buzzing noise interrupts the scene. I look down and realize it's my cell phone. *Private Caller* comes up on the caller ID.

I raise the phone to my ear. "Hello?" I say hesitantly.

"Is this Ted?" asks a pleasant voice. "It's Clark . . . Mr. Kent. I'm going to be going back to Hawaii in a few days and just wondered if you ever remembered anything your great-uncle said."

I look at my friends and mouth the words "Clark Kent."

Isabel and Caleb listen as I continue.

"As a matter of fact, some of it did come back to me. . . .

No, you don't have to come over to the house. My friends and I were just about to get some pizza around the corner. . . . Yeah, it's called Fascati Pizzeria. We can meet there. See you in a bit."

I click off. Caleb and Isabel are staring at me with confused looks on their faces.

"What's with the pizza business?" Caleb asks.

I gather up the box and my great-uncle's pad and put them in my knapsack. "Look, all we know about this guy is that he doesn't really work for the *Honolulu Star-Advertiser*. I don't want him here at the house until I know who he is and what he wants."

"Meeting in a public place. Very smart." Isabel nods. Then her face darkens. "So how are we getting there?"

"Well, we don't get our licenses for four years, so I guess it's bikes," cracks Caleb.

"Well, I don't have a bike. So, what? I guess I'm supposed to catch up on my reading again while you two go gallivanting around?" fumes Isabel.

"*Gallivanting?* Really? You just said 'gallivanting'?" Caleb asks incredulously.

"What's wrong with that?" Isabel asks. "It's a perfectly good word. It means—"

"I know what it means," replies Caleb with a shake of his head. "I just didn't think anyone under the age of seventy used words like that."

I can feel things getting out of hand again. "Guys, listen . . ."

"Fine, from now on I'll only use simple words. Like you find in comic books."

"That is such utter *garbage*," Caleb seethes. "There is some really great writing in comic books. Which you might find out if you weren't such a—"

"*Caleb*. Chill. Isabel, you can use my mom's bike and helmet. They're in the garage."

Caleb and Isabel stand up, and I grab a pen.

"What're you doing?" asks Caleb.

"Leaving my mom a note, letting her know where we're going," I say. "You know how moms worry. . . ."

"Mine doesn't," Caleb mutters.

As we head for the garage, Caleb can't resist. He turns to Isabel.

"So you actually know how to ride a bike? I thought people at private schools only took like limos."

"My mother's family has a place on Long Island. I go there every summer. Well, that is, until this summer, of course," Isabel answers evenly.

I am relieved that she doesn't take the bait.

"So listen, how are we going to handle this?" I ask as we push off in the direction of the pizzeria.

"Simple," says Isabel, easily keeping pace with us. "We just get Mr. Clark Kent to tell us the truth."

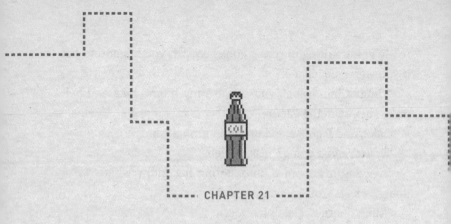

CHAPTER 21

ANOTHER BAD LIAR

As we are about to enter the pizzeria, I turn and notice that the black Jaguar is already parked in front. Clark Kent waves from a corner, where he is sitting with a laptop open in front of him. We approach the table.

"Hey, Ted," Kent says affably. "How nice to meet your friends."

He jumps up and closes his laptop, making room and chatting away, seeming somewhat distracted.

"Aren't you going to introduce me? What is everyone having? A slice? A drink? It's on me."

"No, we're fine," I say coolly. The three of us sit down, facing Kent.

"I thought you wanted to meet here because— Ahem, I see." Kent regards us sitting stone-faced across the table. "All business, well, well!" he jokes, and laughs nervously.

"This is Caleb Grant, and this is Isabel Archer."

"Someone's parents like Henry James!" exclaims Kent, nodding.

Isabel reddens a little. "My father is an English professor."

"Just like Ted, huh? Something in common. That's nice."

Now it's my turn to feel the heat rising in my cheeks. "Look, we're here for a reason, so maybe we could just talk about that."

"Fine," agrees Kent a little too quickly. "So what did you remember?"

"Actually," Caleb says, "that's not why we're here."

"Oh?" Kent sounds less annoyed than nervous.

Isabel takes a breath and then blurts out, "Why do you say you're from the *Honolulu Star-Advertiser* when they've never heard of you?"

Kent looks stricken, his eyes going from one face to another, finally landing on me.

He laughs sheepishly. "You know, they say kids are always the hardest to fool. I'm actually doing this article freelance and was hoping to sell it to the paper—"

"Then why make up a lie so easy to expose?" Isabel insists.

"And why are you so concerned about Ted's great-uncle?" adds Caleb.

"Who are you really?" I ask.

Kent takes out a handkerchief and mops his now sweating brow. "I never was a good liar. It's written all over my face, I guess."

I know how that feels.

"The truth?"

"That would be refreshing," Isabel answers.

"Okay, this is kind of complicated. First, my name isn't really Clark Kent."

I want to say "No duh" but feel that doesn't sound all that mature. What would Isabel say?

"So we gathered," Isabel says coolly.

Great. Now I know.

"My name. I'm actually Stan Kellerman, with the MMFPA." He hands us each a card with a logo of a laurel wreath next to the words *Monuments Men Foundation for the Preservation of Art: Continuing the Work of the Monuments Men.*

"Monuments Men—?" I ask, holding the card.

"It's a long story," says Stan Kellerman, who seems visibly more relaxed now that the truth is out. "And please call me Stan. Actually, I'm glad you other kids are here, as not enough young people know about our work," he continues, opening his laptop.

Stan types an address onto the browser bar, and a website with the same logo appears. There are individual articles trumpeting new finds of artwork, and the discovery of a ledger containing valuable information that turned up in the Library of Congress.

Above these articles is a photo of a group of older men holding out the ledger, with a few younger men behind them. Stan points to one of the older men in the front, stooped and bald.

"That's my dad, Lieutenant Morton Kellerman. He's one of the last remaining original Monuments Men." Behind Lt. Kellerman in the photo, clearly beaming, is Stan.

Stan looks fondly at the photo. Then he seems to remember his guests. "Oh, I still haven't explained who they were. Are you sure I can't get you anything to drink?"

We look at each other.

Isabel smiles. "I'll have a Coke."

Off Caleb's look, I say, "Make that three."

"While I'm gone, feel free to poke around the site—I'll fill you in when I get back," Stan says, getting up and moving toward the counter in front.

We gather around the laptop. Isabel reads from the page:

"'Preserving the legacy of the unprecedented and heroic work of the men and women known as Monuments Men, who served in the Monuments, Fine Arts, and Archives—MFAA—section during World War Two, by raising public awareness of the importance of protecting civilization's most important cultural treasures from armed conflict.'"

Stan returns with the drinks.

"So your dad was in World War Two?" I ask.

"Yep. You see, most of these men and women were museum directors and art historians who went over to Europe during the war to try to help preserve historically important buildings, but some of them were like my dad, who was just a military guy who fell in love with art while working with them."

"Okay, I get that," I say impatiently. "But what does that have to do with my great-uncle?"

"I'm getting to that," Stan continues. "One of the most important parts of the Monument Men's work was after the war, when they set out to discover the hidden locations of all the artwork that had been looted from museums and private citizens in the countries the Nazis had invaded."

Stan takes a sip of his soda.

"We're talking about thousands and thousands of priceless paintings, sculptures, jewelry, some of the greatest works of art ever created, hidden away in castles and even buried in salt mines. Da Vincis, Michelangelos . . . the greatest treasure hunt in history!" Stan concludes, his eyes gleaming.

I realize none of us have touched our drinks, we're so into the story Stan is telling.

"And people like my dad have helped recover most of it," Stan continues proudly.

"And my great-uncle fits in how, exactly?" I ask again. I still can't make a connection from this incredible story to the wooden box, black remote, and key sitting in my knapsack at this moment.

Stan shifts uneasily in his seat.

"You see, I, well . . . a lot of soldiers passed through these areas during the war. And it was quite common for them to take souvenirs home. Or even ship them back."

Isabel has been staring off, lost in thought. "Are you suggesting Ted's great-uncle stole one of these pieces of art?" she finally asks.

"No, not deliberately," Stan says quickly. "I mean, a lot of these guys had no idea of the value of the objects they took. Which is where I come in."

"I don't understand," I say, not meeting Stan's gaze.

"My dad's in his eighties. He can't really do this sort of work anymore. So I go out and see if I can recover anything that might have been, oh . . . how do I say this?"

"You *are* saying my great-uncle stole something from over there, aren't you?"

"It's my job, Ted. I have to determine whether it was a simple mistake or—"

"—or *what*, exactly? Is that why you lied about who you are?" I snap.

Now it's Stan's turn to look uncomfortable. "The thing is, after you do this for a while, you find out that if you come right out and ask about these things, people get very . . . emotional . . . and it's harder to get information about the whereabouts of anything that might have been . . . relocated . . . especially if the person is deceased."

"So you lie and try to trick people who are grieving into giving you what you need," Isabel says, her voice cold and hard.

"Do you think I like to lie?" Stan protests. "You see how bad I am at it? It was my dad who insisted we do it this way, okay? You don't know how much I wanted to do something else, but my dad . . ."

Stan is whining now, sounding more like a kid our age than a grown-up.

I find myself feeling sorry for the guy. Still . . . "But why my great-uncle?"

Stan opens up a small notebook and refers to it, reading from his notes.

"The thing is . . . after the war, your great-uncle had a very prestigious job at one of the top labs in the country. It was about that time that we began this side project of trying to locate American GIs who might have brought these items of value home with them. Up until then, we had concentrated on Europe and hidden caches of artwork there. As soon as we started this operation here in the States, your great-uncle quit his job and went underground. We subsequently discovered that he had been running a liquor store in downtown Los Angeles. By the time we had this information, he had retired. We had no idea where he was living. It wasn't until his obituary appeared in the local paper, written by a"—Stan peers at the page—"Mr. Yamada, and after your great-uncle's will was filed, that we were able to locate where he had been all this time." He sighs.

"We had hoped to find him before his passing, as it would have made things a little easier. I was able to talk to Mr. Yamada and some people at the hospital, but it seems he kept his private life *very* private. I was hoping you'd be able to fill in some of the blanks. But I guess I'll just have to tell my dad this was another dead end."

Stan flips the pages in his notebook and snaps it shut.

Caleb has been staring at the screen of Stan's laptop through much of this.

"So it wasn't you who trashed Ted's great-uncle's apartment?"

"Someone went through the apartment?" Stan asks, a slight quaver in his voice.

"The police think it was just bored kids who saw an open window and decided to have some fun. Who do *you* think it was?" Isabel asks pointedly.

"Yeah . . . kids . . . probably . . . ," Stan says softly. He licks his lips.

Caleb leans in. "Are there . . . other people . . . who might be after something that Ted's great-uncle—"

I cut him off with a glare. Caleb corrects himself. "—that they *think* Ted's great-uncle might have taken?"

"Not this 'enemies' thing again," I sigh.

"I don't know," says Stan, none too convincingly. He takes a napkin from the table and wipes the sweat from his forehead. He looks spooked.

"You really are a bad liar," says Isabel, smiling.

"I really don't. But it's certainly possible that there are . . .

others . . . who would be curious about what your great-uncle did or did not have up there."

I push away from the table and get up. "There's only one thing. My great-uncle didn't take anything."

Stan closes his laptop. I notice his hands are shaking.

"Ted, I'll probably be leaving as soon as I clear up a few loose ends. If you think of anything else, give me a call."

He turns to go, then adds, "And I'd also like you to consider one other thing: how well did you actually know your great-uncle?"

CHAPTER 22

FAMILY MATTERS

We watch as the beautiful black Jaguar oozes out of the parking lot and Stan Kellerman drives off to his hotel.

"Can you believe that guy?" I fume.

"Well . . . you really *didn't* know your great-uncle Ted, did you?" Caleb asks quietly.

"So what are you saying? That he's hidden some treasure for me to find that was stolen from some museum in Europe during the war?"

"Ted's right, Caleb. Why would his great-uncle send him off on this whole chase, figuring out all the puzzles and stuff, knowing that in the end what he found would be taken from him?" Isabel reasons. "He would have asked Ted to keep it a secret."

I look gratefully at Isabel. "Exactly. All he asked me to do was not to give up. To 'Go for broke.'"

"But what if he didn't know it was stolen? What if he just thought it was valuable?" Caleb asks.

"That still doesn't explain why he quit such a prestigious job as a scientist and hid out as an anonymous liquor store owner," Isabel adds. "It's all very mysterious."

We talk as we ride our bikes slowly back to my house, the late-afternoon sun turning the road a brilliant orange.

"I don't have any answers for that. Maybe it's in the notebook."

Isabel holds up the battered paperback. "I'll look through this tonight."

Caleb makes a face. "I guess I have to go through the other notebook you gave me."

"What's wrong with that?" Isabel asks in annoyance.

"It's like having homework," Caleb grumbles.

"You're right! I guess it is!" Isabel answers happily.

"Let me guess," Caleb groans. "You're the one who always does the extra-credit stuff, right?"

Isabel laughs. It's her regular twelve-year-old girl laugh. "What do you think? Hey, there's my ride."

As the Archermobile pulls up to my house, I reach out and touch Isabel's arm, stopping her. "Tell me honestly. Do *you* think my great-uncle was a thief?"

Isabel is silhouetted by the setting sun, and her face is impossible to read, hidden in shadow. "Well," she says after a pause, "I guess that's what we're going to find out, isn't it?"

A shy wave, a small smile, a deep *clunk* of the door and she's gone as the Archermobile roars off to take her back to her palace in Treemont Oaks.

For most of dinner tonight I'm not really paying too much attention.

My mind is on the key we found, what Stan Kellerman said this afternoon, and the new *Game of Ted* that's sure to be on my laptop, which I am going to start as soon as the meal is over.

I get up to help clear the dishes, when I hear Dad call out to my mom, "Amanda, do you remember the name of the lawyer who handled your uncle's estate?"

I turn to see my dad with the local paper in his hands. Nothing strange about that—Dad usually glances through the paper after dinner. But I can't quite read the expression on his face.

"It was Mr. Huang, Dad," I say helpfully. "I don't know how you could forget him—with that tacky office and—"

Dad looks past me. "Is that right, Amanda? Was it Mr. Huang? Ben Huang?"

My mom comes to the kitchen door and leans out. "Yes, Mr. Huang. All I remember is that horrible aftershave and how he had that annoying habit of calling Ted 'Dear Uncle' and—"

My dad motions her over. "Take a look at this."

Mom comes around to the other side of the newspaper and peers down. Her hand flies to her mouth and she lets out a small gasp. I wander over, curious.

There on the page is a photo of Mr. Huang, under the headline:

LOCAL LAWYER DISAPPEARS

"Oh my heavens," my mom murmurs.

"He's been missing for a week," Dad reads from the paper.

"Apparently his office was untouched, though some files are missing, and a lot of his clients' money is missing."

"Ohhh . . . ," Mom says, and she and Dad exchange looks.

"You think he took it?" I ask.

"My uncle sure picked a winner for a lawyer." My mom laughs and shakes her head. "We're lucky he did this after we settled the estate. Who knows what would have been left." She folds the newspaper and sighs. "I guess you never know about people."

"I knew he was bad news when I saw that pinky ring," Dad says.

"You're right about not knowing about people, Mom," I say. "Remember that guy from the paper?"

"Oh, right!" my mom says. "The man from Hawaii. How did that go?"

"Well, it turns out he isn't actually a reporter."

Dad sits down. He doesn't look happy. "Why didn't you tell us this before?"

"Because I only just found out this afternoon!"

"So who is he, exactly?" Mom asks.

"It's a little complicated . . . ," I begin.

"We're listening," Dad says, folding his arms.

"This is unacceptable, Ted. You really needed to tell us the second you knew," Mom admonishes. Before she can finish her lecture, I get up from the table and stalk away.

"You come back here this instant!" Mom calls after me.

I return to the table, carrying my laptop and the business card.

"Isabel was suspicious, so she checked, and no one at the *Honolulu Star-Advertiser* had ever heard of him. This is who he really is."

I throw the business card on the table. My mom picks it up and reads Stan's information out loud.

Then I dramatically turn the laptop around so that she and Dad can see the foundation website (yeah, I checked first this time to make sure it wasn't another senior dating site).

Mom and Dad peer at the screen, absorbing the information in front of them. For some reason, they don't seem all that excited.

"Hmm . . . so this guy was somehow involved with this art restoration thing?" my dad asks.

"No! His *father* was part of the other stuff they were doing. Tracking down missing pieces of art looted by the Nazis."

Mom looks perplexed. "I'm confused. What does this have to do with Uncle Ted?"

"It's pretty simple. It seems some soldiers brought home stuff as souvenirs, and they didn't realize that these were actually priceless treasures," I explain.

"Or . . . more likely, they *knew* they were priceless treasures," suggests Dad.

"Are you accusing my uncle of being a thief?" Mom demands. Her jaw tightens as she glares at Dad.

"I'm just saying you could say a lot of things about your uncle, but he wasn't stupid or naive. If he *did* find something—"

"He would have turned it in," my mom says firmly. "I can't believe you'd think he would—"

"Are you sure?" asks Dad.

"Why would he take anything?" My mom's voice is rising.

Dad speaks calmly and looks directly at Mom. "Hey, I wouldn't blame him. Maybe he thought he deserved it, considering how the Japanese Americans were being treated on the mainland over here."

"My uncle never took a dime that wasn't his. And he was the most generous, giving person—" Mom is now close to tears.

I decide to step in. "Besides, we didn't find anything of value in the apartment."

"Think hard," Dad says, sitting next to me. "No treasure, no paintings or jewelry or anything?"

"Yeah, like I'd keep that from you. All we found was his lighter and some old notebooks and some paperbacks," I answer truthfully.

Dad nods. "So that's that. And you think there's a connection with this disappearance of Mr. Huang?"

"Doesn't it seem weird to you that the apartment was all messed up, and now this?"

Mom looks at me. "Honey, we've gone through that. Those were kids. And Mr. Huang's office was in a terrible part of town. Like your father said, he was dealing with a lot of dangerous people."

I gather up my laptop and head out.

"Yeah, you're probably right," I call over my shoulder, trying to believe it's true.

Once upstairs, I close the door behind me. I sit at my desk and tentatively call up the site where I've bookmarked *The Game of Ted*.

Wouldn't you know it? No more Tom and Barb. Of course, now that I'm alone.

I'm faced with a screen saying: "Coming soon! *The Game of Ted 1.3!*"

I make a sour face. Clearly someone doesn't have their act together here. Where is the "Solve the mystery of the key" game?

I pull open my drawer and examine the key once again. It isn't small and old-looking. It's big and made of a steel-like metal. This isn't a key for a box. On the back is written, in black marker, "P 14."

I wonder where it is. Find the room. Solve the mystery?

My phone buzzes and I see it's Caleb.

"Dude, what's up?" I ask.

"Um, just wanted to ask you something," he begins.

But I figure my news is bigger. "Hey, you remember that creepy lawyer guy my uncle used for the will?"

"The 'Dear Uncle' dude?"

"That's the one. He was in the newspaper. He's been missing for a week."

I hear a swallowing noise from the other end of the phone.

"What? But, but—" Caleb's words are coming out in small gasps.

"Caleb, calm down," I say, as much to myself. "The police think he made off with his clients' money. Nothing to do with us."

"Yeah, I guess so." Caleb sounds unconvinced. He goes on. "But the reason I called is that there's something else."

"Yeah, what?" I yawn. Just by saying it out loud, the story of the lawyer's disappearance is sounding more and more probable.

"Isabel isn't answering her phone. And I've texted her and she hasn't answered those either."

"Hunh," I grunt. So Caleb has gotten over his callingIsabel-phobia?

"Since when have you two been talking?"

"She asked me to recommend some good comics for her to read. I'm sorry, I think she said graphic novels. So I wanted to tell her my picks. Have you spoken to her?" Caleb asks. There's a little fear in his voice.

"No, I haven't. Get a grip, Caleb. What do you think happened to her?"

"It's just not like her to not return a text or a call, that's all."

"You've known her, what? Three days? How do you know what's 'like her' or not?" I say. Now I'm getting annoyed.

"Okay, you're right," Caleb admits. "I don't know about you, but I think I need some sleep. This whole thing is getting to me."

"I'll make you a deal," I promise. "If you still haven't heard from her by tomorrow morning, I'll bike over to her house with you and we'll find out what this is all about. I'll call you when I wake up, and we can meet in front of your house."

"Good plan." Caleb sounds relieved. "Don't stay up playing games, okay?"

"Yes, Mom," I sigh, and click off.

■ ■ ■

As I pull my bike out of the garage, I remember how nice it is to breathe the clear, first-thing-in-the-morning air. Summer here in the San Fernando Valley, it can reach a hundred degrees by noon. At this hour, though, it's comfortable and almost cool. My favorite time to go for a ride.

The only sound in the stillness is the ticking of my bike coasting down the hill to Caleb's house. Caleb waves from the top of the drive, and I join him.

"Man, I've never biked all the way to Treemont Oaks. You know where we're going?"

"I printed these out last night." I show Caleb a map with our route highlighted on it. "If we follow the service roads along the 101, we should be able to get there in less than an hour."

"Right on. Let's roll," Caleb says.

What feels like a hundred miles later, I gesture to the right, and Caleb nods. A sleepy, tree-lined street with large stately houses behind neatly cultivated yards, La Quiñata Boulevard stretches out forever in front of us.

I count off the cross streets as we ride, and finally we spot the welcome street sign announcing Treemont Drive.

My legs are aching by now, and the sun is higher in the sky, making the air heavier and wetter.

I spot a familiar shape parked next to a house.

"Archermobile ho!" Caleb cries out, clearly seeing the same thing.

We prop our bikes against a tree in the front yard and, after a quick swig of water, walk up to the front door.

I press the button next to the ornate, Mission-style wooden door. A chiming sound can be heard deep within the house. A short while later, the door opens.

It's Mr. Archer, looking a little less cheery than usual. "Well, hello, Ted, this is a surprise! I do wish you had called first."

"Well, we were just on a bike ride and remembered that Isabel lives around here, so we just thought—"

"I'm so sorry, boys, but I can't let you in just now."

There is the sound of movement upstairs. "Is Isabel home?" asks Caleb. "She hasn't been answering my calls or texts."

"We just wanted to make sure she was all right," I add, trying to sound casual.

Mr. Archer's eyes dart quickly toward the upstairs and then back to us.

"Isabel is here, but she's very busy packing."

"Don't you mean unpacking?" I ask, craning my neck to look past Mr. Archer, who pulls the door a little more closed.

"No, I mean *packing*," Mr. Archer says firmly. "Isabel is returning to New York the day after tomorrow."

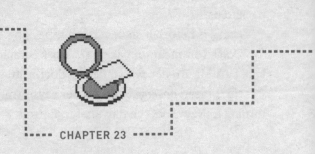

CHAPTER 23

THE CAPTIVE

Mr. Archer finally moves slightly out of the way, and behind him in the hall sits a large suitcase. It's bright red, and clearly Isabel's.

I'm at a total loss for words. I'm trying to figure out what's going on. Nothing is making sense.

"That's really . . . random . . . ," Caleb begins. "I mean, it's not like her to—"

Mr. Archer's face hardens. He seems to be on the verge of saying something, then changes his mind.

"You will have to forgive me, boys. It's just that . . . things have changed for Isabel and me, and we think it best that she return to New York and continue her schooling there."

I let this sink in. "We?"

"Yes, Isabel agrees with me. She misses her friends."

"Uh-huh . . . ," says Caleb. He looks down at the ground, frowning.

"May we at least say goodbye to her?" I ask.

Mr. Archer moves into the doorway again, blocking our view. "I'm sorry to have to tell you this, but Isabel feels that she'd rather not speak to either of you again."

"What?" Caleb exclaims. "We haven't done anything!"

"There must be some misunderstanding," I insist. "If we could talk to her—"

"No!" Mr. Archer says a little too loudly. Quickly, he tries his best to adopt the charming smile we're so used to. "I don't know what to tell you, but once Isabel makes up her mind, there's no convincing her otherwise. If you knew her like I do, you'd know I'm right."

I sense this is a losing battle. Mr. Archer puts his hands on our shoulders and gently guides us away from the house.

"I can't believe my little girl is becoming a teenager," Mr. Archer continues as he gives each of our arms a gentle squeeze. "You boys will have to face it, this sort of drama is only going to get worse as you get older. I wish I could explain it, but it's basically just—well, the mind of a teenage girl is a mystery that would baffle even the world's greatest scientists."

He laughs again, a little more easily this time.

I see where his daughter gets it.

"Will you at least let her know we stopped by?" Caleb asks.

"Of course, and I wouldn't be surprised if you hear from her once she's back in New York." Mr. Archer shakes his head in wonder. "You know, if it were up to me, I'd let you see her. I just do what I'm told."

I put out my hand. "Thanks, Mr. Archer, and please let her know we're sorry if it was anything we said or did."

Mr. Archer looks sincere and grasps my hand firmly, like

always. "I sure will, Ted. And please be careful biking home. It's a pretty long trip."

"We'll be fine," I assure him.

There's an uncomfortable pause; then Mr. Graham slips away from us and hurries back to the house.

He turns to us at the door. "Thanks for stopping by, and send my best to your parents," says Mr. Archer, backing away from the door as he closes it.

We stand there for a moment.

"What just happened?" asks Caleb, looking at me with a stunned expression on his face.

"Beats me. Part of me thinks he's lying, but part of me knows that I don't know squat about girls, so maybe he's not," I admit.

We turn to walk back to our bikes.

Thump.

The sound comes from somewhere above us.

We look up but see nothing.

"A bird?" Caleb asks, none too convincingly.

"Or a squirrel?" I suggest, although neither of us believes it.

Thump.

I'm able to determine that the sound is coming from the side of the house. "Go back and see if Mr. Archer is watching us," I tell Caleb.

Caleb heads back to the front door. Halfway there, he turns around. "What if he's right there, looking out the window at me?"

"Tell him you need to use the bathroom," I say impatiently.

Caleb goes the rest of the way and peers in a side window by the door. He turns and gives me the thumbs-up.

"The coast is clear," he calls back.

"Wait there and signal me if he comes back."

Thump thump.

Now it's clear that the sound is coming from someone tapping on an upstairs window.

I cautiously follow the path around to the side of the house and look up.

Isabel is in the window, looking down with frustration. Her body language is clearly saying, *What took you so long?*

"We were—" I call out, but Isabel immediately raises her finger to her lips and turns her head. She then makes a "wait a minute" gesture and disappears.

I look around, knowing that Mr. Archer could come out a back door or appear at the window at any moment. I see Isabel's window open a crack and then hear her voice.

"I just wanted some air. God! Fine! I'll close it!"

Just before Isabel closes her window, something small and round is tossed out and falls close to my feet. I grab it and stuff it in my pocket, turn, and run back to my bike, motioning Caleb to join me.

Caleb starts to lope over. With a start, I see the large frame of Mr. Archer fill Isabel's window, looking out at us. I frantically wave at Caleb to pick up his pace. Caleb breaks into a sprint. I'm holding his bike for him and he jumps on.

A few blocks down the street, I pull over.

"Jeez, I almost sprained an ankle. What was the rush?" Caleb demands.

"Mr. Archer was in the window. Something is definitely going on," I say, and we start the long trip back to my house.

It's close to lunchtime when Caleb and I drag ourselves up the driveway to my house. Peeling ourselves off our bikes, we throw our helmets in the general direction of the garage and collapse on the lawn.

As I lie there, my hand brushes against my pocket and I'm reminded of the object Isabel threw to me from the second-floor window.

I fish it out. Caleb turns over and rests on his elbows, and we regard what is sitting in my outstretched palm.

It's a small round case made of green marbleized plastic, with a hinged lid and a clear top. At one point it contained eye shadow or face powder. But clearly visible under the transparent lid is a piece of paper, folded many times and wedged inside.

We both look at it in disbelief.

"Dude, are you thinking what I'm thinking?" Caleb asks, gazing at the case in wonder.

"Yeah," I answer, shaking my head in amazement.

"Isabel wears makeup?" we say in unison.

I pry off the top, and the paper falls to the ground. Caleb grabs it and starts to unfold it.

"Careful, your hands are all sweaty!" I warn. "If it's a message, you might smudge it!"

"We'll bring it inside and wash up first," Caleb suggests.

I nod in agreement. Besides, since we don't know what it says, better to read it in private.

A few minutes later, we're cleaned up and ready to examine Isabel's message, whatever it is.

I carefully put it on the bed.

"Maybe it's just a goodbye note," Caleb says, frowning.

"Maybe. We'll know soon enough," I answer, pulling at the corners and revealing what is on the page:

Hi, guys. I guess you know by now that my father has gone totally psychotic or something. He's been really crazy overprotective of me since my mother died, but I thought he was over that when he let me hang out with you two. And then last night this man I've never seen before came over and asked my father to talk to him in private about something important. They talked for maybe fifteen minutes, and that's when my father went nuts. He started going on and on about how he never should have brought me here and I had to leave as soon as possible. I told him he was acting crazy and he told me I didn't know what I was getting myself into and he wanted me to promise I would never talk to or see either of you again. I said he was being ridiculous, as he was the one who wanted me to make friends and everything, and he went even further around the bend. That's when he took my phone and my laptop and said he couldn't trust me. That really got me nervous, but then it just got worse. He came back into my room and took all my paper and pens and pencils! Like I was going to mail you guys a letter or something? What he forgot was that I had my journal— that's like a diary, Caleb, in case you didn't know—

"I know what a journal is, you stuck-up—" Caleb mutters.

"You can tell her if we ever see her again," I say, going back
to the note.

> So I was able to tear out a page and use that.
> And I still have the typewriter I got for my
> eighth birthday. Ha ha!
>
> Anyhow, he also took The Maltese Falcon,
> which is bad for two reasons: 1. I didn't finish
> it. 2. It's REALLY GOOD!!
>
> So basically, can you guys figure out a way
> to GET ME OUT OF HERE? My father will be
> gone from tomorrow morning until dinner.
> He's got conferences. The problem is that he
> turns on the perimeter alarm when he leaves
> the house, so I can't go out through the door or
> even any of the windows because if I break the
> beam, the alarm will go off. And he's changed
> the code, obviously. Anyhow, I don't want to go
> back to NY right now. I want to see you two,
> even if only for the day. Maybe one of your
> parents can talk to him or something.
>
> Isabel

"I love how she signed it. Like we wouldn't know who it was
from otherwise," grouses Caleb.

"Shut up. This is really serious," I say.

Caleb looks into my eyes. "Yeah, I know. I wish we knew
who that dude was who visited Isabel's dad. And what could
the guy have said that freaked him out like that?"

I sit down on the bed. "Something to do with the Monuments Men?"

Caleb sits next to me. "Yeah, those 'other people' Stan was talking about?"

"I don't know. But the first thing we have to figure out is if there's any way of getting Isabel out of there tomorrow."

Caleb stands up, stretches, and walks to the door. "That's your department, Ted. You're the one who knows every trick to escaping a room. Maybe you can even dream up another 'game' to help you. Or you could always ask Tom and Barb."

He expertly dodges the pillow I throw at his head and yawns. "Man, those last few miles really wore me out. I think I need a nap."

I laugh and wave as Caleb leaves, closing the door behind him.

I go back to my desk, flip open my laptop, and wait impatiently for it to boot up.

It finally does, and I open my browser and navigate to a familiar link.

This time, I know what I'm going to find there. It would have been a surprise if it *weren't* there. And now it has a name.

But there it is: "Coming Tonight: *The Game of Ted 1.3—Escape the House!*"

CHAPTER 24

MOVIE DAD TO THE RESCUE

It seems that Lila called from Harvard this morning, so the dinner conversation is all about how she is clearly the most incredibly talented, smartest person to ever go to Harvard, blah blah blah. I tune in and out, playing with my food as my mind turns over the one problem I need to solve.

"Let's say Isabel *does* escape her dad's house? What do we do then?" Caleb asked when I called before heading down to dinner, to tell him I'm pretty sure I'll have the solution to getting Isabel out by the morning.

That stopped me cold.

"I mean," Caleb continued, "she doesn't have a bike here. And there's no way you and I can lug your mom's bike up that hill."

"Yeah," I agreed, "and I don't see her riding on either of our handlebars."

For some reason, the image of that, with Isabel perched there like a scene from some corny movie, made both of us crack up. It's clearly something that would never happen.

"I can just see it. She's up there, you're going downhill, hit a bump and—"

"Don't go there," I implored. "We need a real answer to this. I'm just glad you thought about this before we got there."

We agreed to try and find a solution by morning.

I tune back in to discover that the dinner conversation is winding down.

I get up with my dishes, when my dad's question stops me in my tracks.

"You really didn't find any 'treasure' in Ted's apartment, right?"

I keep my back to my dad. I try to keep my voice as even as possible. "Yeah. Like I told you. All we found were some paperbacks that Isabel took, and his lighter."

Dad turns me around. His eyes catch mine and hold them. He's clearly not finished. Mom is watching me as well. "I mean, if you did find something valuable, you'd tell us, right?"

It's not a lie, I tell myself. *We haven't found anything. Yet.* "Of course, Dad. There's nothing to find. We've gone through all this."

My dad hugs me. I can feel the worry as he holds me tightly. "Teddy, we trust you. You really are a very smart kid."

"Please be careful," my mother adds.

"Sure, Mom," I say. "Dad, could we let up on the hug? I'm starting to have a hard time breathing here."

Dad laughs and relaxes his death grip. "Sorry about that. Guess I don't know my own strength, huh?"

Dad sounds relieved. I know as soon as the corny jokes come out, things are back to normal.

As I move to head upstairs, a thought occurs to me. It's risky, but it's a plan. And it just might work. I look and see that Mom has gone into the kitchen and I'm all alone with Dad. Now is my chance. I pause, wondering if I really have the— well, let's just say the nerve to do this.

I know it's the only way, and I have to make it convincing. I turn to Dad.

"I need to ask a favor," I say, hoping my face looks appropriately desperate.

"What . . . kind of favor?" my dad asks, looking slightly worried.

"The thing is," I look away, figuring this is what I would do if I were actually telling the truth, "this has to do with Isabel."

My dad licks his lips. Clearly he's no more ready for this conversation than I am.

"We aren't doing anything . . . you know . . . anything," I stammer, "We're just hanging out, you know?"

"Of course. That's what I thought." Dad lets out a big breath, relieved. Even though we've entered uncharted territory (like they say on those old maps, Here Be Dragons), this is going even better than I hoped.

Then, I kid you not, he jingles the coins in his pocket. Like some corny dad from a movie. All he needs is the pipe and sweater. Movie Dad nods wisely.

"Ted, I just don't want you to get hurt. Isabel's not like the girls around here. And I know she's really pretty, so it's no wonder that—"

"That's not the reason I like being with her. The truth is,

what I like about her the most is that she's so smart . . . kind of like Mom."

I look at Dad at this point. I know I've taken a calculated risk with this one. For a moment I can't tell if he's going to burst out laughing or roll his eyes.

But instead, his eyes are glistening.

Oh, man. I've really hit a home run.

Dad leans in conspiratorially. "So what's the big favor?"

"Apparently Mr. Archer feels strongly that Isabel should go back to New York and her old school."

"That's too bad—" my dad starts.

"And what's worse, she's leaving the day after tomorrow. And as you know, tomorrow's that big all-day conference for new faculty members—so I was wondering if you'd drive me over there tomorrow morning. Otherwise we won't have a chance to say goodbye."

Dad stands up. "Can't he drop Isabel here? I really have things to do."

"She has to finish packing," I say quickly. "Caleb would be coming too. We'll meet her there and then you can pick us up like in an hour."

"An hour at most," Dad says. "I think there's a coffee place near there where I can get some reading done. But it can't be much longer. I have some students coming in to see me at noon."

"That would be so cool. We'll just be on the corner of Treemont and Alameda. You can meet us there."

"Well . . . I'll think about it," says my dad in that voice that usually means yes.

"Awesome!" I yelp happily, and give him a huge hug. I leave before he can return the favor.

When I walk into my room, I look achingly at the bed. I could really use some sleep around now, but I'm not sure how long this game is going to take. Well, the sooner I finish it, the sooner I can get some shut-eye.

I go to my desk, feeling good. By now, I know the score. The game will pop up. I'll play it, playing will give me clues about how to get Isabel out, and then I can go to bed. My laptop boots up, and I see the familiar game logo. Here we go.

I peer at the screen.

I see a bedroom with boxes on the floor. I click around the room. There's a bookshelf partially filled with books. A desk with more books stacked on it. The spines read *Jane Austen, F. Scott Fitzgerald.* . . . I'm clicking everywhere, trying to get something, anything, to pop into my inventory, going about my regular gaming routine.

Then it hits me. This is Isabel's room. This isn't just a *regular* game room to escape. It's her actual bedroom on the screen.

And I'm in it.

I have the uncomfortable feeling that I'm doing something wrong, that I'm somewhere I shouldn't be.

This is wrong. I have to get out of here before she comes back.

I sit back in my chair, panic-stricken. And then realize with enormous relief that I am completely insane.

This is just a game. I'm only in Isabel's room in a game.

And then another realization: I'm not me. I'm playing as Isabel. I have to be. It's *her* escape.

This has now become twice as hard. I don't have to just

figure out how to win the game; I have to get Isabel to follow the steps in order to get out of her father's house.

I sigh. That bike ride really took it out of me, and it's getting hard to concentrate. I rub my eyes to clear the cobwebs. Time to get to work.

I find a wallet on the desk. I click on it, and it opens, revealing a neat stack of cards. I click on them and a library card slides out and presents itself into my inventory. Clicking around the room, I find nothing else useful, and thankfully nothing embarrassing.

Isabel is not a slob, like me.

My next click takes me in front of Isabel's bathroom.

I grimace. Is this necessary? I know this is the last place in the world Isabel would want me to go. But at the same time, I have no choice. As I gear myself up, my eyes droop a little, and the screen is looking a little fuzzy. I clear my head by taking a few deep breaths, and dive in.

The door opens, and I enter. Again, it's all perfect, of course, with makeup and shampoo bottles lined up in rows. I click on each of them, finding nothing.

As I absent-mindedly click on the screen, I arrive at the mirror above the sink and to my shock see Isabel's face staring back at me.

I gotta tell you, I almost close the game right then, before remembering that it's "my" reflection.

It's still an incredibly weird sensation, as if I am in her body, doing what she would need to do. I click down to the sink, and with triumph click on a tube of lip gloss, which makes a welcome *plink* and now sits in my inventory, next to the library card.

I click through to the door of Isabel's room, which brings me to the stairway. This takes me down to a set of locked double doors behind which I assume is Mr. Archer's study.

I grab the library card and click on it, bringing it up on the screen. I drag the lip gloss over to it and smile as the gloss spreads over one side of the card—to make it slippery, I've already figured. I take the card and put it next to the doors. It slides into the small crack between them, stopping at the lock, where it eases itself between the latch and the plate. They open, and I am—or rather Isabel is—in.

It's only a matter of time . . . time. . . . Couldn't hurt to just put my head down for a few minutes. . . .

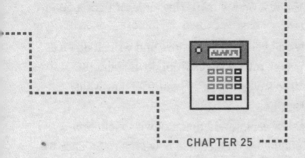

CHAPTER 25

THE GAME OF ISABEL

"Ted! *Ted!*"

I open my eyes and gape in horror at the light streaming in through my window. My dad is shaking my shoulders. I quickly check the laptop and see that it's in sleep mode.

Sleep. *Argh!* How long did I sleep?

"I'm really sorry, Ted, but we've got to get going," my dad says. "Brush your teeth or do whatever you have to do to make yourself presentable. We're leaving in five minutes." He turns. "And later we'll talk about this obsession with those games. Falling asleep in front of the computer is *not* acceptable."

"Riiight," I say thickly, wiping the drool from my face with my sleeve. Five minutes? That's crazy! I can't solve the game in five minutes! I run to the bathroom while the laptop is waking up, trying to think of anything that will clear up this mess. I figure I'll tell Isabel the few things I've learned and hope that

I can figure out the rest on my own. Hey, at least I got a good night's rest!

As I frantically go over what I do know, and write it down as instructions for Isabel, my dad calls from downstairs.

"Ted, you want to say goodbye to your friend or what?"

"Be right there, Dad."

I grab the sheet of paper and book it down to join him.

Caleb is just pulling up on his bike as we open the door to the car. He hops in and we're on our way.

The trip is a whole lot faster this way, let me tell you.

Dad stops at the corner of Treemont. He turns and looks at me.

"Noon. Right?"

"Actually, we said eleven," I remind him. "You're meeting students at noon, remember?" Mom may not be right about everything, but boy, is she right about the not-listening part.

Caleb and I jump out.

"Maybe I'll go to the office instead," my dad mutters, and drives off.

As we approach the house, Caleb stops.

"Now, I know you've got this all figured out and everything, but I still don't know how you're going to get the instructions to Isabel. If anything breaks that beam, going in or out, it sets off the alarm, right?"

"You're forgetting one place," I say with a smile as we walk up the stone steps leading to the front door.

I point.

"Of course," marvels Caleb. "The mail slot. The mail has to be able to get in."

I lift the slot and peer inside. No sign of Isabel. The house looks still and cold.

"Isabel!" I call. No response.

"Maybe she's in her room," Caleb suggests.

We move around to the side of the house.

Up in the window, there is no sign of movement. But I can just imagine her on her bed, lying there, looking up at the ceiling. How odd to know a room so well and never have been inside.

"Isabel!" Caleb yells.

A familiar face appears in the window and breaks into a smile. I wave and gesture for her to come downstairs. Once again we station ourselves by the mail slot.

Soon we hear a rustle, and then it's clear that Isabel is on the other side of the door.

I lift the slot again.

"I don't believe you guys! It's so great to see you!" Isabel sounds genuinely happy.

"You too," I say, proving once again my gift for smooth-talking the ladies.

"I wish I could get out of here," Isabel sighs. "But it's nice that you came."

"'O ye of little faith,'" says Caleb, and points in my direction.

"You don't mean—" Isabel begins, staring wide-eyed at me.

"That's from the Bible, by the way. I looked it up," Caleb adds proudly.

"I know it's from the Bible. Matthew chapter eight, verse twenty-six," Isabel says impatiently.

I remove the sheet of instructions from my pocket. I go into the speech I've so carefully worked out to convince Isabel to follow the walkthrough.

"Here's the thing. I sat and thought through your problem

as if it were an escape game. I put together what I observed about your house and my best guesses as to what to do to get you out of there *and* get back the book. I've got an idea for the first few steps. But, ummm . . . I may need your help on the other stuff."

"I figured out that the perimeter alarm was only for the windows and the doors, not the mail slot. Pretty slick, huh?" Caleb adds.

Isabel isn't listening. She looks at me expectantly. "So what do I do first?"

"Get your library card."

Isabel looks at me like I'm demented. "My library card?"

Before I can stop myself, I blurt out, "Your library card! The one in your wallet on your desk! Then get some lip gloss from your bathroom and come downstairs."

There is a *long* pause as Isabel takes this in.

"Look, do you want to get out or not?" I ask firmly.

Her eyes are locked on mine through the slot. I'm getting a little creeped out.

Finally: "Yes. I do. So I'll get my library card and some lip gloss."

We hear her footsteps echo on the stone floor of the entry and then up the wooden stairs to her room.

A few moments pass, and we can see her with her library card in one hand, lip gloss in the other.

"Just put some lip gloss on one side, slide it down the door until you reach the lock, and pull," I coach her through the slot.

"I figured," Isabel calls back. "We used to do this all the time at school to get into the library when it was closed. It wouldn't have occurred to me to do it to my dad's office."

There's a click, and Isabel cries, "I'm in!"

She comes back to the mail slot and stares at me. "I checked my dad's desk. I'm pretty sure that's where he's put the book, because the drawer is locked, and it normally isn't, and the book isn't on any of the shelves in there. So now what?"

I forget that Isabel is getting pretty good at this too. Great. I need all the help I can get. The fact that her dad put the book under lock and key has to mean something. I'm guessing the book has something to do with the numbers on the house alarm system's keypad.

"Okay, so first we need to find the key to that drawer. . . ."

I begin to mull it over. It's a lot harder than the game, because on-screen I can just click until I have pieces to use. I remind myself that Graham Archer is a person, not a computer game designer. "He must have hidden it in there somewhere. Would he have left a reminder to himself about where it is?"

"I don't want to be the one to say it," says Caleb, "but seriously, Ted. You play too many of those games. Wouldn't he just take it with him?"

I glare at Caleb. I hate him for being right. Is all this just a waste of time? Is the key with Mr. Archer?

"Actually, I don't think so," Isabel says excitedly. "My father hates having too many keys in his pocket. He says it ruins the line of his pants. He usually just has the car key when he leaves, and comes in the house through the garage."

"Well, that's something!"

Isabel thinks for a minute. "Shouldn't we start in the obvious places? Hold on." She rushes away, and we hear her rummaging in different parts of the house, before she goes back to the study and searches in there. When she comes back, she looks defeated.

"No desk key anywhere that I can think of, at least nowhere it'd make sense. It's got to be hidden somewhere pretty obscure."

"So where do we start?" Caleb jumps in. "He doesn't have a calendar, does he? Like Great-Uncle Ted?"

"No . . . ," says Isabel, "but he does have a datebook. He says he doesn't trust computers with his appointments and things. Should I look in there?"

"Couldn't hurt," I answer.

Isabel comes back with a small leather-bound notebook. She flips through the pages, then stops and holds the book up to the slot. We see a date circled in red ink. September 21.

"Father's written something below it," Isabel says. " 'Deliver paper to Shakespeare Conference, LASS.' LASS?"

"Los Angeles . . . ," I begin.

"—Shakespeare Society!" Isabel cuts in. "Father said he was delivering a paper there in the fall. I think I saw a draft of it on his desk." Before I can say anything, she's run back into the study and returns with a packet of papers that has a Post-it on it, marked "9/21."

The title of the lecture is *What Fools These Mortals Be—The Great Clowns of Shakespeare.*

Isabel flips quickly through the paper. "Nothing in here mentions a key. Now what?"

"That's okay. Dead ends happen all the time. We'll just try something else." I try to picture the game in my head. I remember noticing something on the desk just before I conked out.

"Does your father have a laptop on his desk?"

"Yes," Isabel says.

"Can you get onto his computer? That's a good place to start," I suggest.

Off Isabel goes. A shout reaches us. "It's asking for a password! He's never had a password before!"

If he's never had a password before, then whatever it is will reference something recent. I think of her father's paper. *What Fools These Mortals Be.* Maybe it wasn't a dead end after all? "Try '*WFTMB*'!" I shout back.

"Of course!" Isabel answers. Then she comes back to the door, looking dejected.

"It didn't work. Any other ideas?"

Normally at this point, if I were playing the game, I'd go to Wikipedia. But I realize I have something else just as good right in front of me.

Isapedia.

The Great Clowns of Shakespeare. "So who would you say is the most famous Shakespearean clown?" I ask.

"Will Kempe, of course," Isabel says immediately. "I mean, he was the original clown who Shakespeare wrote all his comic roles for."

"Try adding *'Kempe'* to the *'WFTMB'* for the password," I suggest.

Off she goes.

And back she comes, looking irritated. "Still nothing. We're missing something." Then her face brightens. "Wait! After Kempe quit Shakespeare's company, he was replaced by Robert Armin, who created some of the most famous fools! Should I try him?"

"Sure," I say. "'*WFTMBArmin.*' If that doesn't work, try

'*WFTMBKempeArmin.*' Or '*GreatClownsKempeArmin.*' You have to try every combination—"

"That one worked! I'm in!" says Isabel. I hear a note of triumph in her voice.

"Now you know how Ted feels when he's solved one of his games!" Caleb calls.

"We haven't solved it yet," I remind him.

An excited squeal comes from the study. "I found a folder on the computer desktop marked 'September 21.'"

Then silence. Caleb and I run around to the side of the house where the study is. We push through the rosebushes to get a better view of the room.

We see Isabel through the study window as she heads toward the back wall of the room, where there is a series of three framed pictures.

The one on the left is a photograph of a beautiful woman on a beach, in a thick woolen sweater. I know at once this has to be Isabel's mom.

On the right is a family portrait of three skiers. Graham is on one side, his wife is on the other, and Isabel is in the middle, about ten years old. The two adults are laughing, and Isabel is looking up at them.

Between these two photos is an odd picture.

It's a painting of a man with a donkey's head, stretching his arms as if waking from a long sleep. Looking at him with adoration is a beautiful woman, her hands stroking the fur on his muzzle.

Isabel marches over to the middle picture and reaches behind it, feeling around. When she pulls her hand out, she waves a key victoriously.

We watch as she goes to the desk. The key opens the drawer, and she holds the copy of *The Maltese Falcon* up to show us with a big thumbs-up.

She leaves the room and we meet her back at the door. She's laughing.

"Of course my father would hide the key behind his Bottom."

Now it's my turn to look confused. What the heck is she talking about? Happily, I can always count on Caleb to bail me out.

Caleb has a baffled look on his face. "What? He hid the key in his butt?"

Isabel laughs. It's not her grown-up laugh. More like a "stupid me" laugh. I like it better.

"Sorry. Family joke. Father got that painting when I was three, and we always called it his Bottom."

Now it's our turn to stare through the slot. Isabel sighs.

"You guys, Bottom is the name of the comic character in Shakespeare's *A Midsummer Night's Dream* who is given the head of a donkey by the king of the fairies."

"Uh-huh . . . ," says Caleb, looking dubious.

Then it dawns on me.

"The man with the donkey head in the painting!" I say.

"Right!" Isabel says. "And Titania, queen of the fairies, is enchanted to fall in love with him."

"A guy named Bottom gets a donkey head," Caleb says skeptically. "It sounds like a real laugh riot."

"At least it's not about some guy who dresses up like a bat and is supposed to scare bad guys," Isabel snaps back.

"I think we're getting off track," I say. "We need the code.

It's clear that your dad locked up the book for a reason. It has to have something to do with the code."

"Of course!" Isabel crows. "We just need to find four numbers in here."

"Hunh. How about a year?" suggests Caleb.

My eyes widen. He's got it. I know he's got it.

"Isabel," I instruct. "Check the publication date. It's on the—"

"Ted! I think I know where the pub date of a book is!" Isabel says, actually rolling her eyes. She opens the book and reads out: " 'First paperback edition, 1948.' You really think this is it?"

Our eyes meet. "Yes. I'm pretty sure. Only one way to find out."

Standing on the steps, we hear her slowly and carefully enter the four numbers into the number pad. *BEEP BEEP BEEP BEEP.*

I hold my breath.

Two corresponding beeps are heard. She's deactivated the alarm.

The door slowly opens. Isabel stands there, eyes bright with excitement, holding *The Maltese Falcon.*

She steps carefully over the threshold to the outside.

We all stand stock-still, waiting to hear a siren, or any other sign that the plan has failed.

After ten long seconds of silence, Isabel breaks into a grin, and Caleb and I cheer.

She is about to leave, and turns around.

"What are you doing?" Caleb hisses.

"Resetting the alarm," Isabel says, her usual calm demeanor having returned. "Just being a responsible daughter."

Slowly, the three of us walk down the stone walkway, saying nothing, as if at any moment, Graham Archer will reappear and foil the whole elaborate scheme.

We walk along, our bodies beginning to relax as the truth dawns on us.

"We really did it," Isabel marvels. She turns and gives a surprised Caleb a huge hug.

"It . . . it was mostly Ted," Caleb splutters.

I wait for my hug, a big smile on my face. I can't help it. Things are working out perfectly. I've rescued Isabel, and soon we'll solve the riddle of where the key belongs, and then—

That's when Isabel punches me in the face.

CHAPTER 26

FALLING APART, COMING TOGETHER

At that exact moment, two thoughts go through my mind simultaneously.

First, as a middle-class half-Asian, half-Jewish kid, I've never punched anyone in the face in the entire twelve years of my life.

And second, Isabel Archer packs a mean punch.

Her fist lands squarely—perfectly, of course—on my cheek, sending me reeling.

"What the heck did you do that for?" I screech.

"I come from New York, so let me tell you, I've known some creeps in my time," Isabel spits out, "but you are without a doubt the creepiest, most disgusting excuse for a—"

"You're *mad* at him? But he just got you—" Caleb tries to get between Isabel and her prey, but she swings hard and gets me in the gut this time.

She stands over me, her face red with what looks like a combination of rage and disbelief.

"How did you know what was in my bathroom? That my wallet was on my desk? God! It's too gross to even think about! Did you climb into that tree and stare at me at night or something? You . . . you . . ."

"I never thought I'd see it," Caleb says. "Isabel Archer is actually speechless."

Isabel whirls and faces Caleb, her hands still balled into tight fists.

"Hey! Don't get mad at me! I wasn't the one spying on you!" Caleb quickly adds.

"Caleb!" I moan from the ground. "You're not helping. . . ."

"I mean, Ted wasn't spying on you either! Ted wouldn't do that. It would be—"

Caleb talking is good, I think through the pain as I prop myself up on one arm. *It gives me a chance to gather my thoughts.*

"Sick! He's a *sicko!*" Isabel screams.

Caleb talking is bad, I think. *It gives* Isabel *a chance to gather* her *thoughts.*

"I mean, I'm glad you got me out, but just the thought of you—"

Isabel pushes me back down again, this time with her foot.

As I writhe on the ground in agony, it occurs to me that perhaps I haven't thought this through completely. Clearly I shouldn't have mentioned her wallet and the desk. I should have thought of that. Of course, she would have—*ow!*

Isabel has just elbowed me hard in the ribs.

Now, this part, with her hitting me, this is definitely new information.

I hold up my hands, flinching. "Let me explain. . . ."

Isabel crosses her arms. "Okay, I'm waiting. And please don't insult me with any more talk about some game on your laptop telling you what to do."

I wince. "Give me a second." I'm trying to buy a little time. Nothing is coming.

I have to make it good. Isabel is too smart.

A look of contempt passes over her face. "All along, I thought you were kind of a cool guy, and now I find out you're a . . . a . . ."

"A what?" I ask, starting to get a little angry myself.

"You want me to say it? Okay, a *pervert*! God, spying on me like that! No wonder my dad didn't want me to have any contact with you!"

"Are you on drugs? How does that even make any sense?"

Isabel is pacing now. "Sure. That man who came and visited my father and upset him so much, he's probably a neighbor, and he saw you outside my window and told my father. And you concocted this whole thing to make yourself look like a hero or something."

Isabel has worked herself up again, and runs at me.

Seeing her coming, I put Caleb between me and another blow to the head.

Isabel pulls up short and stands there panting. "You're so smart, huh? Let's see you escape *this*!" Just as she reaches to push Caleb out of the way, there's a buzz from my phone.

"Hold that thought," I say. "I think that's my dad."

It is indeed a text from Dad. *Oh, perfect.*

Checking in. We said noon, right?

Just once, I wish Mom were wrong about the not listening. This is perfect.

Isabel is staring at me, with fire still in her eyes. "So?"

"That was our ride," I say simply. "My dad isn't coming for another hour."

"What? But that means—" Isabel begins.

The three of us freeze as a familiar heart-churning sound comes from up the street.

The unmistakable sound of a throaty engine returning.

I turn accusingly to Isabel. "You said your father was gone for the day!"

"He's supposed to be," she says, her hand rising to her mouth. "Maybe the conference has been canceled?"

Too soon, a large, expensive car turns onto the road. But it's the Jaguar XJ6 sedan, with a welcome familiar face at the wheel.

Stan opens the door and gestures to us to come over. Scarcely believing it, we run over.

"What are you doing here?" I ask.

"I went by your house this morning to try to talk to you again and saw you guys on your bikes. I guess I hoped that maybe you were going to get whatever your great-uncle left you."

"So you thought Ted had buried it in the woods or something?" Isabel asks.

"I've seen it happen," Stan says. "But then I saw you guys kind of dusting it up back there, and wondered what was going on, so—"

"It wasn't anything about his great-uncle," Isabel says, brushing herself off. "It was . . . a misunderstanding."

Great! I think I'm off the hook, until I see the look she shoots me.

"So, do you guys need a lift?" Stan asks.

We look at each other in relief.

"Could you possibly drop us off at my house?" I say.

"Sure, no problem. Hop in!" Stan says happily.

Isabel goes back, picks up *The Maltese Falcon* from the ground where she flung it after punching me, and brushes it off. She heads to the car without so much as a backward glance at me and Caleb.

I note darkly that Isabel immediately chooses to ride up front with Stan, relegating me and Caleb to the backseat.

Stan asks her how long she's lived in the neighborhood, how she likes California, stuff like that. Since neither of them seems to want to include us, I text my dad to tell him we got a lift from Stan, and turn to Caleb.

"How are you gonna explain this to her?" he asks me. "I mean, I know you're a genius with these games, but you have to admit, it is a little wild that you knew her wallet was on her desk and—"

"It was all deduction," I sigh. "I swear to God."

"Hey, I believe you, but Isabel's the one you have to convince."

For a while we ride in silence. The two up front continue to chat away like old friends.

This is good for me. As we near my block, I've worked out my entire defense. I just have to pray that it will work.

We're about to turn into my driveway when I hear Isabel say, "Thanks so much. When we heard the car, we got a little spooked that you might be my father."

"What's the matter?" jokes Stan. "Your dad doesn't want you to hang around with these clowns?"

"Something like that," Isabel says. "Some guy visited him last night, and after that, Father freaked out and tried to keep me locked in the house."

There's a squealing sound and we're thrown forward as Stan slams on the brakes.

"Your fa-father had a visitor last night?" Even from the back-seat, I can see that his knuckles are white as he grips the steering wheel. "Someone from the college?" he asks hopefully.

Isabel frowns. "I don't think so. It was someone he didn't know. And it was a pretty intense conversation."

"Fu-Fudgie the Whale!" Stan exclaims.

"Excuse me?" I ask, trying to figure out what's going on.

"I was going to say something else, but then I remembered there were kids in the car," Stan explains.

"It's okay, I go to private school—our teachers curse all the time," Isabel remarks.

It seems like all the blood has drained from Stan's face.

"You don't think this has anything to do with my great-uncle?" I ask.

"Er, no, of course not," Stan says, in that way that means *Absolutely I do.*

He pulls the car up to our driveway and we get out.

"So what do we do now?" asks Caleb.

"We?" says Stan, who seems in a hurry to get the heck out of here. "Well, I've got a lot of errands to do . . . and like I said, I'll be leaving LA today. It's been great meeting you kids. . . ."

"Are you running away?" asks Isabel, using her best "let's be real" voice.

Stan is visibly sweating now. "The thing is . . . I didn't sign up for this. I'm just supposed to find stuff and report back to my father and the other Monuments Men. I promise as soon as I get home I'll get him to call someone and they can come out and—"

He doesn't even finish the sentence before he's slammed the door and backed out onto the street. He's going so fast he almost hits two garbage cans on the curb.

We watch him drive away.

"Our hero," mutters Caleb.

As soon as we hit the kitchen and before Isabel can open her mouth, I hold up my hand.

"You said you wanted an explanation, and I guess I owe you one," I announce.

Isabel looks at me. She starts to say something but changes her mind. Then, with a defiant look in her eye, she sits on one of the stools by the counter.

"I'm waiting," she finally says.

I clear my throat. "Okay, let's take one thing at a time. You have to understand that a lot of what I guessed comes from hours and hours of playing these games, and learning where things usually are in houses and how people think of passwords and stuff like that."

Isabel cuts in. "That doesn't explain—"

"Let me finish. Is it that weird that I knew you'd have a library card? You already told us you got that book from the library, remember? I mean, where else would it be but your wallet? I guessed it would be on your desk. You seem like the kind of girl who would have a place for everything. And I knew that the houses in your neighborhood were built in the seventies, when the room locks all worked the same way, with a button lock you could disable with the old credit card trick."

"He's right!" Caleb interjects. "Our house was built then, and we always do that if someone locks the bathroom door accidentally."

"Exactly," I continue. "I'm sorry you got freaked out about the lip gloss, but you really jumped to some conclusions there. I have an older sister. And before she went to college, we shared a bathroom. She always kept her lip gloss in there. There were like a hundred tubes or something. So that was an educated guess."

Isabel's face falls. She winces and puts her hand to her mouth, as if she wishes she could somehow take back everything she's said and done.

"So, you didn't . . . ," she struggles. "I mean, it wasn't like you—"

"First of all, I would never do anything like that. Second of all, don't you think your dad would call my parents, if not the police, if he thought that was the case? And third of all, I'm not that good at climbing trees."

Isabel gets up and crosses to me. For a moment, I'm not sure what she's going to do. She leans in close to my face. It's funny—I can smell the conditioner in her hair.

Isabel winces. "I think you're going to get a bruise there." She pulls away and goes to the refrigerator. "Can I get some orange juice or something? I'm really thirsty."

I look at Caleb, who's grinning from ear to ear. Crisis averted!

"I think we all could use something to drink," I say, reaching into the open fridge and grabbing the container. I pour three glasses, and we move into the living room.

It's time to get to work.

"Listen, Isabel, this guy—the one who freaked your dad out so much. Could you describe him?"

Isabel makes a face. "Sure, I guess so. Why? Do you think you know him?"

"I doubt it," I say. "But just the idea of him spooked Stan so much. What did he look like?"

Caleb turns to a fresh sheet of paper in his sketchbook, and as Isabel begins to describe the man, he deftly fills in the contours.

"He had kind of a squat face, with a double chin. And a big, broad nose, and a—what do you call it? A unibrow. And he was bald, except for a little fringe of black hair around his ears."

"How about his eyes? Were they big and bulging? Deep-set under a big caveman brow?" Caleb is firing questions as he rushes to keep up with Isabel's description.

"Big, I guess. Hard to tell. He had thick black glasses."

"Hipster glasses? Like he was wearing them as a joke?" I ask.

"No, this guy didn't look like he joked about anything. I think he had them because they were practical."

Caleb holds the pad at arm's length, appraising his work. He adds a few more details and turns it around. Isabel gasps.

"Oh my gosh! That's him! You're amazing!"

I stare at the man in the picture. He looks dangerous. What did he tell Mr. Archer? What would make a father lock up his daughter?

"So now all we've got is a key to somewhere and a book that doesn't seem to mean anything," I sum up.

Caleb and Isabel look at each other. Caleb grins like an idiot, and there's even a small smile on Isabel's face. She turns back to me.

"Actually, I think that book *does* mean something. I had a lot of time, so I read it while you two were—"

"Gallivanting around?" Caleb interrupts helpfully.

"Hey, someone learned a new vocabulary word!" Isabel exclaims. "And he used it correctly!"

Suddenly, there's the click of the back door opening and closing and the welcome sound of Mom's voice. "Is that Isabel and Caleb I hear?"

My mom bursts into the living room and gives us each a quick hug.

I note with approval that Isabel has hidden the copy of *The Maltese Falcon* behind her back before Mom gets to her.

"Please excuse the mess, Isabel. I've been working all week, and it's not like anyone else here seems to notice."

Isabel gives my mom her best "I hear you" laugh.

"I'm just going to get dinner ready. I'm afraid I can't stay and chat. I'm covering for a friend tonight, so I don't have that much time," Mom explains to Isabel, and then sweeps out.

My mom hums, opening and closing doors and drawers in the kitchen. I lean in and say in a low voice: "So—about the book?"

"Right!" Isabel says excitedly. "It's about this detective—"

"The one who's named after you," Caleb throws in.

"Miles Archer gets killed in the second chapter, actually. Can I finish, or are you going to keep interrupting with smart remarks?" Isabel asks sharply.

"So it turns out there are a whole bunch of people after the same thing—this statue of a falcon made right after the Crusades. These Crusader knights—you know who they were?"

Caleb rolls his eyes. "Yes, we know who the Crusader knights were. The ones who went to try to liberate the Holy Land from the Moors."

"According to this book, some of them took enormous amounts of wealth with them when they left," Isabel continues. "And as a gesture of thanks to the Spanish king, they sent him a falcon statue each year. The first year it was encrusted with every type of priceless jewel, and probably made of solid gold."

I pick up the old paperback and flip through the pages. "So this is a history book?"

Isabel sighs. "No! It's fiction! It's all made up! It's not like the Maltese Falcon ever really existed. But I think it's kind of a message from your great-uncle."

"Like what?" I ask.

"Well, these people were all looking for this incredibly valuable thing and were willing to kill for it."

"So what happens in the end?" demands Caleb.

"So," says Isabel, "the bad guys finally get it—well, they think they do—and it turns out to be fake. Well, that's not really the part I think your great-uncle was trying to tell you. I think it was more about the search for this thing of great value. That you can be fooled into thinking you've found it when you haven't."

Caleb put his head in his hands. "I have no idea what you're talking about."

There is a pause.

Isabel purses her lips. "Okay, maybe that wasn't it either."

I suddenly feel very tired. "So basically you're saying we're back where we started. I'm glad it was a cool book, but you really don't know what it has to do with figuring out what the key goes to."

"Well ...," Isabel says slowly. "We *are* back where we started. But that's a good thing. Because while I had all that time, I figured something else out as well."

"How can being back where we started be a good thing?" Caleb gripes.

"Think about it," Isabel continues. "Your great-uncle didn't know what room he would be in in the hospital until he got there, right? So how could he have scratched the number into the box in his apartment? An apartment he never went back to before he died?"

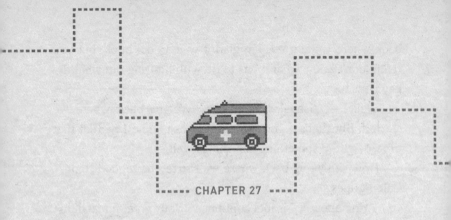

CHAPTER 27

ONE LAST VISIT

The only sound we hear is my mom in the kitchen closing the refrigerator door. Caleb and I stare at Isabel with a mixture of admiration and shock.

"How come I didn't see that?" I say, almost to myself.

"You were a little busy, you know . . . ," Isabel replies, absent-mindedly flipping through the pages of *The Maltese Falcon*.

"But it was right in front of my face!" I protest.

"So who was it, already?" Caleb asked, moving over to the book Isabel is holding and looking at it as if the clue were in there.

"There was only one person Great-Uncle Ted would trust to go into his apartment and set up that whole thing."

"Your mom!" Caleb exclaims. "I always knew she was hiding something!"

"No, you dimwit," I snap. "It's—"

"Mr. Yamada!" Isabel yells, unable to hold it in any longer.

"Mr. Yamada. Of course! So he knew all along!" Caleb laughs. "He probably knows everything!"

"He certainly knows more than he's told us," I reason.

"I think we need to pay him a visit as soon as possible," Isabel says. "Because if my father comes home tonight and finds out I'm gone, he's going to go completely mental and I'm definitely on that plane tomorrow."

I look at the kitchen. "If we're going to see Mr. Yamada, it needs to be now."

Isabel pushes open the door. My mom is sitting at the kitchen table, writing something. She looks up and smiles.

"I'm leaving a note for your dad. I left some lasagna in the fridge. Just nuke it for two minutes a portion."

"Sounds great," I begin in my most cheerful voice. "Listen, Mom. I need you to do me a favor. A big favor."

Mom has a wary look on her face. "Oh, Ted. I hope it isn't driving you somewhere."

I sit down on the chair next to her. Isabel takes the chair on her other side.

Good move, Isabel, I think. *Surround the enemy. Leave her no escape route.*

"I wouldn't normally ask you, but—"

Mom immediately softens. She regards Isabel with what I can only describe as a look usually reserved for pictures you find on the Internet of kittens in teacups or YouTube videos of kids saying adorable things.

"Isabel, if it's really that important . . ."

Isabel looks away, as if she doesn't know quite how to bring it up. I marvel at her ability to pull emotional strings like this. It's almost Jedi-like. Or Sith-like.

"It's Mr. Yamada. We were going through some old magazines Ted took from the apartment and this fell out."

Isabel holds out *The Maltese Falcon.*

"My gosh!" remarks Mom, examining the book. "This was one of my uncle's favorites. He loved the movie too. He was always quoting from it."

"We thought this would be the perfect thing for Mr. Yamada to remember him by," continues little Miss Sweetness and Light.

My mom looks from one of us to the other. "So what exactly do you want me to do? Drive all the way over Laurel Canyon now to drop this off for him?"

I hear the fatigue in her voice. This will take all of Isabel's powers.

"Mr. Yamada spoke to us about it. He told us about how he used to read it to your uncle when he would visit and how your uncle's eyes would light up . . ." Isabel sighs.

An award-winning performance. She sticks the landing. A perfect ten.

"All right. But we really have to go right now or I'll never get back in time for my shift with all the traffic on the Canyon."

My mom calls Donna Yamada, who says her dad would be happy to see us again.

Caleb bounds in happily from the living room, sketchbook in hand.

As we head out to the car, I turn to Isabel. "That was amazing. I think I speak for all the civilized world when I say how grateful we are that you have decided to use your powers for good instead of evil."

"You never know," Isabel says, fixing me with a wicked grin.

This time, Isabel sits next to me and Caleb in the backseat. And this time, the traffic is more problematic. The trip seems to take much longer than it did the first time. We sit in silence, each of us thinking how best to approach Mr. Yamada.

"I say we bust the guy," Caleb finally decrees as he absent-mindedly draws a large caped superhero standing over a cowering elderly Asian man. The caped man has scissors in one hand and a bonsai tree in the other. A speech balloon is coming from the avenging hero, who's saying, "One false move and I snip!" Isabel looks over and giggles.

"I like the idea of taking his teeny tree hostage," she says. "But I don't think that will be necessary."

She turns to me with a look of unmistakable admiration and continues. "I bet your great-uncle told him that once you passed the test and found the key, he could tell you everything."

"We'll know soon enough," I say as we finally turn onto Mr. Yamada's street.

It takes a moment to register. First there is the crackling sound of a two-way radio. Then the flashing lights, the ambulance.

Donna Yamada stands by the open doors, looking like the sky has fallen on her.

"Oh my gosh!" Mom cries, and pulls the car over to the side of the road. Clawing off her seat belt, she races ahead of us. We follow as fast as we can.

"You don't think . . . ," Caleb gasps. We stop at a respectful distance to watch the two women talk in hushed voices. My mom has her hand on Donna's shoulder.

"It wasn't anything violent," I say, "if that's what you're asking."

"And how do you know that?" Isabel asks.

I gesture up and down the street. "No police cars. It has to be something else."

Isabel looks toward the door. "The gurney's inside. So either he can't walk . . . or—"

Mom walks slowly back to us. "It seems that Mr. Yamada might have had a stroke. The paramedics are bringing him out now."

"Would it be all right if we go over with you and talk to Donna?" I ask.

Mom looks at me for a moment. "I'm going to hope that you will simply tell her your thoughts are with her and leave it at that."

"Sure, Mom, of course," I agree, and we walk over to join the anxious woman. Donna Yamada looks like she's somewhere else.

"We're so sorry to hear about your father," I begin.

"It happened so suddenly. It was after the visit . . ." Donna is looking away.

"*Our* visit?" asks Isabel in surprise.

Donna seems to notice us for the first time. She looks up with a small smile.

"Oh no, not you. He seemed so happy after you left. He was so fond of your great-uncle, you know," she adds to me.

"He's a very special man," Isabel offers. I know that if any one of us can reach Donna, it's Isabel. "How is he doing?"

"It's too early to tell," Donna says, her voice trembling, "but with all of our thoughts and prayers—" She stops and gasps.

Her eyes are a mix of surprise and fear. "Th-that's him! Where did you get that?"

She is pointing at Caleb's sketchbook. It's open to the page where Caleb drew the picture of the man who visited Isabel's dad.

"What do you mean, 'that's him'?" asks Isabel gently.

"That face! It's the man who visited my father this morning!"

"Are you sure?" I press.

"Positive. He said he had something important to discuss with my father, and I left them alone together. I heard raised voices, and when I came back, the man was about to leave. My father became very agitated. He collapsed and I called 911 immediately."

There is a flurry of commotion at the front door of the neat little house. Two burly EMTs are carefully guiding a gurney over the doorstep.

Isabel, Caleb, and I exchange anxious glances as we recognize the inert form of Mr. Yamada strapped on top.

"He has an oxygen mask," whispers Isabel. "That's a good sign, right?"

One of the EMTs is holding an IV bag over Mr. Yamada's head; the other end is attached to the arm of the old man.

The other EMT jumps into the ambulance to prepare to load Mr. Yamada.

The gurney sits for a moment directly in front of us. I can see Mr. Yamada's pale face, his closed eyes, his damp hair clinging to his forehead. His daughter reaches out to hold his hand. I turn to Donna. "I really hope he gets better soon."

Upon hearing my voice, Mr. Yamada's eyes pop open.

His eyes find my eyes and lock onto them. Then he reaches out and grabs my wrist.

"Ghh . . . yrrghh." Mr. Yamada is struggling to say something to me. It seems like the most important thing in the world to him. "M . . . m . . ." He is desperately trying to find the words to impart something to me.

"Yes? M . . . ?"

Mr. Yamada shakes his head. "M . . . M . . ." And then, with one last effort, he shouts out what sounds like "Shee guy mass!"

The old man's eyes close, and he falls back into unconsciousness. My mom puts her arms around his poor daughter.

"Donna, what does that mean? 'Shee guy mass'?" I ask, but Mom glares at me.

"Leave her alone, Ted. She's doesn't need your questions right now," she says in a flat, even tone that means no talking back.

After the gurney has been loaded into the ambulance, Mom helps Donna over to the truck, then turns to the EMTs.

"Where are you taking him? Cedars?"

"Cedars" is Cedars Sinai, the best hospital in Los Angeles.

"Yes, ma'am."

My mom turns to Donna. "He's going to get excellent care. As soon as my shift is over, I'll come and see how you're doing."

Donna nods, unable to speak. The EMTs help her into the back, where she sits looking at her father as they close the two doors with a slam. The siren whoops, and the ambulance takes off at top speed.

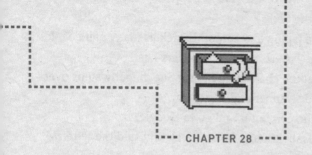

CHAPTER 28

NOT THE SAME

No one says much of anything on the ride back to the house, and we're all shaken after my mom drops us off at home.

Caleb looks down at the burly man staring back at him from the sketchbook sitting on the hall table.

"Whoever you are, you sure have lousy people skills," he says.

Wearily, the three of us troop up the stairs and down the hall to my room.

My room.

I have the sickening realization that Isabel has never seen my room.

Or smelled it.

I run to open a window.

Isabel gives a weak smile as she looks around the collected debris that makes up my bedroom. "Well, this is certainly cozy. . . ."

"Yep, this is where the magic happens," says Caleb, flopping down on the bed.

I turn on the laptop and smoothly kick as many pairs of old underwear and T-shirts under the bed as I can.

I offer Isabel the chair by the desk. She gingerly steps over an old fast-food wrapper and sits down.

I lean into the computer and go to Google.

"First off," Isabel finally says, "he clearly said the letter *M*. More than once."

"Yeah, that's got to have something to do with it," I agree.

"What starts with *M*?" Isabel asks in a slightly smug tone.

"Is that a rhetorical question?" snipes Caleb from the bed.

"How about . . . *Maltese Falcon*?" Isabel practically shouts. "He was trying to give you message about the book."

"Maybe," I say. "But I'll feel a lot better when I can figure out what 'Shee guy mass' means."

"You're pretty proud of yourself, aren't you?" asks Caleb.

"You didn't think of it," Isabel says with a smirk.

"Yeah, but I also didn't miss something right in front of me," Caleb says as he riffles the pages of the book in his hands.

Isabel and I turn at the same time. "What?"

We jump on the bed and look over Caleb's shoulder as he opens the paperback. He stops on page two. It's been lightly circled in purple pencil.

He raises an eyebrow and turns to page fifty-four. Also circled in purple.

"They're the only two pages circled," he tells us.

Isabel scans the pages.

"There's nothing important on these pages, is there? I don't see any numbers or anything about a key," Isabel reasons. "Although the detective does hide the falcon in a storage locker and mail the key to himself."

"And you never told us this?" I ask incredulously.

"We'd already found the key, and it wasn't mailed, so I didn't think it was important," Isabel snaps back.

"You guys are missing something," Caleb sings in a *nyah-nyah* voice.

I glare at him. "Okay, big shot. Let us in on it."

"Sorry, it's just not so often I figure out something before the great Ted Gerson, so I wanted to enjoy the moment," Caleb says.

"Okay, you've had your moment. Now tell us or I'm taking a pair of Ted's old underpants that he tried to hide under the bed and pulling them down over your head," Isabel replies calmly.

I'm not sure which is worse, that Isabel saw me do it, or hearing her say "Ted's old underpants."

"Two numbers are circled. Two and fifty-four. And in what color?"

"Purple?" I say. Then it dawns on me.

"Remember the blank piece of paper back in Great-Uncle Ted's apartment?"

"Violet," Isabel laughs. "Ultraviolet."

I turn from my Google search. "Purple . . . well, 254 nanometers falls in the spectrum for ultraviolet light, right?"

"But we don't have the lamp," Isabel says, bummed. "How are we going to—"

Caleb sits up. "Ted, you still have that UV pen, I bet!"

I nod. "Somewhere in my desk."

Isabel looks at me strangely. "You have a UV pen?"

"Sure," Caleb explains. "It's a spymaster kit thing. You write notes in invisible ink to each other that can only be read under UV light. We both got them for Christmas."

"I see," Isabel says, nodding. "Like, when you were eight or something."

"Actually," Caleb answers proudly, "it was last year."

I don't have to turn back from the desk to know that Isabel is suppressing a giggle. She clears her throat.

"Well, that's one advantage of being a ner—I mean, liking that kind of thing, I guess," she says.

I pull out my desk drawer. I remove random Pokémon cards, Lego pieces, an old *Transformers* toy from a Happy Meal, and a plastic Slinky from a birthday party I probably went to in third grade.

Finally, after what seems like every embarrassing thing I've ever owned has been taken out and put on display, I find the pen. Miraculously, the battery still works.

I hand the pen to Caleb.

"We just run this UV bulb on top of the pen over the pages in the book and see if anything pops up," Caleb tells Isabel, and they set to work.

I turn back to my computer. I type in "shee guy mass" and get nothing.

Well, I do get someone Chinese whose name is Shi Gai.

"Bull's-eye!" Caleb cries. "We've got a winner!" He crosses his arms in triumph.

"I don't see anything," Isabel sniffs. "There isn't anything written."

"We're not just looking for words," he reminds her. "See? That letter is underlined." He grabs his sketchbook. "This is going to take some time. We have to be really careful not to miss anything." He writes down the letter *M*.

"A coincidence?" asks Isabel. She leans in and watches Caleb run the UV light from the pen over the page. They turn the page and she points excitedly.

"Another one!" Caleb writes the letter *O* next to the *M*.

"Have you checked the page numbers too?" I ask as I try yet another spelling of "shi gai mas."

Caleb looks sheepish. "That's the kind of thing he asks me when I get stuck in an escape game."

Sure enough, one of the page numbers turns out to be circled under the UV light.

I'm having a lot less luck.

Nothing is coming up for me. I try putting "shi gai mas" into a Japanese-to-English translation program and it shows nothing.

Isabel takes a break from the book and looks over my shoulder.

"Maybe Japanese uses another letter for the *sh* sound?" she suggests.

"Maybe," I say. So I try "chi gai mass" as Isabel returns to help Caleb.

The closest thing I find is "chi gai massage," a business with a sexy-looking woman smiling out from the Web page. Don't hold me to this, but I'm reasonably sure that wasn't what Mr. Yamada had in mind.

"How's it going over there?" I call.

"We're halfway through," Isabel reports. "We've got a whole bunch of letters and numbers, but I'm not sure it's making sense."

I turn back to the screen. I quickly type "chigai mass," and before I can correct my mistake, Google suggests "chigaimasu."

I feel that familiar jolt go through me, like whenever I solve a killer game.

"I got it," I say, pumping my fist.

Caleb and Isabel look down at the laptop as I press the button to reveal what the word means.

"'*Chigaimasu:* Not the same, mistake, or wrong, or incorrect,'" I read.

"So he was saying *M* is incorrect or wrong?" asks Caleb.

"Great. Now all we have to figure out is who or what *M* is," Isabel says sourly, sitting back on the bed and going back to tracing the pen's light over the pages.

"Okay. Let's think," I suggest. "*M* could mean *Maltese Falcon*. Was he telling us *The Maltese Falcon* was the wrong book?"

"That doesn't seem right," Caleb reasons.

"*M* . . . is there a person named M?" My eyes catch the sketch of the burly man in Caleb's sketchbook that upset Donna Yamada so much.

I look over at the man. "Are you Mr. M? Are you wrong? Incorrect?"

Caleb closes the old paperback. "We've got all the numbers and letters."

"Let's see what you have," I say, and proceed to write them neatly on a new sheet of paper. "The numbers are 23, 44, 57. The letters are *M, O, R, P, O, A, R, K, S, R, T, E, T, E.*"

"It *has* to be an anagram. But what are the numbers?"

"There are too few to be a phone number," I say, "unless you missed one."

Isabel throws the book at me. "You look, then. I checked Caleb and he checked me. That's all we found."

"It could be an address," suggests Caleb.

I nod. "Of course. Look at the letters. If you rearrange them, they make the words *Moorpark Street.*"

"Is that near here?" Isabel asks.

"Not too far. 234457 Moorpark Street."

I turn and enter the information into the computer.

"Wait," says Isabel. "You hit the *M* twice. It says *MMoorpark.*"

"Right," I answer. "Hey, don't hate on mistyping. That's how I found out what *chigaimasu* means."

I'm about to retype the address, when I stop.

"What's up, dude?" Caleb asks. "Come on, let's find out where 234457 Moorpark Street is."

"Mr. Yamada didn't say 'M, *chigaimasu,*'" I say slowly as my mind turns this over. "He kept saying 'M . . . M . . . *chigaimasu.*'"

I look up at them. "What if he *meant* 'M.M. *chigaimasu*'?"

"So?" Caleb says impatiently. "So it's M.M. We don't know any M.M., do we?"

"Maybe we do." I begin typing something into the browser. "M.M.? Monuments Men?"

The Monuments Men site loads in. But somehow, it looks slightly different.

"Isabel, do you know how identity thieves get you to enter your private information online?"

"I think so," Isabel answers. "My dad warned me about this before I could buy anything on the Web. They set up sites that look exactly like the real sites, only they're phony. And the Web address is the same except for one small change."

"Exactly. Like dot com instead of dot org." I scroll up and come to the page Stan showed us on his laptop.

But it isn't that page. Instead of copying the address from Stan's business card, I find the site through Google.

It's www.monumentsmen.org, not www.monumentsmen .com.

All the difference in the world.

"What are we looking at?" asks Caleb in a small voice, like he knows what it is.

"This is the real Monuments Men site," I say as we look at the photo. It's identical to the one Stan showed us, but he's not in the picture.

Behind the old man holding the ledger is a different smiling man.

He has a broad, bald head, a unibrow, big black plastic glasses, and a fringe of hair around his ears.

"And that," I say, indicating the man whose face we've come to know so well, "is the real Stanley Kellerman."

"Nicely done!" says a voice behind us.

CHAPTER 29

DOUK-DOUK

I've felt a lot of things in my gut—the lurch of nausea before a big test, butterflies before giving a presentation at school, even the whomping up-and-down of a roller coaster.

But this is different.

For the first time in my life, I feel real fear.

Fear in the pit of my stomach.

A cold, small thing that slowly begins to grow as I turn with the others and see the man we've come to know as Stanley Kellerman standing there.

"How did you get in?" I ask. I'm buying time, trying to process what's happening.

"Oh, I let myself in," Kellerman says easily. "It's not hard if you know how."

Isabel opens her mouth as if to yell, but quicker than I would have thought was possible, Kellerman bounds across the room, grabs her wrists in one hand, and squeezes.

"Ouch! That hurts!" Isabel gasps.

"Well, it's supposed to, isn't it?" he says genially, like a gym teacher at your school explaining the rules of a new game.

"How long have you been here?" I demand.

"Long enough. I stood outside the door for a while. You were doing so well decoding your great-uncle's little game, I didn't want to interrupt you."

I try to casually put my arm over the paper.

Kellerman laughs. "Oh, Ted. That's so silly, isn't it? Let's just go back to your work and find out where that building on Moorpark Street is, okay?"

He's still holding Isabel's wrists in a viselike grip.

Caleb sounds like he's hyperventilating. "Are you . . . going to kill us?"

Kellerman regards Caleb for a second and then looks at me. "Kill you? Whatever gave you that idea? I just want what Ted's great-uncle found."

"So you promise you won't kill us?" Caleb pleads.

"Yes, I promise," Kellerman says soothingly. "As long as Ted cooperates. He's quite good at these games, as you know. His great-uncle was right to trust him to solve his little amusements." He pulls Isabel toward the door, then leans against it, as relaxed as if he's just popped by to hang out and shoot the breeze. "So, first things first. Where's the key?"

"What key?" I ask, trying to stall as long as I can. I desperately wonder if there's a walkthrough on the laptop for this: *The Game of Ted 1.4: Escape the Fake Kellerman.*

"Okay, Ted, we'll play it your way." Kellerman sighs. "I think it's time for you to meet Douk-Douk."

"Douk-Douk?" asks Caleb, who is curled up on the bed.

"A Frenchman named Gaspard Cognet made the first douk-douk in 1929," Kellerman says. "It was supposed to be just for the colonial workmen, you know, to use in their daily jobs."

There's a click. A small folding knife appears in Kellerman's other hand. It has an engraved blade and a blue hilt.

"But in the fifties, the Algerians who were trying to liberate themselves from France found a whole new use for douk-douks. They're very sharp, you see. Razor sharp."

The silence in the room is total. No one moves. The only sound is Caleb's labored breathing.

"I'd like the key now, please," Kellerman repeats in the same pleasant tone.

A small red dot appears on Isabel's arm. At first I can't figure out what it is.

But to my horror, I watch the dot grow larger, and I realize: Isabel is bleeding.

The douk-douk has pricked her. Isabel tries to wriggle free, a look of panic in her eyes.

"Oops. Guess my friend Douk-Douk slipped. Accidents happen, huh?" says Kellerman, in the same maddeningly pleasant voice. "I guess by now you should have figured it out, Ted," he continues. "As your 'Dear Uncle's' lawyer found out, this is not a game."

Kellerman reaches into his pocket with his knife hand, pulls something out, and throws it at Caleb, who looks frozen with fear.

"There's a Band-Aid—be a good boy and open it for me, Caleb?"

Caleb stares at the wrapped Band-Aid and slowly begins to peel it open.

"Go to the bathroom, Ted, and get a tissue. And if you're not back in five seconds, Douk-Douk might slip again. You understand, don't you?"

I nod. I race to the bathroom and return with the tissue.

I head over to Kellerman, who tightens his grip on Isabel.

"No need to come closer, Ted. Just put it on the edge of the desk. Now, Caleb, take the tissue and dab it on Isabel's arm. That's good."

Caleb does what he's told, then carefully applies the Band-Aid to Isabel's wound. His hands are shaking.

"You're not still scared, are you?" asks Kellerman. "Nothing needs to happen. It's all up to Ted. Right, Ted? Now let's have that key."

I look at Caleb and Isabel. Both have fear like I've never seen in their eyes.

I slowly walk around the room.

"So where do we think he hid it, kids?" Kellerman asks lightly. "Behind a poster? Taped under a drawer in his desk? I can't wait to find out!"

I go to my desk chair and turn it over.

"I do hope Ted isn't thinking of throwing that at me. That would be a very foolish thing to do, wouldn't it, Isabel?"

Isabel stares straight ahead, mute.

"I said, wouldn't it, Isabel?" Kellerman says, a slight menace apparent behind the jolly voice.

"Yes, it would," Isabel replies mechanically.

I stare at Kellerman with contempt. I carefully unscrew one of the wheels from the legs on the chair and then turn it right-side up. The key falls into my hand from the tube.

"Excellent!" Kellerman says. "That's a new one on me! Ted, slowly place the key on the table and back away."

I do as I'm told. It all seems so dreamlike, as if it's happening to someone else.

"Now we're all going to go on a little trip. But first, I need you to take out your phones."

"My father took my phone," Isabel says, in a voice barely above a whisper.

"Then I guess it's just the boys. Let's go, fellas. Phones, please."

We both reach into our pockets.

"Put them in the desk drawer and close it."

My heart sinks. Without our phones, we can't be traced. We do what he says, and I watch our chance of rescue disappear as I push the drawer shut.

"There's just one more piece of the puzzle, right?" Kellerman continues, casually shifting so that he can view the laptop while still holding tight to Isabel's wrists. "I believe you were going to look up an address."

I move to the laptop and sit down. I reach for the keyboard, but Kellerman calls out: "Ted, please don't do anything stupid, like typing a different address into the search bar. I can see it from here. Just press Enter, and we'll all see where we're going."

"We?" Isabel asks softly.

"I can't exactly leave you here, can I?" reasons Kellerman. "Besides, who knows? I might need Ted's genius at solving games. Great-Uncle Ted was certainly a clever man, wasn't he?"

"Then just take me."

I'm a little surprised to hear these words coming from my mouth. "As long as you have me, they won't say a thing, right, guys?"

"You may be a wizard at figuring out clues, but when it comes to people, you've got some growing up to do," snorts Kellerman. "If I just take you, who knows what little scheme you might cook up? But with your friends along, you're not about to put them in danger. And whether they are in danger depends solely on how well you cooperate. For example, just press the Enter key, please."

I do what I'm told.

We all stare at the screen.

234457 Moorpark Street is a storage facility.

Kellerman's face lights up. Almost to himself, he murmurs, "That's the ticket! You've done it. Only a matter of time now . . ."

As he stands momentarily mesmerized, Isabel wrenches herself out of his grasp and pulls at the bedroom door, trying to get out.

Caleb and I immediately spring forward, reaching for the knife in Kellerman's hand.

With one move, Kellerman pushes us out of the way and slams the door on Isabel's arm. With a cry of pain, she pulls her arm back in.

Kellerman grabs her, roughly this time.

"All right, we could have done this the easy way, but I see you have other ideas. Any of you try anything like that again, I can make one of you disappear just like that lawyer. Don't think it can't happen. I've done it before, but only when I had to. Do I make myself clear?"

The three of us stand there frozen, dumb with terror.

We all nod.

Kellerman's demeanor changes, and the good cheer returns

to his voice. It's chilling how easily he can go from one to the other.

"Now we're going to all go downstairs and into my car. Let's make this nice and simple. I apologize for losing my temper. You honestly have no idea what you're dealing with here. But once this is over, as long as everyone plays along, you'll have a great story to tell your friends and I'll have what I want. Deal?"

We nod again. Kellerman reaches behind him and with his knife hand opens the door.

He backs into the hallway, still holding Isabel.

We reach the landing, a weird procession, Kellerman walking backward with Isabel, with us facing them. At the head of the stairs, Kellerman motions with his head for Caleb and me to go first.

"I'm sure we don't want me to trip on the stairs, do we? It'd be terribly unsafe while I'm holding a knife." Isabel's eyes are staring straight ahead, as if she's willing herself to get through this.

We walk carefully down the stairs, with Kellerman and Isabel close behind.

Just as they reach the bottom step, we freeze.

There is the unmistakable sound of a key turning in the lock.

CHAPTER 30

ROAD TRIP

The door opens and Dad is standing there, looking through some papers. He looks up, distracted.

"Oh, hello! I didn't realize we had visitors."

Kellerman turns to me. There is a clear warning in his eyes. "Ted, would you do the honors?"

"Dad, you remember Mr. Kellerman," I say tonelessly. "He's the guy with that organization that's tracking down lost treasures the Nazis looted during World War Two."

"Oh, right. Nice to see you," Dad says, barely paying attention.

Kellerman smiles. "I'd shake your hand, but I'm just getting over a cold. Wouldn't want to give it to you."

"Mom said you weren't coming home till dinner," I say, trying to send a message with my eyes.

Dad shrugs. "The meeting finished early." He turns to

Kellerman. "So you're the guy who thinks Uncle Ted was a master criminal."

"Oh, I guess I didn't really explain very well what this has to do with your wife's uncle," Kellerman laughs. "We were never accusing him of anything. We just thought he might have had some information about a very valuable artifact, and Ted was showing me a pad containing his last words. I had hoped he might have said something."

"Was it helpful?" Dad asks.

"No, I'm afraid it was a dead end," Kellerman replies. "But Ted and his friends were so *cooperative and helpful* I want to take them out for pizza before I leave LA."

"That's very nice of you!" says Dad, completely oblivious to the tension. He turns to Isabel, her face full of concern.

"Ted tells me you're going to be leaving us! I'm so sorry."

"Me too," Isabel says, pale as a ghost.

"You are planning on coming back soon, aren't you?" asks Dad.

"I really want to," Isabel almost whispers as Kellerman keeps close to her. "But it's really not up to me." Her eyes dart at Kellerman and then back to Dad.

"Well, I've got a plane to catch at five, so I'd better get these kids their pizza," Kellerman says, winking. "But it was very nice to see you again."

We head out the door.

"Wait!" Dad calls.

Kellerman stops and turns slowly to Dad.

Yes, the brain cells have finally kicked in.

"You know what's a shame, Isabel? I never got to talk about *The Portrait of a Lady* with you."

This is what he cares about? *Great, Dad.*

"I know," Isabel said, her eyes locked on Dad's. "I think my favorite part is where Isabel decides to stay in London and not return to that idiot Osmond."

Dad looks confused.

"But—" he starts, but Kellerman cuts him off.

"I don't mean to be rude, but we really have to go," he says over his shoulder as he gently but firmly pushes us kids in front of him. "And don't worry, I'll have Ted back for dinner."

We head down the front walk as Dad looks after us.

The street is deserted, and my heart sinks when I see the black Jaguar parked on the street. Kellerman switches the douk-douk into the hand that holds Isabel, fishes out his key fob, and unlocks the doors with a beep. He motions to me.

"Open the back door and get in. Just remember, play along and all this will be nothing but a good story later."

Caleb and I slide into the spacious leather backseat of the luxury automobile.

He's going to need his hands to drive, and he'll be distracted. That's when we can make our move.

Kellerman reaches into his pocket and fishes out two strips of what look like thin plastic.

"Aren't zip ties wonderful?" he asks, tossing them into the backseat. "You can use them for so many things, like keeping your computer cords all neat and tidy. Now, first, Caleb, if you'll just pull that edge through the other end, and, Ted, you can put your wrists behind your back, and then, Caleb, slip the loop over Ted's hands. Now pull it tight. Atta boy!"

I hear the *ziiip* as the plastic cord tightens around my wrists. It's locked into position. I struggle but quickly realize that nothing I can do will break the band.

Kellerman has Isabel reach behind and do the same thing to Caleb, but he isn't as pleased with her work.

"You can pull harder than that!" he admonishes. Kellerman yanks Caleb's band and Caleb lets out a yelp of pain.

Isabel glares at Kellerman. "You didn't have to do that."

"And you didn't have to try to deliberately leave it loose either," Kellerman retorts as he slips a third band roughly around Isabel's wrists and pushes her back into the front seat. "So we're even."

Kellerman pulls the seat belt around Isabel's body, clicks it in place, then leaps out of the car and does the same to us.

"Now we're all buckled up," he says, once again the cheerful uncle. "Wouldn't want to be pulled over for not wearing seat belts, would we?"

He settles back into his seat and starts the car. He's visibly relaxed now.

"Everyone comfy?" he says. "No one has to go to the bathroom, right? Because I told you to go before we left!" Chuckling at his little joke, Kellerman pulls out a phone.

"What was that address again?" he asks, consulting the paper he took from my room. "234457 Moorpark Street. Let's find the cross street, shall we?"

He gestures at us with the phone.

"Nice phone, right? Brand-new. Just in case you were wondering. I gave my other cell phone number to so many people, you know. It would be easy to trace the GPS on it, if anyone was going to try. Like that gentleman in your picture, Caleb. Such a good likeness!"

I look out the window.

Kellerman continues, "That one is in my hotel room right now. If anyone tries to trace my phone, they'll think I'm sitting in my hotel. This one, well . . . no one knows about it. Pretty untraceable. That sounds like something you would have thought of, right, Ted?"

I just glare.

Kellerman shakes his head and looks down at the screen. "Okay, so we're off to Moorpark and Valencia."

"Can I ask you a question?" I finally say to the man in the driver's seat.

Kellerman looks at me in the rearview mirror. He's driving slowly through local streets. "Sure, Ted, fire away."

"What's your real name? We can't call you Stan anymore, now that we know—"

"Oh, I don't think my real name matters," Kellerman answers lightly as he speeds up after a stop sign. "Notice I came to a complete stop before moving forward. I know you won't be taking driver's ed for a few years, but listen to me, you'll want to form these habits early."

"I thought it was because you didn't want the police to pull you over for running a stop sign," I say.

Keep him talking, I'm thinking. *Maybe something will come to you.*

I'm running through every possible scenario I've ever played in every game, trying to figure out how to loosen or cut through the plastic that's biting into my skin. I look over at Caleb.

Caleb looks down at the zip ties. He almost imperceptibly moves his head to indicate that we should shift our bodies.

I make an elaborate show of moving my shoulder around. Soon we're back to back.

"Getting comfortable, are you?" asks Kellerman.

"Yeah, it's kind of hard on your back to sit too long in one position with these on," Caleb says.

I feel something tickling my hands. It's Caleb's fingers trying to reach for my zip tie. I hold my breath.

I look up at the front seat. Isabel sits immobile, pressed against the door, as far away from Kellerman as possible. Meanwhile, Kellerman seems distracted by the traffic. There's an accident in front of us, and flashing lights.

Caleb's fingers find my zip tie. He grabs it and pulls. Nothing. He pulls harder, and I nearly fall off the seat.

Guiding the car expertly as the police wave him past the accident, Kellerman casually turns his head. "You know what's also great about those plastic zip ties? You can't undo them. Not like rope or handcuffs. You can't slip out of them or release someone from them." He smiles. "The only way to get them off is to cut them."

Caleb and I slump down, defeated.

"And I'm glad no one was silly enough to try to jump out of the car when we passed the police. I control all the door locks, of course."

In the front, Isabel comes to life. Her eyes lock on Kellerman with hatred.

"The one thing I don't understand is what you're planning to do with whatever you hope to find in this storage unit."

"That's a good question, Isabel," Kellerman says. "You kids are so smart! You know that there's no way I could sell it on the open market. But that's only true if it's a painting or a piece of sculpture. And even then, there are buyers—anonymous buyers in Asia, for instance, with whom I deal quite a bit. They give me lots of money for all sorts of things, no questions asked."

"Why are you so sure it's going to be there?" Isabel presses. "It could just be another clue."

"Let's hope it's not," says Kellerman, the smile frozen on his face. "Ah! Valencia! Moorpark should be coming up any minute now. . . ."

We turn and cruise out of the shaded residential area.

The street is beginning to look more and more industrial. Low warehouses and small factories sit behind gates and barbed-wire fences baking in the sun. There are no more shops or malls or houses.

Kellerman finds the address, and the car is suddenly in front of a nondescript gate with a rusted sign that reads VALLEYVIEW LONG-TERM STORAGE FACILITIES. OPEN BY APPOINTMENT ONLY.

Underneath is a phone number. Apparently no one is here right now, as there is a thick chain attached to a formidable lock holding the gate tightly shut.

Kellerman gets out of the car and looks at the gate, hands on hips. He takes a pair of sunglasses out of his pocket. For a brief moment, his back is turned.

Isabel immediately wheels around in her seat and whispers to me, "So what's the plan?"

I look back her blankly. "Plan?"

"Yes! What do we do?"

I realize that Caleb is also looking intently at me, glancing outside every couple of seconds to check on Kellerman.

"I . . . don't know," I reply flatly.

"You—but you have to know!" insists Isabel annoyingly. "All this time you've been sitting back there. I just assumed—"

"Look, it's not that simple!" I snap.

"Obviously," Isabel hisses. "But I tipped off your father. Now all you have to do is get us away from Kellerman."

"How did you tip off Dad?" I ask in amazement.

"Remember what I said about the ending of *The Portrait of a Lady*? It was completely incorrect! He'll figure out that something's wrong, and—"

"What are you talking about?" I groan.

"I told him how cool it was that Isabel stayed in London, when in fact she actually did return to her horrible husband. Everybody knows that," Isabel says proudly.

I hang my head. "Let me get this straight. You think my dad—who never listens to anyone—is going to hear you make a mistake about the ending of some book and figure out that we're being kidnapped by this guy? And then convince the other parents or the police to find us?"

Isabel's face reddens. "It wasn't a mistake. He would know I was deliberately saying something wrong. I know you don't think so, but he really seemed to notice—"

"—that you made some mistake about a book . . . yadda yadda yadda. I know," I reply through gritted teeth.

"Okay. Forget it. You get us out of here, Mr. Master of Exit Games. You always seem to know exactly how to get out of things. So prove it."

"First of all, they're called escape games, not exit games," I say.

"Guys! Guys! He's coming back!" Caleb whimpers.

Kellerman has returned to the car. I'm surprised to see him walking past the driver's door and going around to the back. I hear a click and the trunk pops open. Kellerman takes something out and slams the top down.

Suddenly my door opens and I'm blinking in the blistering midday heat.

Kellerman pulls me out of the car, and then Caleb. He's

holding a large mallet with a rubber-coated head. He then goes around to the front and opens the door for Isabel. He smiles broadly as he escorts her to stand with us.

"Now, Ted, let's say this was one of your games," Kellerman begins. "How would you get past this lock?"

"I thought you said this isn't a game," I say sourly.

"Right you are!" Kellerman laughs. "Just trying to make things interesting for you." He takes a small leather case out of his pocket and unzips it. "You know, most people would think a bolt cutter would work on that chain, but that's hard work. Or you could just cut a hole in the fence, but that leaves sharp pokey things, and I'd hate for you to rip your clothes getting inside."

Kellerman holds out a key.

"Have you ever seen one of these?" he asks.

"A key? Yeah, I think I've seen a few." I smirk.

Kellerman's face hardens. "I'm disappointed in you, Ted. This is a particular kind of key. Have you heard of a bump key?"

I shake my head.

"They're very useful. If you look carefully, they're cut in a very particular way. Each one matches a certain type of lock. I think this one should be perfect. Okay, here's the tricky part."

Kellerman walks over to the locked gate and carefully inserts the key.

"You see, if you do this just right, you fool the lock into thinking the tumblers are lined up properly, for just enough time to—"

Kellerman takes the mallet and gives the key a sharp tap, simultaneously turning it to the right. There's a pop and the lock springs open.

"Hey! Got it on the first try. Not too shabby, huh?" Kellerman crows. "Let's get out of this hot sun, shall we?"

Kellerman pushes the heavy gate open, kicking up a cloud of dust.

I cough as I feel my mouth go dry.

Kellerman pushes us toward the hulking warehouse, lying silent and dark.

We approach the entrance and Kellerman reaches into his little leather case and finds a different bump key. Again he expertly turns the key, and the door opens.

"You know where I learned how to do this? YouTube!" laughs Kellerman. "You can find anything there, right?"

Kellerman pushes us into the building and closes the door.

Holding the key he took from me in front of him, Kellerman looks at the letter and number written on it. He motions to a bench by the door.

I peer into the blackness, which appears to hold hundreds of storage units. This could be it.

If we run in different directions and find something sharp to cut the zip ties, he'll never find us.

Kellerman is looking at a map of the various units on the wall, trying to locate Great-Uncle Ted's. Now is our chance.

Maybe our last chance.

"Run for it!" I yell, and the three of us break for the darkness.

I sprint ahead and find myself in a huge warehouse, corridor after corridor stretching in front of me, each one filled with sliding doors to storage units. I run, not daring to look back, praying that my friends have managed to make their way into the welcoming shadows.

I can hear Kellerman cursing and running somewhere in the distance. I turn a corner and sit down, my lungs bursting.

I need time.

I need to gather my thoughts.

I need to escape.

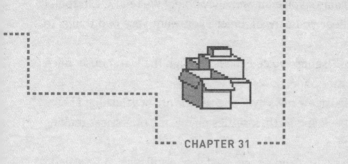

CHAPTER 31

THE BLACK BIRD

As I sit in the cool, empty warehouse, my eyes now completely accustomed to the dark, I can feel myself calm down.

So long as Caleb and Isabel are also hiding, I'll think of something. I look at the unit closest to me and note with satisfaction that the handle to pull up the door has a sharp edge. Something to avoid, normally ("Those things are dangerous! What were they thinking?"—every mother), but perfect for one thing: cutting plastic.

I position myself and begin to feel for the handle.

"Ted?"

My heart sinks. Somewhere a few rows over, I hear Caleb's tremulous voice.

"He's got me, Ted." I think of Stan's knife and what he's threatened to do with it.

"Okay, okay!" I call out. "Where are you?"

Kellerman's voice answers, icy cold. "We're at C4. Isabel, I have to hear you as well, unless you want very bad things to happen."

"Stop!" Isabel's voice echoes through the warehouse, filled with frustration.

I trudge a few rows over and see the arc of a flashlight beam shining back and forth. It settles on me, the brightness making me wince.

"Turn around and let me see if you're still nice and zip-tied," Kellerman's voice commands. I do as I'm told. The light moves off me and finds Isabel. Her hair is coated in dust, and she stares back defiantly.

We rejoin Kellerman, who has his arm hooked around Caleb, the douk-douk open and ready. He does not look happy.

"That was a rookie move, Ted. Really stupid. You have a nice long life ahead of you unless you try something like that again."

There is no trace of humor or "Uncle Stan" left in his voice. It's cold and hard.

Somehow, I like it better. I know where I stand with the person in front of me.

Kellerman marches us over to the side of the structure, walking along the wall until we come to a large metal box. He opens it and pulls a large switch.

Instantly, the warehouse floods with light from above. Kellerman flicks off his flashlight. He looks grimly at me. "Okay, let's do this. We're going to row P, unit 14."

Sorry, Caleb mouths at me.

Not your fault, I mouth back, and bump shoulders with him. I'm just glad he's okay.

Counting over to the fourteenth door, Kellerman marches

us over and puts the key into the lock at the bottom. He pulls at the door, and there's a deafening screech as the protesting steel grate eases up, revealing a small room. Clearly no one's been here in ages.

Like all the other units, this is nothing more than a concrete bunker, a simple windowless room made of concrete cinder blocks with a thin coat of paint slapped onto them.

Boxes are stacked all around, and signs from forgotten brands of snack foods and beer from the seventies lean against the walls. Shelving units rise high above our heads, holding cartons of old glassware and what look like plumbing supplies. A few cardboard signs advertise snack foods.

"He must have used this to keep the stuff from his store after he closed it down," I observe, looking around to see if I can spot something—anything—before Kellerman does.

Kellerman pushes us rudely into the unit, flicks on the light switch, and pulls down the grate.

"In the unlikely event someone does decide to come and visit their belongings while we're here, this way we'll have some . . . privacy," he states.

He turns to us and motions to the floor.

"Sit. The three of you. And not a word between you. Am I understood?"

We all nod meekly. My heart is thumping.

"This time, Ted. I asked nicely before, but now I'm not going to be so nice," Kellerman said. "For the last time, what did your great-uncle tell you before he died?"

"It wasn't anything!" I plead. "I swear! I think it was never give up, never stop learning, there's always an answer . . . and . . . go for broke!"

" 'Go for Broke'—that was the motto of the 442nd Regiment,"

Kellerman muses, scanning the contents of the room. "His unit, the one that made it to Austria. And then to Berlin. Where he acquired the thing we're looking for today."

"Which is what, exactly?" asks Caleb.

"Ask your friend Ted," Kellerman says impatiently. He walks over to a few cartons and pulls them open.

"Nothing but old liquor bottles," he says. "It's got to be in one of these."

Isabel turns to me. "What's he talking about? What did your great-uncle find?"

I look over with a scowl of frustration. "Look, if I knew, I'd tell him! All I know is what you know! He said there was treasure for me to find, but he never said what it was!"

Kellerman studies my face. "Say that again. And look me in the eye."

I glare at Kellerman and repeat what I said.

Kellerman regards me for a long time. Then a faint grin comes to his lips. "You . . . you really don't know, then?"

Isabel studies my face for a moment and smiles despite herself. "You know he doesn't. I haven't known Ted that long, but I know he's a lousy liar. Unlike some people."

"True enough, Isabel. I am a good liar. It comes in handy in my business."

"I'm assuming it's a work of art of some sort," I reason. "And something Great-Uncle Ted could move easily. That rules out a painting."

"Not necessarily," Isabel counters. "You can roll up a painting. Art thieves do it all the time. Right, Mr. Kellerman, or whatever your name is?"

"Paintings are quite portable, Ted, as your charming friend

suggests," Kellerman responds. "But we're not looking for a painting."

He moves quickly around the room, tapping the walls, peering into the overhead shelves.

Then he turns to me and bends down. When he speaks, his voice has changed. All of a sudden he's speaking in an English accent, in a low, gruff voice, with a hint of a chuckle. "Mr. Gerson, have you any conception of how much money could be made from the object your great-uncle found?" Either Kellerman is imitating someone, a famous actor I've never heard of . . . or he's gone around the bend into crazyland.

Best thing, I think, is to play along. "No."

Kellerman leans in even closer, so I can feel his breath on my face. "Well, sir, if I told you—by gad, if I told you half!—you'd call me a liar!" Kellerman looks from face to face, seeking something. Approval? "Nothing? No one? I guess we have no movie fans here. Isabel, I would have thought you—"

A gasping sound comes from the back of Isabel's throat. She stares in disbelief at our captor. "But . . . that's a quote from *The Maltese Falcon*. I mean, I knew that. But you're not suggesting . . . ?"

"There was evidence. There were witnesses. People saw it. Even as careful as your great-uncle was, there were some who saw what he had."

"But the falcon, it's not . . . It was just a story . . . ," Isabel stammers.

My fear is undermined by my irritation. "What are you talking about?"

Kellerman bows to Isabel. "The floor is yours, Miss Archer."

"I told you guys back in the room, remember? In the book,

the thing everybody is trying to find is a statue of a falcon, solid gold and covered in priceless jewels of every kind. But the writer of the book made that up!"

"Yes, he did," agrees Kellerman. "You're absolutely right about that. There was no falcon—"

"So if there is no falcon, how could my great-uncle have taken it?" I demand.

"There was no falcon until 1941. The man Adolf Hitler trusted to loot the treasures of the invaded countries, his right-hand man, Hermann Goering, was a huge fan of mystery novels. *The Maltese Falcon* was one of his favorites. It has been rumored in certain circles that he came up with an audacious little scheme to enrich himself while acquiring items for the Reich. He made his own Maltese Falcon, encrusted with diamonds, rubies, sapphires, and whatever else he could pry out of jewelry intended for the Nazi cause."

Kellerman pauses to let this sink in. Then, as he goes on opening cartons and peering inside, he continues: "If anyone noticed a few gems missing here or there, well, things get lost in transit. Over time, he amassed quite a collection, and he knew it wouldn't look very good if they were found in his possession. So he had the falcon made, of solid gold, like the one in the book, and had jewelers encrust the object. As a final piece of insurance, he coated the bird in black paint and then hid it among the other treasures in the salt mines of Altaussee."

"How did you learn all this?" Isabel asks as Kellerman methodically moves two boxes aside to get to what's behind them. All of a sudden we see a display case, glass intact, which I guess once held candy, salty snacks, and cigarettes. Now it's coated in a fine layer of dust. Kellerman picks up a rag and begins to clean it.

"Good question. The jewelers he used were some of the finest in all of Europe."

"So one of the jewelers talked?" Isabel says.

"Not exactly. You see, Goering made a deal with them: if they did the work, he'd fly them secretly to the United States. Instead, after they finished, he had them killed. Which wasn't so hard in wartime Germany."

I'm getting tired of the history lesson, but I look over at Isabel, and it dawns on me what she's doing. She knows that every minute we can keep Kellerman talking is a minute in our favor.

Maybe my dad did figure out that something was wrong. Or if we stall long enough, maybe someone will come into the facility, notice the lights are on, and call the police. Anything is possible as long as we keep asking questions.

"So where does my great-uncle figure into all of this?" I ask.

Kellerman has most of the glass cleaned by now. Behind it, clearly visible, is a series of tiles set into the wall. Kellerman peers at them curiously.

"You have to understand, Ted," Kellerman says as he pushes against the cabinet. "The Nazis were meticulous record keepers. That's one of the gifts they left to the Monuments Men. Every item, every painting and piece of sculpture, every tapestry and necklace was listed and cataloged in giant ledgers. All except one. The falcon. No one knew of its existence."

The display case won't budge. Kellerman tries pushing harder, but it doesn't give an inch. His forehead is beaded with sweat. He kneels down, his chest heaving.

At last, he catches his breath. He turns to me with a smile.

"Goering was clever, but it didn't occur to him that the jewelers had wives, and children, and that the creation of this extraordinary thing would make for lively dinner conversations and bedtime stories. And even if he had thought of it, he would have assumed those people had perished in the death camps. But even though Goering himself died after the war, some of his victims survived. And rumors began to spread."

Kellerman mops his forehead with a handkerchief. We look up at him like eager pupils. He's clearly pleased, and continues.

"Meanwhile, a German soldier takes the bird from the salt mines and brings it with him to Berlin. He is killed in combat, and a young American soldier finds a black statue of a bird that has fallen from the dead man's backpack and takes it as a souvenir. Just like thousands of other soldiers take Luger pistols or cigarette lighters or other trinkets."

"And that man was my great-uncle," I conclude.

Kellerman takes out his flashlight and peers under the display case. He feels around with his hand.

"Actually, that man was named Howard Brennan. He lost the bird to your great-uncle in a craps game."

"A *what* game?" Caleb looks up. It's the first thing he's said since we've been brought into the unit. Clearly the word "craps" has sparked something in him.

"A dice game, Caleb. It's called craps. Don't ask me why," Kellerman says, with a hint of the pleasantness that his voice contained before. Being this close to the end of his quest is obviously putting him in a better mood.

"There were witnesses. Other men in the game. It meant little to them, but once word began to spread that a statue of a bird had changed hands, those who were already searching for it tried to locate the new owner. Finding him was not easy. It took years and years to identify even his first name. Since, of course, he was known in the army as Ted, but was registered under his legal name, Takateru."

Kellerman pauses for a moment, pulls a small water bottle out of his pocket, and takes a swig. "And then somewhere along the line, your great-uncle began to suspect that what he had was worth a tremendous amount. Perhaps that's when he quit his job and opened his liquor store, hoping to disappear from prying eyes in the best way possible. And he succeeded all too well."

Kellerman takes another sip of water, showing no intention of sharing it with us.

"So it was not until one of my colleagues spotted your great-uncle's obituary, detailing his name and his history, that we put two and two together. In talking with Mr. Yamada, I confirmed that indeed, he was the very person I was looking for."

Kellerman puts his hand under the counter of the display case.

When he pulls it out, it's covered in old grime and grease. He wipes it carefully on his handkerchief.

"Which brings us," he says with a touch of satisfaction in his voice, "to today. And so here we are."

By now, my legs have fallen asleep, and I know that even if there is a chance of escape, I'll be useless.

"Which also brings us, Ted Gerson, to you."

Kellerman pulls out the douk-douk and it snaps open once again, the click of the razor-sharp steel echoing in the tiny room.

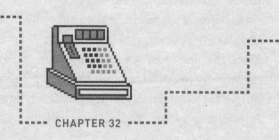

CHAPTER 32

ONLY FOR DEATH IS THERE NO SOLUTION

To my amazement, I feel the knife slice cleanly through the plastic band on my wrists, releasing me. I stare at Kellerman, trying to figure out what has just happened.

"Feels good to be free, doesn't it?" asks Kellerman solicitously as he watches me rub my hands together and flex my fingers. "Wouldn't you like your friends to be free too?"

"Of course," I reply as Kellerman helps me to my feet.

"Upsy-daisy!" Kellerman says in his maddeningly cheerful way. "Walk it off, now."

I can feel tingling in my legs as the blood rushes back into them. I pace around the small room, never taking my eyes off Kellerman.

"So what do you plan on doing with me?" I finally ask.

"I think the question really is what are you going to do for me?" Kellerman replies, leaning against the display case. "It looks like I need your help. Clearly we have to get to the tiles behind this case, but it won't budge. There's got to be a solution, and I have a feeling your great-uncle thought you were just the young man to figure it out."

I think about this. It's the only way. "Let Caleb and Isabel go and I'll help you."

Kellerman lets out a short, unpleasant laugh. "That's not going to happen. Saying something like that might sound noble, and it might impress Miss Archer. Did it?" he asks, looking coyly at Isabel.

"I don't think he has any intention of letting us go," she says in a quiet voice, flat and defeated.

"That's a trifle melodramatic, but you are that age," Kellerman sighs. "No, I simply need a little, shall we say, insurance. This can work out for everyone, really. I get what I want, and you get to go home. Sounds like a good deal to me. How about you?"

I swallow and think of my options. When Kellerman says things like this, it sounds so reasonable. And if I can distract him even for a minute, is there some way to disarm him? What if I somehow manage to get the knife away from him, only to find out he also has a gun?

It's getting too hard to think. I make a decision.

"I'll do it. I can't promise you you'll find what you're looking for, but I'll try to help figure out how to solve this."

Kellerman breaks into a huge smile. "I knew you couldn't resist a challenge."

I bend down and look at the display case. I then hoist myself up on top of it. One of the advantages of being a little guy is that I'm light enough to perch there without breaking the thin wood countertop. It's at an angle to the wall, and from this vantage point, I can see a space.

"There's a place down there where I can fit between the wall and the case," I announce. "Should I do it?"

"As your great-uncle would say, 'Go for broke!'" Kellerman answers eagerly.

As three pairs of eyes watch me, I carefully position myself over the tiny triangular opening and lower myself. I'm now wedged between the wall and the display case, but I can reach my hand down and feel under the shelving unit.

There, below the shelves of the case, is a hidden shelf, invisible from the front.

"Have you found anything?" Kellerman calls out, craning his neck.

"Not quite sure," I lie. I feel around and grasp something cold and metal. For a brief moment I have a flash of hope. I remember Mr. Yamada's words: *"The only thing I remember seeing that he brought back from the war was a Colt .45 automatic, which he always kept behind the counter."*

But it's nothing like a gun.

It's a boxlike object with buttons. I grab it, and slowly work it over to the part of the opening where I can reach in with both hands and pull it out.

Kellerman leans forward. He looks at the thing in my hand with a mixture of curiosity and frustration.

"Just an old cash register," he grumbles.

I place it on the counter. It is, as Kellerman has said, an electric cash register from back in the seventies, by the looks of it. I wipe off the grime and check the plug.

"This is here for a reason," I say coolly, looking around the counter. My hands are feeling around the edge.

"I've already done that," Kellerman says impatiently.

"Yes, but you were looking for a switch. I'm looking for something else," I answer, carefully examining every inch of the underside of the counter with my fingers.

I stop, and smile.

"There's an outlet here," I say, reaching for the cord from the cash register. I snake it under the cabinet and, with a little wiggling and pushing, plug it in.

With a buzz, the cash register comes to life, a digital display on its ancient screen showing "0.00." I press the No Sale button and the drawer springs open.

Kellerman, forgetting himself, rushes over to look.

"Empty," he spits out. "Any more bright ideas?"

"This is it," I say simply. "We just have to know how to use it."

I type a number into the cash register and press Enter. Again the drawer opens, but nothing else happens.

"What was that?" asks Kellerman.

"I tried 1405, his hospital room number. But that was a long shot. We have to enter a number here. I'm sure of it."

"But it could be any number," Kellerman says, sounding less easygoing by the minute.

"If it was a seven- or ten-digit number, it would have been a phone number," I say. "It has to be shorter. But something significant. A date, maybe."

"Try 12741," says Kellerman excitedly,

I nod and put the numbers in. Once more the drawer pops out, revealing itself to be still empty.

"Why 12741?" asks Caleb.

"December 7, 1941." Kellerman shakes his head in astonishment. "The bombing of Pearl Harbor. Don't they teach you anything?"

All of a sudden, Isabel blurts out, "Try 9066."

Where did that come from?

Kellerman rubs his chin. "Why does that number sound so familiar?"

"It was the number of the executive order Roosevelt signed sending the Japanese Americans into internment camps," Isabel explains.

"How the heck do you know that?" Caleb asks.

"Remember I told you I read that book *Farewell to Manzanar* at school? I did a whole report on the Japanese internment camps."

"Let me guess. You got an A, right?"

"Our school doesn't believe in grades. They think it makes kids too competitive."

Caleb snorts.

"Guys!" I call out. "Later. What was that number again, Isabel?"

I input 9066. There's a deep *kachunk* like a lever being released, and the display case suddenly swings outward. Behind it, embedded in the back wall, is a series of three rotating wheels with numbers on them next to a small panel.

The wheels are numbered from one to ten. The panel holds a picture familiar to all of us by now. It's identical to the one on Great-Uncle Ted's lighter. The shield with the hand holding the torch—the insignia of the 442nd Regiment of the U.S. Army.

Kellerman rushes forward and pushes past me. He confidently rotates the wheels until the numbers on top read "442."

Nothing happens. He does it again.

The panel remains shut.

Kellerman mutters to himself "Not 442? Wait! It was also the 100th Battalion!" He has remembered that the original Hawaiian unit of Japanese American soldiers was the 100th Battalion.

"1-0-0." The panel remains stubbornly closed, mocking him.

I am turning numbers over in my head. I know Kellerman isn't going to simply sit there and try every combination of three numbers he knows.

"It's got to be something about the regiment. It has to be." Kellerman is now pacing.

Then he lunges at the panel and stabs at it with the douk-douk, trying to pry it open.

But the panel holds firm.

I brace myself, knowing what's coming. Kellerman wheels around and faces me full on. I get the feeling he's no longer going to be someone to reason with.

"He was *your* great-uncle!" Kellerman screams. "It has to be something he thought you would know!"

Combinations of numbers whirl around in my head. As I'm desperately thinking, I scratch my knee absentmindedly. It's still prickly from sitting on the floor so long. I can only imagine what Isabel's and Caleb's legs must feel like now.

Kellerman is standing over me, chest heaving, but I barely notice him.

I scratch my knee again. I'm back in my room, puzzling through a game no one else can solve.

"What was it she said . . . ?" the others hear me mutter.

And then, just like that, I burst out laughing.

I know. I *know*.

I've had this feeling before, when I solved the fourth and hardest level of the hardest room escape game I ever played.

But this is even better.

"Okay, I've got it," I announce.

Kellerman eyes me warily. "Just like that?"

"Just like that." I smile. "Five four zero."

"Five four zero . . . ," whispers Kellerman softly as he crosses to the panel, as if he's reciting a prayer.

He turns the wheels. Five. Four. Zero. There's a pause, and then the panel slides over to the right.

I go to join the others, crouching down as Kellerman, with trembling hands, removes a velvet drawstring bag from the hole that has been revealed in the concrete wall.

Kellerman looks inside the bag and allows himself a small smile before he carefully puts the bag on the counter.

He turns toward us, the douk-douk in his hands.

But before he can do anything more, out of nowhere, the floor begins to tremble.

I watch in fascination as the cartons all around us dance and jitter, the rumbling getting louder and louder.

Kellerman whirls around and around, trying to locate the source of the vibrations that seem to come from every side. A pipe from one of the shelves rolls onto the display case, smashing the glass. The floor is bumping and bucking, the walls of the room swaying as if the concrete were made of paper.

It's just as I see a stack of cartons falling directly on top of Kellerman that the lights go out.

CHAPTER 33

SHAKEN

I can remember my first earthquake. I must have been five years old, and my parents carried me out of my bed. It seemed like some kind of hilarious game to me, the whole family huddled together in a doorway.

But since then, even the smallest earthquakes have been terrifying. You never really get used to the feeling of the Earth shifting under your feet, giving way, the seconds passing like hours.

In the darkness, I feel the swaying stop, and the room settles into a strange sort of quietness.

To my immense relief, I hear a voice squeak, "What the heck was *that*?"

And then Caleb's slightly calmer voice: "I think, Isabel, you've just survived your first California earthquake."

I call, "You guys all right?"

"I think so." Isabel's voice has regained some of its usual coolness, though there's still a totally understandable edge of panic.

"Yeah, but . . ." Caleb doesn't need to finish the sentence. We all saw the boxes fall on the man we knew as Kellerman, heard a strangled scream escaping, and then nothing.

I get to my feet. I almost fall back as I realize the floor has shifted to a crazy angle, like some sort of fun-house room. I reach down and realize that a small cylindrical object is rolling around at my feet. It's Kellerman's flashlight.

I switch it on and play the beam around the room. First, I see the very welcome sight of two pale but unhurt faces, followed by debris of every kind that has fallen into the center of the tipping room. I then move the light over to the gate.

Great. It's completely blocked. The display case has rammed into it, making a huge dent in the center. It'll be impossible to raise that thing, even if the stuff around it is removed.

Finally, gritting my teeth, I focus the flashlight on the boxes that have toppled onto Kellerman. What I can see of him is still, and the hand holding the knife is thankfully clear of the debris.

I carefully make my way over to him.

Cringing, I gingerly touch the hand and pull the knife from its grasp.

Fighting nausea, I go back to Isabel and Caleb and quickly cut them free from the plastic cords.

Caleb looks with distaste at the pile in the corner and asks, "Is he . . . ?"

"I don't know," I admit.

Isabel is rubbing her wrists and stomping her feet to get the feeling back in them. "We've got to check."

"Fine," says Caleb. "Ted, you have the flashlight. Go ahead."

"Hey, you want the flashlight, tough guy, you can have it," I say.

"My feet are still all tingly," Caleb whines.

"Look, I went over there to the get the knife. Now it's your turn."

We look at each other in the beam of the flashlight.

"Rock paper scissors?" suggests Caleb.

"Okay," I agree.

Isabel grabs the flashlight. "You two are pathetic." She goes over and pulls the boxes off Kellerman. "They're not even all that heavy. It's weird."

Well, she *does* come from New York City.

She kneels over the figure sprawled on the floor.

"He's still breathing," she announces. "Would one of you big babies come over here and help?"

Caleb and I scramble over as Isabel reaches into Kellerman's jacket pocket and pulls out a handful of the hated zip ties. She holds them up gleefully.

We go about our merry task quickly. I pull his arms behind his back, and Isabel puts two zip ties around his wrists and pulls tight while Caleb does the same with his ankles.

"There," Caleb says, wiping his hands on his pants. "He's not going anywhere."

Isabel looks around. "Neither are we, by the looks of it." She turns to me with a worried expression. "How bad do you think it was?"

I wander around the unit, the others following close by. "Well, we're nowhere near the epicenter, or this whole building would have come down, probably. So we can be grateful for that. But who knows what kind of damage is out there? For all we know, this area might have been hit pretty bad."

There's a low moaning from the corner.

I smile with satisfaction as Kellerman struggles against his bonds and slowly realizes the situation he's in. Then he spits out a series of words that are about as nasty as anyone can say. He curses me, Isabel and Caleb, Great-Uncle Ted, his bad luck, and the greater Los Angeles area.

Yes, no more Fudgie the Whale. Fudgie has left the building. His vocabulary now seems to consist entirely of words for body parts and bodily functions—words my parents would ground me for a week for using.

Isabel calmly goes over to him and kneels down until she's at his eye level.

She punches him as hard as she can.

"OWWWW!" protests Kellerman.

Caleb winces. "She really is surprisingly strong for a twelve-year-old."

"Tell me about it," I say.

Isabel looks at Kellerman with contempt. "He doesn't deserve good manners."

Brrrrrr. There's a rattling sound as broken glasses and bottles vibrate against the hard floor. Isabel's eyes widen.

"Aftershocks," Kellerman says grimly. "They can be just as bad as the original quake."

"That one wasn't too bad," I say as it subsides.

"Look, you kids need me," Kellerman continues. "Your only chance of getting out of here is by moving those boxes and somehow prying that gate up. You've got my knife. You're not strong enough to do it alone. Admit it."

I look around the small room. It's pretty bad, with the toppled display case and the boxes everywhere. We could move everything out of the way without Kellerman, but it might take hours.

Sensing my unease, Kellerman presses his case. "Ted, you're a smart kid. We have no way of knowing how structurally sound this place is. The next aftershock, even a small one, could bring the whole ceiling down on us."

Caleb feels along the walls. He turns to me, a worried look on his face. "He's right, Ted. We've got to get out of here, and—"

"And what?" Isabel protests. "We're supposed to trust him? As soon as you let him up, he's going to do whatever it takes to leave here alone."

There is another tremor. The look in Kellerman's eyes goes from an easy calm to an edge of panic.

"Ted, you've got a choice. You let me help you, or we all could very easily die."

"Shut up!" I close my eyes and try to think.

The words on my great-uncle's pad call out to me. *Keep looking for the answers!*

I turn to Kellerman. "You were so determined to find out what my great-uncle's last words were. Well, he did say something. The one word he said, with one of his last breaths, was 'Promise.' He was making me promise to never give up. I made that promise. And I can't break it."

I turn my back on the man trussed in the corner. "Isabel, can I have the flashlight?"

Isabel tosses it to me, and I run the beam around the room one more time.

Maybe there's something I've missed. I look up, and I can feel the smile spread across my face.

"So? You're letting me go, right?" whines Kellerman, trying to catch my eye.

"Just be quiet and let me work this out," I order. I hand the flashlight to Caleb. "Keep this light on me, okay?"

There is one area of the floor that has stayed perfectly flat, right in the center of the room. I slowly take two of the cartons that fell and carefully place them next to each other. I then clear away the broken bottles with my foot and stack two more cartons on top of the first two.

Caleb and Isabel watch me, fascinated.

"Caleb, what's the first thing I say to you whenever you're stuck?"

"You mean like in a game?" Caleb asks.

"No, when your zipper's stuck. Of course in a game," I sigh, and move three more cartons next to the pile I've started. "Whenever you call me as soon as you run out of ideas . . ."

"Ohh . . . right." Caleb thinks, and his hand moves the light up. He follows the light and says something that sounds like "Huh!"

"You don't think . . ." His face is set in disbelief.

"Only one way to find out," I say. I move two more boxes onto the floor, making a pattern of three-two-one, piles of three, two, and one boxes in a row.

Caleb hands the flashlight to Isabel and joins me in arranging the boxes.

"You're wasting time!" whimpers Kellerman.

As we continue to move the boxes around, Caleb turns to Isabel.

"When you play an escape game, you have to look everywhere for clues. The one place people always forget to look is the ceiling. Ted always has to remind me to check there."

Isabel moves the beam of light onto the ceiling, where a pattern of boxes has clearly been drawn in chalk. If you didn't know any better, you'd think it was simply a decorative design, or something drawn by a bored workman.

Caleb and I have finished. We exchange looks.

"You're missing two boxes, aren't you?" Isabel asks anxiously.

I take the flashlight and look up at the ceiling. If it *is* a pattern, Isabel is correct. We're two boxes short.

Kellerman struggles against his bonds. "What did you think you could accomplish with that? You didn't seriously think that piling up a bunch of boxes was going to do anything, did you?"

Ignoring Kellerman, I rack my brain. I go through every strategy I've ever played, every solution that seemed impossible but turned out to be right there if you knew where to look. I make an inventory of the room's contents once more.

And then my eyes settle on the cardboard signs leaning against the wall.

"Isabel, point the light over there," I say.

I carefully make my way over to the signs and, to my satisfaction, see that they're scored.

They aren't signs at all. They're flattened boxes. Two of them.

I hand one to Caleb and take one myself. Quickly, we fold the boxes and assemble them. Then we put them in the right place in the pattern.

Nothing happens.

"I told you!" Kellerman laughs. "Now why don't you be smart about this and cut these things off me."

I reach down and find some of the bottles that have rolled out of a box and put them into one of the empty cartons. I then put a pipe that has fallen off one of the shelves into the other. There's a grinding noise.

"We need just a little more weight," I tell Caleb.

Caleb looks around and disappears out of the circle of light. There's a cry of delight and he reappears. "How about these?" he asks, indicating the stack in his arms.

"Uncle Peter's comic books!" I laugh. "So Great-Uncle Ted didn't throw them out!"

What happens next is even more amazing.

I gently lower the comics into the boxes, half in one and half in the other. There's an earsplitting grinding sound as the floor begins to shift again, magically leveling itself, while the display case pulls away from the gate.

We watch in fascination as the gate automatically, slowly, rises to reveal . . .

The world outside. The beautiful, real world. Untouched.

CHAPTER 34

THE END OF THE GAME

Kellerman still lies hog-tied on the floor of the unit, staring from one face to another, uncomprehending. He looks like he's in shock.

"I don't get it," he keeps repeating over and over.

Isabel looks at me and shakes her head.

"I don't either," she admits. "What just went on in there?"

"May I?" asks Caleb with a hint of pride.

"Be my guest," I say.

"Ted's great-uncle left one more test before someone could take the falcon. You had to arrange the boxes in the storage unit to match the diagram on the ceiling. Otherwise, if you tried to open the compartment and remove the bird, well . . . you saw what happened."

"But how?" demands Isabel.

"There's some sort of pistons or springs set underneath

the unit," I explain. "If the weight wasn't distributed properly, opening the panel would trigger them—"

"—tilting the whole room and trapping whoever was in it inside!" Caleb finishes triumphantly.

"So the only way out . . . ," Isabel reasons, "was to put the boxes in the right pattern and hope it reset the mechanism?"

"I figured there had to be a reset," I say. "In case of some sort of accidental triggering, or if we'd placed the boxes wrong the first time and had to try again."

Isabel stiffens. She looks wildly at me. "Did you hear that?"

In the distance, the sounds of shouts and running feet.

"No one knows we're here," Caleb says anxiously. "But someone sounds like they're in an awful hurry."

I kneel down next to Kellerman. Now I'm the one who's not playing. "Do you have friends? Are there people who were going to meet you here?"

Kellerman just looks at me and smiles. "Why don't we find out?"

I spin around. The voices are getting closer. There's shouting, but it's indistinct.

Isabel grabs my hand. "We have to get the falcon and hide."

I look down and raise my eyebrows. Isabel drops my hand.

"I don't think so," I say as the voices grow clearer.

The words are becoming easier to make out in the echoes of the big warehouse.

They're calling, "Ted! Isabel! Caleb!"

"It's a trap!" Caleb shouts.

"No, it's not, you idiot. That's your mom's voice."

"I know." Caleb grins. "But I've *always* wanted to say that."

We yell back, and the excited cries of the rescue party let us know that they're only a few rows away.

"Row P, row P!" I call, and Caleb and Isabel join me in a sort of improvised school cheer. "Row P! Row P!"

And now here they are.

My mom, running in her scrubs, followed closely by Graham Archer, with Caleb's parents, followed by the now-familiar form of a squat, burly man with a fringe of black hair around his ears, chunky black glasses, and a unibrow.

Behind them, taking his time, ambles good old Dad.

"Man, your mom can book it," Caleb says.

"She used to run track in school," I remind him proudly.

And then we're crushed in an avalanche of hugs and kisses as each of us is tackled in turn.

Graham Archer holds Isabel in his arms, tears streaming down his face as he strokes her hair.

Isabel looks uncomfortable at first, patting her loving father awkwardly on his shoulder. Then she grabs him as hard as she can.

"I'm okay, Daddy, really. . . . I'm okay now. . . ." But looking over, I can see that her eyes are glistening too.

And she called him Daddy.

Looking over isn't easy; Mom seems permanently attached to me, like a giant squid, sucking the life out of me with her hugs. She's also openly sobbing.

I note with satisfaction that Dad is doing his best to hold it together by talking to the burly man as the two of them peer into the structure.

Doris and Gene Grant are trying to concentrate on their son.

"By the way, Doris, I didn't mention it before, but you're looking good. Have you been working out?" says his dad.

"As a matter of fact, I have. Thank you for noticing," Doris says proudly, flexing her biceps.

Caleb pulls himself away and joins Isabel and me, once we've both pried our respective parents off our bodies.

Dad comes over with a big smile on his face.

"I know . . . I never listen . . . but I *knew* something was wrong when you said Isabel didn't return to Osmond," Dad tells Isabel. "I just didn't know *what*."

"I knew you'd get my clue," Isabel replies, nodding vigorously. "*Ted,* of course, thought it was a stupid thing to say."

"Well, Ted should trust his Dear Father. So I told your mom, who kind of freaked out—"

"Why did Mom freak out?" I ask.

Before Dad can answer, my mom turns to the burly man, who is having a one-sided conversation with Kellerman, who is glaring at him.

"Kellerman!" Mom shouts.

"Yes?" both men answer.

My mom marches over, sheer fury in her eyes. The fake Kellerman looks terrified.

She reaches back and wallops . . .

. . . the real Kellerman, who falls over, coughing.

"Amanda!" Dad rushes over but freezes as she glares at him.

The real Kellerman has gotten to his feet, looking baleful.

Then Mom says, through gritted teeth, "You *promised* us! You #$%# liar!"

Whoa.

I did *not* see that coming.

Wait, this is my mom? The "for heaven's sake" mom?

He must have messed up big-time to get her this mad.

"Everything we were told suggested he was not violent or

capable of doing what he did." The real Kellerman speaks with a thick New York accent, kind of like he could be Mrs. Krausz's son.

Mom smacks him again, hard. "Our children could have *died.* We trusted you when you said he was just a harmless antiques dealer. You said to say nothing to them, that he'd show himself and you'd take care of it."

The real Kellerman raises his hands. "Whaddaya want me to do? I'm not the FBI, for God's sake. We're just an organization looking for artwork."

"That is *unacceptable.*" My mom is fuming. "I am writing a letter to whoever runs your organization."

"Fine! Write a letter!" the real Kellerman shoots back. "Get a lawyer! Sue them! See if I care! I didn't even want to do this! I wanted to be an orthodontist, but *no,* I had to run around the world looking for artwork, because that's what Kellermans do. Seriously, go ahead."

This stops Mom for a moment.

"HE KIDNAPPED OUR KIDS!" she screams at him.

I walk over to Dad. "Wait, so you *knew* that Kellerman was a phony and you let him take us?"

"I wasn't there when that guy talked to your mom. I kind of wasn't paying attention when she told me," Dad answers.

"But you put two and two together when Isabel said something wrong about a book?" I ask incredulously.

"Well, that's different," Dad says, impossible as ever. "I mean, if it weren't for Isabel—"

"I know, *I know,*" I say.

As Mom continues to beat the living daylights out of the real Kellerman, Caleb joins us.

"Okay," he says. "Your mom. Isabel. Steel cage match. Your thoughts?"

"Well," I say appraisingly, "Isabel definitely has the height and the reach. . . ."

"Yeah, but your mom has age and experience," counters Dad.

"That's true." Caleb nods.

"Definitely," I agree. "You know what they say: Asian blood is *strong* in that one!"

The real Kellerman then turns to the other parents, who by now have gathered around him, and is once again telling anyone who will listen that they should go ahead and do whatever they want, it's fine with him.

Dad turns back to Isabel as if nothing has happened.

"So, as I was saying," Dad goes on, as if this is a funny story from his class. "Ted's mom went a little nuts. I guess your father went a little crazy too when this Kellerman fellow showed up and mentioned that *other* guy pretending to be him."

One thing doesn't make sense. "But how did you find us?"

"I know you don't think so, but I'm not completely stupid." Dad smiles. "I went to your room to see if I could discover anything, and you'd left your laptop on. I hit the History button, and it pulled up Google with the address on it."

I nod. "You are definitely not completely stupid. You teach college and everything."

"Wait. If you had the address, what took you guys so long?" Having gotten bored with watching the real Kellerman being berated, Caleb is now part of the conversation.

"We've been here for a half an hour looking for you guys," Dad explains. "Do you know how big this place is? How many floors? It wasn't until Graham heard the noise of the gate opening down here that we had an idea of the general direction to follow."

I turn and see something out of the corner of my eye that makes my stomach drop into my shoes.

During all the yelling and catching up, no one has kept an eye on the fake Kellerman.

There on the floor are four zip ties, neatly cut. He has somehow managed to find his douk-douk in the rubble and release himself.

"Kellerman's gone!" I shout.

"Whaddaya mean? I'm right here!" yells the real Kellerman. He looks around and, as the realization sinks in, says simply, "Oh . . ."

He turns to my mom. "See? *This* is what happens when you get angry at the wrong person. *He's* the one who threatened your children. I didn't see you beating *him* up."

Before Mom can answer, a deep voice calls out, "Anyone looking for this?" We're met with the welcome sight of half a dozen LAPD uniformed police turning the corner, one of them pulling a disheveled fake Kellerman with him.

"Well, you certainly took your time," Graham Archer says.

"It would have helped if you'd given us some idea *where* in the building you were," the officer answers coolly.

The police need a statement, so Caleb, Isabel, and I go with one of the officers to file a report. As we turn to leave, I see the real Kellerman emerge from the dust and debris of the storage unit, clutching the velvet drawstring bag.

I stop.

"Can we see it, please?"

All eyes are on the real Kellerman as he carefully undoes the string and lowers the bag.

There in his hand is a statue of a falcon covered in black paint, looking just like the one on the cover of the book Isabel Archer read and told me and Caleb about, what feels like a lifetime ago.

There's silence in the room.

"It don't look like much, right?" the real Kellerman says softly. "But it'll clean up real good. . . ."

He takes a small penknife out of his pocket. Unlike the douk-douk, this knife looks friendly and cute, like one you might use to sharpen a pencil. He opens it and scraps the blade against the black paint.

In the bright lights of the Valleyview Long-Term Storage Facilities (open by appointment only), there is the unmistakable glitter of gold beneath the black.

■ ■ ■

It's a couple of days later and things have finally quieted down to something remotely resembling normal.

It turns out the man who was the fake Kellerman is a rogue antiques dealer (my dad particularly loved the idea of a rogue antiques dealer—"That's like being a homicidal Scrabble player!" he keeps saying, to no one's amusement) named Francis Chamberlain.

"Francis?" Caleb exclaims. "We were afraid of a guy named *Francis*?"

"Oh, like *Stan* is such a terrifying name," Isabel shoots back.

The real Stan Kellerman has gathered the families together

to explain that the process of locating the rightful owners of the jewels found in what the media are calling the Nazi Falcon might take years. The gold, however, will belong to me if I want to sell it or melt it down.

"Where did the gold come from?" I ask. Then I quickly add, "I don't really want to know the answer, do I?"

"No, I don't think you really want to know the answer," Kellerman says. But then, of course, he can't resist telling. "When the Jews were killed in the concentration camps, their bodies were burned, and then gold was taken from the fillings in their teeth. So—"

I hold up my hand. "I don't want it. It's so gross and horrible."

Kellerman shrugs. "You're half Jewish, right? We are the people of the Book, no? So maybe it would be kind of nice if the money went, let's say, to your education?"

I promise to think about it.

After talking to Caleb and Isabel (and my folks), and doing a little research, I reach a decision.

Most of the money will be split between the Japanese American National Museum in Los Angeles, the 442nd Veterans Club in Honolulu (which is still keeping the memory and history of the famed 442nd Regimental Combat Team alive), and the United States Holocaust Memorial Museum.

I should mention that someone lobbied very hard for some of the money to go toward the purchase of a French farmhouse table but was outvoted. Although I have to admit that his compelling argument that as a half-Jewish family we would be honoring the brave French Resistance fighters who stood up to the Nazis was both creative and pathetic.

Now that the whole story has been told, and retold, and

arguments settled over who did exactly what, there's one question everyone still has: how did I come up with the proper three-number sequence to open the panel and discover the falcon?

"I knew it had to be something to do with being Japanese," I finally tell them. "When I scratched my knee, I remembered Mom telling us that the only Japanese she knew was a silly phrase Great-Uncle Ted had taught her to learn the first five numbers.

"If you get a mosquito bite on your knee, it itches, and if you rub sand on it, the itch goes away. So . . . *'Ichi ni san shi go.'* *Go* is 'five' in Japanese. And what's another way of saying you have no money?"

"Broke," Caleb suggests.

"Right, so being broke means you have *zero* money, right?" I continue.

Isabel shakes her head in admiration. "Oh my gosh, that's brilliant."

"Five-four-zero . . . *Go for broke.*"

EPILOGUE

They are sitting cross-legged on the brown late-summer grass outside Caleb's house when I pull up on my bike.

Isabel is looking over Caleb's shoulder at a book of drawings he's done.

"Hey, welcome back!" I call out as I get off and join my friends.

"Hello, stranger." Isabel smiles and motions with her head for me to see what Caleb has done. "Have you seen these?"

Caleb clears his throat. "I, uh . . . well, Ted, I *was* going to show you, but I wasn't sure how you'd feel, but then Isabel insisted, so—"

"It's okay," I say. "Now I know what he's been doing all summer. I thought he was just avoiding me."

Soon after the first news reports of the discovery of the falcon, our story went viral on the Internet. Interviews on morning talk shows followed, which, as Lila so delicately put it, "will look *awesome* on Ted's college applications!"

There was more happy news.

Mr. Yamada, it turns out, suffered a stroke when he realized that the man he had talked to wasn't the real Stan Kellerman. But he's slowly getting better. We wanted desperately to see him, but Donna insisted that as long as his health was still fragile, we'd have to wait until fall.

As for Isabel, Graham had already been planning a trip for her to visit all the cities of Europe she had read about that summer, and a decision was made to go ahead with it, since he felt getting her away from all this was the best thing.

And it would give them some really nice father/daughter time together.

Isabel sent dispatches back, emailing pictures and descriptions, with quotes from books I had never heard of, let alone read.

The one topic she didn't address was whether she was going back to her old school or staying here.

It was clear from her emails that as much as Graham loved having his daughter with him, he felt La Purisma had too many awful memories for her, and she belonged back in her world of New York City, with her old friends and teachers.

And now, with a week to go before school starts, Caleb calls and asks if I can come over.

And here is Isabel, sitting with Caleb.

Is she saying goodbye?

Caleb, as I said, has made himself scarce for most of the summer, not telling me what he was doing, simply making vague comments about "working on something."

As for me, I managed to convince my parents that because of what happened, instead of going off to computer camp in August like we'd originally planned, I could spend the rest of the summer basically hanging out. I had it all planned that I would spend as much time as possible time playing my favorite escape games, but things didn't really work out that way.

After discovering that I'd "borrowed" Mom's ID and biked to the hospital in the middle of the night, my parents decided the best punishment was to confiscate my laptop for two months.

I think anyone would agree that this was totally unfair.

But since I had nothing else to do, I picked up *The Maltese Falcon* and ended up reading it from cover to cover. I actually got so into it that I went to the library and found other books by the same author, Dashiell Hammett, and read those as well.

As Dad says, it's not Henry James, but it's a good start.

I squat down to sit next to Isabel.

Caleb passes me his sketchbook.

Instead of the usual superheroes, he's worked out an entire story called "Three Kids and a Falcon." The heroes are a tall blond boy, a pretty blond girl, and a short skinny kid with spiky hair named, well, Ted.

It's in a new style—nothing like the superheroes I saw in Caleb's bedroom when I visited and we called Isabel for the first time, before Kellerman and the douk-douk and the whole crazy experience that almost cost us our lives.

The story of our adventure, in comic-book form. And right under the title, he's written "Amazing Adventure #1." I guess if he couldn't find a copy of the real comic, he'd make one himself.

"Isn't it great?" Isabel exclaims, looking proudly at Caleb.

"Yeah, but . . . I'm not really that short, right?"

Isabel and Caleb shoot me a look.

"Dude, you are," Caleb says.

"Yeah, dude. You totally are," says Isabel, without a trace of irony.

I clutch my chest. "Did . . . did . . . Isabel Archer just 'dude' me? Have aliens from the planet California infected her brain?"

"Shut up and tell Caleb what a genius he is," Isabel says, smacking me. Gently.

"I can't do both," I say.

"You know what I mean, Ted. Be nice," answers Isabel as Caleb chews on the corner of his thumb. I guess he actually does care what I think.

"You still made me look like some manga or something," I add, "with those big eyes."

I point to a picture of Isabel's body and remark, "And you gave Isabel—"

Isabel's eyes narrow. "He gave me *what*?"

I open my mouth and then shut it. "Nothing. It's great, just like you said."

"It *is* great. And I was about to tell Caleb that as soon as I get back to St. Anselm's, I want to show it to these guys I know who have a webzine and see if they'll put it on their site. And who knows? One of their dads is a big guy in the graphic novel field—"

St. Anselm's.

I see Caleb's face fall, and I'm pretty sure the same expression is on mine.

"So . . . you're going back to St. Anselm's?" I ask.

"Yeah," Isabel says simply.

She looks for a long time out at the traffic snaking past Caleb's house. It's impossible to read her face. We all sit silently for what feels like forever.

Finally, Isabel turns to us.

"Of course I'll go back to St. Anselm's—at Thanksgiving, when I go to New York to see my friends and family."

"Does that mean you're going to La Purisma this year?" Caleb practically yelps like a puppy.

"Yeah." Isabel grins.

"Wow." I'm speechless. "I mean . . . that's nice."

"I'm glad you're so pleased, Ted," Isabel snaps.

"I'm completely stoked," I say. "I just didn't expect you to give up such a great school, and all your friends, and—"

"That's going to be hard, but you know what was harder?" Isabel asks.

Somehow, Caleb and I know enough to just let her talk.

"When I was at St. Anselm's last year, I was the girl who lost her mother to cancer. That's how everyone saw me. And it's not their fault. It's not anybody's fault. But you have to understand. My mother was *loved* at that school. She was one of the school librarians and volunteered for everything, and she's . . . well, she's everywhere in that place. I need to be somewhere else now."

Isabel rubs her eyes with the back of her hand. I don't know how to comfort her. I'm pretty sure if I try to hug her I'll get punched. Or maybe not. It's so confusing.

"And La Purisma is just as good as anyplace else."

Isabel sees Caleb and me looking at her with such sad eyes she shakes her head.

"Let's change the subject, please. I wanted to talk to Ted about his great-uncle."

"Sure," I agree quickly. "He seems like he was an amazing dude."

"Yeaah ..." Isabel draws out the word, as if she's going through something in her mind. Then she adds, "Sounds like he was. But there's something I don't get."

"What's that?" I ask.

"The notebooks. He left you the notebooks. And yet there weren't any clues or hints about the falcon in them, were there?"

"There was the key," Caleb reminds her. "He did hide the key in one of them."

"He could have hidden the key *anywhere*," Isabel insists. "He could have taped it inside *The Maltese Falcon*."

"That's true," I admit. "Maybe he just thought the note-books were interesting."

"There's some pretty cool stuff in there, I bet," adds Caleb.

Isabel looks like she's about to burst. "Here's what I think," she says, then continues all in one breath. "Your great-uncle *knew* that even if you found the falcon, it wouldn't belong to you. He had to know that. So what if that *wasn't* the treasure he was referring to? What if finding the falcon was just a test? What if the treasure is something else? Something to do with those notebooks?"

I try my best to look like this is possible. Caleb is less chari-table.

"I hate to state the obvious, but you read too many books," he says.

"I didn't get that from a book!" fumes Isabel. "It could be true."

"I guess . . . so . . . ," I say, trying to sound positive. "I think the treasure was something else too. But not necessarily the notebooks."

"What, then, Mr. Know-It-All?" asks Isabel.

"Since you've been gone, and Caleb hasn't been hanging out with me, I've had a lot of time alone to think about things. Maybe the treasure was the *search*. The discovery. I don't know . . . the adventure, I guess. Learning to not give up. Learning to go for broke."

Isabel and Caleb look at me without saying anything.

"I guess that sounds pretty stupid," I finally say.

"Yeah, it kinda does," Caleb agrees, going back to his drawing.

Isabel kicks him.

"Maybe it's both things," Isabel suggests. "Maybe you're right *and* I'm right."

"That doesn't make sense," says Caleb. "It's either one or the other. He didn't say 'treasures.' He said 'treasure.'"

Isabel shakes her head. "You're thinking so literally. No wonder you're so bad at escape games."

"I am *not* so bad," Caleb grouses. "We're talking about being consistent, here."

"Well, you know what Emerson said," Isabel sniffs.

"I have *no idea* what Emerson said," Caleb shoots back.

"'A foolish consistency is the hobgoblin of little minds,'" recites Isabel.

"Who is Emerson, anyway? One of the Muppets on *Sesame Street*?" Caleb asks.

"Ralph Waldo Emerson! *God!*" Isabel seethes.

And just like that, I happily see my future. Days to come filled with bickering, clues, and discoveries, with the three of of us looking into what's in those notebooks the mysterious Great-Uncle Ted left me. And maybe finally finding out exactly who created those games I SWEAR were on my computer.

Amazing Adventure #2?

I guess life can be like that.

And looking at my two friends, I realize that there are some places you don't want to escape from.

This is one walkthrough I'll happily do myself.

ACKNOWLEDGMENTS

Getting from a manuscript to a book takes a lot of people, a lot of patience, and a whole lot of support. Especially a debut novel.

Some people who helped early on include freelance editor JillEllyn Riley, whose enthusiasm for the project and savvy notes helped to remove some of the most egregious faults and traps I had gotten into.

Joanna Volpe, Stephen Malk, Steve Meltzer, and Christi Ottaviano read early drafts and said helpful things that moved the manuscript forward and taught me what was missing. Sometimes those one or two notes can make a difference in getting it right. Or at least a whole lot better

When I wondered if I would ever find an agent who would represent this project, Colson Whitehead, brilliant author and fellow school parent, provided invaluable help. He asked his wife, Julie Barer, who provided me with a list of names, one of which was Holly Root.

Since the moment Holly signed on to be my agent, she has put up with all my questions, my occasional tantrums, and my general cluelessness with extraordinary good humor and smart and levelheaded advice. She has yet to steer me wrong, and every day with her is like a Hollyday. (She no doubt rolled her eyes at that, as she should.) She sold the manuscript to the right people—Delacorte Press was my first choice, so I was delighted when I found out that an editor there was actively pursuing the book.

That editor, to my eternal gratitude, is Kate Sullivan, who combines an unerring eye to spot the smallest flaw in logic or clumsy sentence with the vocabulary of a Teamster, and who in all honesty is the person most responsible for taking the manuscript and turning it into a *book*.

Yes, I hear her say, that's my *job,* stupid. (She would probably edit out the word "stupid.") But doing your job and doing it brilliantly are two very different things. I think she's one of the greats, and I sincerely hope we continue to do this together for a long time.

To Kate's name I must add a few more: the folks from Random House/Delacorte Press, who were essential in making this book look as good as it does.

A huge thank-you to:

The patient and brilliant art director Katrina Damkoehler, who found our astounding artist.

Octavi Navarro, who provided the kind of masterful cover and interior illustrations that make the twelve-year-old in all of us joyful.

Stephanie Moss, who designed the book so beautifully.

Copy editors Colleen Fellingham and Alison Kolani, who seemed to catch every errant "was" and missing "to" with incredible precision. I hope they will read these acknowledgments with equal attention!

Now to the personal.

No one has been more helpful in providing support, email addresses, and insight into the process than Mary Pender-Coplan. She is one of those "behind-the-scenes" people in publishing, and I am delighted to tell you for a change to pay attention to the person behind the curtain.

Special thanks to:

Matteo Bologna, typographer *straordinario* for his always wise advice, his friendship, and his inspirational fonts.

Melissa Kantor, who read the book early, gave brilliant and incisive notes, and encouraged me when no one I wasn't married to or related to by blood believed in me.

My mother-in-law, Alice Iwai, who has been a source of emotional support for her daughter and for me as long as we've been together.

My father-in-law, Chuck Iwai, and his lovely wife, Sherry, who have never once questioned his daughter's decision to marry a journeyman writer with nothing to give her but love and respect. They have always been in my corner, and I thank them for all they've given us.

My Aunt Cecille Markell has read more mysteries than anyone I know and passed her love of them on to me.

My sister, Dr. Mariana Markell, and her husband, Dr. Jody Blanco, and their children, Miranda, Max, and Peter, who have always provided a place for me and later my wife and son in their home and their hearts.

My brother-in-law, Jeff Iwai, and his wife, Wendy, and their three kids, Sam, Nick, and Emily, who have been an endless source of joy, laughter, and love when we have needed it (and when *don't* you need it?).

My parents, Robert and Joan Markell, who raised me in a house filled with music, art, great conversation (and listening), and of course a love of reading and good books, which they possess to this day. I love them more than I can ever express, and their unwavering support for their son and his often-wavering career has meant everything to me.

Every single day has been made richer, funnier, more delightful, and better in every way since Melissa Iwai agreed to go through life with me. I am constantly amazed by her love, loyalty, beauty (inside and out), wit, intelligence, and abundant gifts as an artist. By the way, she's also a great cook and mom.

Just ask the incredible, surprising, hilarious, and (in my humble opinion) adorable and brilliant person who is our son, Jamie. He is, and will always be, the greatest thing I've ever helped create.

This is Denis Markell's first novel, and he took writing it very seriously, playing hours and hours worth of escape-the-room games for research (or so he told his family). He also wrote or cowrote the following: an award-winning Off-Broadway musical revue; a few musical comedies for the stage; various and sundry sitcoms; a play with Joan Rivers; an episode of *ThunderCats;* and two picture books illustrated by his wife, Melissa Iwai—*The Great Stroller Adventure* and *Hush, Little Monster.* He is currently working on a new novel for kids about an RPG adventure gone terribly awry, called *The Game Masters of Garden Place.* Denis lives in a small apartment in Brooklyn with Melissa and their son, Jamie.